March 1

P9-DMG-014

118 Falconer St

Frewsburg N. Y.

Song of Deborah

Song of Deborah

A NOVEL

Bette M. Ross

Fleming H. Revell Company
Old Tappan, New Jersey

Library of Congress Cataloging in Publication Data
Ross Bette M
Song of Deborah.
1. Deborah, judge of Israel—Fiction. I. Title.
PS356.O846   813'.54   80-283551
ISBN 0-8007-1263-3
Copyright © 1981 by Bette M. Ross
Published by Fleming H. Revell Company

For my husband, Guy

ACKNOWLEDGMENTS

WITH GRATITUDE, I wish to acknowledge help from the following people: the Reverend Larry Boles, for sharing his fascination with ancient political history; Paula de Jonge, for maps, materials, and travel recollections from the Holy Land; Leta Fischer, for research materials; and Dr. Victor L. Oliver, for the original inspiration to capture Deborah in fiction.

B.M.R.
West Covina, CA

Song of Deborah

1

"You! YOUNG WOMAN!"

The girl stopped singing. "Me, lord?" She waded out of the water. Her headcloth slipped, spilling a radiant mass of red hair about her shoulders. The sodden hem of her pale garment clung to her slim ankles. A glossy piece of green leather girded her waist.

His eyes swept her slender figure. She was like a willow with fire in its crown.

She tilted her head back to address the man on the horse. "Yes, lord?"

"Aren't you a little far from town to be alone?"

"Oh, I am not alone."

King Sisera glanced around. He'd sat the ridge for an hour and seen only a caravan snaking between brown foothills. The girl was watching him. "I was informed Shamer the tanner works hereabouts."

"That is true, lord. At present he is at work catching fish. But a storm is coming, so he may be back soon."

Sisera laughed. "And how is it that you know so much about the tanner?"

"I know about you, too," she said, inviting him to share the pleasant afternoon, the banter.

He shot her a quick glance. "In truth now!"

"You are King Sisera, from the Canaanite camp. And the leather vest you are wearing is nearly new, and it is the finest, toughest vest you have ever had." Her lips turned up saucily.

In a moment, Sisera was off the horse. He was powerfully built. Under the bronze helmet, his tanned face was clean-shaven. His deep-set eyes were guarded by a network of lines: eyes used to gauging distances. He seized her arm. "Who are you, wench?"

"Let me go!" She was stronger than he realized, for she nearly succeeded in wrenching her arm free. "I am only Deborah, the tanner's daughter. Your vest came from my father's tannery. He has made dozens of them for your officers."

"Let me see your hands." Her hand lay quietly in his, like a strong, brown bird. He turned it over. The nails were worn off smoothly, with crescents of dye ingrained around the edges. Sisera pressed her hand gently before releasing it. "I could wish for such hands among Canaanite women," he murmured. "Very well, Deborah. Do not be so playful in the future. It will get you only trouble."

As she stepped back, he caught a scent of her. It was not perfume, but a spicy scent, as though in her striding through fields, the wild mustard and sage weeds had caught her skirts and gifted them with fragrance.

"I am not a slave, lord." Her gaze matched the quiet intensity of her voice. "Our home is but a short distance." Deborah pointed out the direction. "You may await him or return later. Please yourself."

Sisera yielded a slight bow. "I will see your father later." He remounted and looked down at her. She did not move. The wind was picking up, and strands of red hair blew across her face. He stared boldly at her, as if unwilling to break the moment. Finally he said, "A caravan is coming." Turning the horse, he started for Hammath, breaking into a gallop as he left the shore.

A caravan! Deborah shaded her eyes against the whiteness of sand and water. All she could make out was a low cloud of dust at the southern curve of the Sea of Galilee, also known as the Sea of Chinnereth. Oh, if only Gemalli were here to take her into town! But why wait for her brother and perhaps miss the caravan? She tugged her sandals over her wet feet. If she hurried, she could reach the gates in time to see it pass through!

By the time Deborah reached Hammath, out of breath, the first asses were being guided inside. She was sure the caravan was from Damascus. What treasures were hidden in those packs, in the baskets piled high on the backs of camels and asses! She shrank against a limestone wall, still close enough to smell the sweating horses. The wild-appearing men on their backs were heavily armed and dressed in flamboyant colors. Suddenly she saw a man on a huge roan stallion.

"It's Lapidoth the Philistine!" a man exclaimed. "It's Lapidoth's caravan!"

Lapidoth pulled up only a few paces from Deborah. His eyes were a piercing blue. A leather helmet strapped beneath his chin framed hair and beard the color of parched barley. Deborah had never seen shoulders so broad, thrusting out from a leather vest, and below his tunic legs like cordwood were laced into leather leggings from thigh to sandal.

"Lapidoth!" called a woman beside Deborah. Her headcloth was pushed brazenly back; the fullness of her robe, tucked into her girdle, revealed the outline of well-shaped breasts.

Lapidoth's eyes swept the pressing crowd. "Ho, Bithia!" His smile flashed. "Have your wineskins brimming tonight!"

"Anything else, lord?" Her voice carried a tone Deborah knew, and yet did not know.

With a low laugh, Lapidoth leaned over the horse's flank and swept Bithia to him with a loud, smacking kiss. As he pulled away, he surprised Deborah's eyes upon him. His glance flickered over her and back to her intent stare. The inflection in his voice changed. "Is this a new one, Bithia?"

A shiver curled somewhere in Deborah's stomach.

Bithia threw her a contemptuous glance. "That skinny one? You've been in the desert too long, Lapidoth."

Deborah flushed and crept away. Her ears burned with the woman's laughter. She imagined the same contemptuous smile on the face of the man. Her father would be angry that she'd ventured into town alone. Surely they would be back from fishing by now. She had better get home and start the cooking fire.

2

AT FIFTEEN, Deborah had not yet begun to round out in the manner of most of her friends. She was often alone now, since most of them had married. Even last year, while her friends were content to sit with mothers and aunts in the pleasant shade of date palms, Deborah was happier going hunting. She loved her forays into the hills with Gemalli. The wind seemed to whisper to her. Often she would forget they were stalking the red hind and simply stop and lift her face to the wind. Then her arms would raise, and she would feel Yahweh's presence. A silent song would rise on her lips in praise of him who made the world.

Deborah was humming as she reached the tannery. She set about arranging brush and dung chips in the stone fire pit before the house. That the tannery lay so far beyond the walls of the city was the fault of the elders. Convening, as was their habit, upon seats near the gates of Hammath, they had decided one fine morning that the odor of hides in various stages of preparation was polluting the town's air. They prevailed upon Shamer to relocate.

Deborah did not mind. Beyond the walls, she had more freedom than other young women. She loved her brother and her father dearly. Not for all the wealth of Hammath would she trade them for a husband in a different household. Since her mother's death three years earlier, her chores seemed endless, yet she took joy in them. Her father gratefully allowed her free rein with household matters.

The tanner's house was a wide, squat building of sun-dried bricks. Steps formed along an outside wall led to a smaller room on the roof. Here they would sit of an evening to catch the wisps of breeze off Galilee. On very hot nights, they sometimes brought their pallets up and laid them out on the flat roof for sleeping.

Behind their home Shamer had built the tannery, using the long

15

rear wall of the house for support and extending the roof to form an open-sided shed.

By dusk, Deborah's fire was glowing brightly. She heard Gemalli's voice and looked up. He was bringing a string of fish.

"Look, father. That's faith. Deborah has the fire ready before the fish are brought."

Deborah embraced her father and took Gemalli's fish. "I was afraid you would be caught in the storm."

"It blew over, daughter. No rain for us, I'm afraid." Shamer was a short, stout man with heavy features. His shoulders and arms were powerfully muscled from years of working the tough hides, and his fingertips were smoothed to the sheen of marble from the harsh chemical compounds.

"Did you see the caravan, father? It's come all the way from Babylon! Father, maybe we can get some new dyes, or some of those hard, metal stamps to put designs on our leathers. I'm sure we could sell—"

"Ah, daughter, can't it wait? Your poor father is hungry! Now go, feed us!" Shamer slapped her playfully on the backside.

As she left, he said wistfully to Gemalli, "Other girls would beg for new cloth and fancy bangles."

Gemalli had fetched water for washing from the covered crock they filled from the village well and pulled off his tunic. He was stocky, like his father. "She has a point, father. The Egyptians send leatherwork off on the caravans, and people fall all over themselves to buy it. With proper tools, why could not we do the same?"

"We could." Shamer began to wash.

With a glance toward the house, Gemalli added, "Also, I think Deborah should have a new gown. She's too old to be unmarried."

Shamer laughed. "You think a new gown will help? I expect she will tell *me* when there is someone she's willing to marry."

"You shouldn't allow that! It was a mistake to give in to her before, when someone wanted her."

Thoughtfully, Shamer wiped his hands. "Your mother always loved that blue cloth from Phoenicia. She said it didn't fade. Do you think Deborah would look good in a blue gown?"

"Well, maybe then she wouldn't look so skinny and tall. We've got to do something."

Shamer bellowed a laugh. "But then who will cook us fine meals?

Or are you bringing home a wife?"

Gemalli looked at his smiling father. It was hopeless. Shamer obviously didn't care if Deborah ever married.

After supper, they sat around the trench table in the lower room. Shamer selected a long fishbone and began to pick his teeth. "Bless Yahweh for such a fine catch. And bless you, too, daughter. A woman who can prepare an excellent meal is a blessing indeed."

"Did Moses say that too, father?"

Shamer chuckled. "He probably did."

"He probably said 'A woman praised is a woman silenced,' " put in Gemalli.

Deborah punched him. "You wouldn't have said that before supper!"

Gemalli laughed. "Deborah, you should have gone fishing with us."

"I went walking. I wanted to be alone."

"You always want to be alone. How do you expect to get a husband?"

"Maybe my own company is better than some I know!" Suddenly Deborah remembered the solitary rider. "Father, a soldier came to see you today. He wanted to see you right away. As though you have nothing better to do than wait upon soldiers!"

"A soldier?"

"Yes. It was—"

A brisk rap sounded on the door. Gemalli climbed over the bench to answer. Two soldiers loomed in the darkness. Without invitation they stepped inside and looked around, then stepped outside again with the announcement, "King Sisera!"

Hastily Shamer got up. He drew his sleeve across his mouth. "My lord Sisera!"

Sisera strode inside. "You are Shamer the tanner?"

"Your servant. My house is yours. Deborah," he motioned her to clear the table, "bring some wine."

Ignoring them, Sisera moved to the rear wall, where hung bundles of tanned hides. He gathered a soft piece of chamois in his fist and rubbed it. "Truly you are a master of your craft, Shamer."

"I am most grateful that it pleases my lord."

"It is the purpose of my call." Suddenly Sisera seemed to realize that all were still on their feet. "Please sit," he said graciously.

Gemalli drew a bench a respectful distance from where the king now sat at table with his father. Deborah served the wine, then sat beside her brother. Watching her, Sisera frowned.

"Does something offend you, my lord?"

"Canaanite women do not listen when business is at hand."

"We are Israelites. My daughter serves in her mother's stead. She who works as hard as any, shall she not also be consulted?"

Deborah lowered her eyes to the hands nested in her lap. It was not her wish to embarrass a guest in her father's house.

Sisera's face became a mask. Gracefully, he lifted his cup. When he had tasted, he said, "Shamer, I have decided you should move your tannery."

"What? Again?" cried Shamer. "Who is complaining now? When the elders complained of the stench—and I do not blame them, noble Sisera; the treatment of hides is a noxious one—did we not move outside the protection of the city? Were we not careful to locate downwind? Though this is certainly not the most desirable location, with no level patch for Deborah's vegetable garden. . . ."

Sisera's hand waved impatiently. "No, no. Complaints are not my concern, Shamer. I have use for you."

Shamer's manner changed abruptly. A guardedness crept into his voice. "What do you mean?"

"Simply that I desire that you relocate in Taanach, my capital."

In the stunned silence, Sisera felt Deborah's gaze. He was compelled to meet it. Once again he felt its burning intensity. He'd give a day's tax revenue to know what lay behind those spice-brown eyes.

"To Taanach!" Shamer spluttered. "But that is beyond Mount Tabor, beyond the Plain of Jezreel. We would be surrounded by Canaanite cities—by Canaanite gods! It is impossible!"

"Why can we not serve you here, my lord?" asked Deborah.

Pointedly ignoring her, Sisera addressed Shamer. "You may freely serve your god there. You will be charged with the royal tannery, supervising all leather goods for my armies. Is that not reason and honor enough?"

A bewildered smile tugged at Shamer's mouth. "Oh, yes, a great honor! But Yahweh is here. Yahweh gave this land into the hands of the tribe of Naphtali, by his servant Joshua. Joshua decreed that we should live on Yahweh's land. I have heard that your city on the plains is of surpassing beauty, King Sisera, and . . . and wealth. But

I can't go there!" His voice was beseeching. "My father built this trade. I have taught my son and daughter. Yahweh would be exceedingly angry if we were to move among the baals you worship."

Sisera smiled. His eyes remained hard. "Shamer, you will find we are much more tolerant in that respect than you Israelites. Our gods do not whisper to us to demolish other gods, as yours is rumored to do. No one will interfere with your worship. My word upon it."

"Why couldn't I go to Taanach, father?" Gemalli cried. "There is scarcely enough business here to keep all three of us busy. I could go, and Deborah could help you. She knows as much as I!"

Sisera pursed his lips, as though considering this. He flicked a glance at Deborah. "Let Shamer and the daughter go."

"No, father!" Deborah's hands flew together. "Taanach is an evil in the sight of Yahweh. Their gods demand unspeakable things, and they do not value human life!"

"Oh, come now," laughed Sisera pleasantly. "The people of Taanach are hardly uncivilized." *The sheer gall of these peasants in this stinking hovel!* Sisera cleared his throat and said casually, "Tell me, Shamer, is your daughter betrothed?"

Shamer's breath caught. "Why do you ask?"

His upper lip curled slightly. "She may not be sold unless she learns to keep quiet."

Deborah rose. "No one sells me! Or buys me!"

"Young maidens who are too particular may find themselves serving the temple," Sisera said coldly. "Temple virgins are kept quite occupied, with little time to engage their betters in verbal battle!" Sisera rose from the bench as his voice rose in pitch. Deliberately, he turned his back on her and addressed her father. "Had you goods on the caravan from Babylon?"

"Not this time."

"Just as well. Caravans can be risky these days. I expect to hear from you tomorrow, Shamer." With a curt nod, he left.

They stared after him in disbelief.

"Father," said Gemalli, "he can't force us to go, can he?"

"Well I'll not go! I'd sooner marry Nabal than live in Taanach!" Deborah exclaimed.

"But, child of my heart, your brother and I would protect you!"

"Yahweh does not want me in Taanach yet!" A sob clutched her throat.

Shamer stared at her. "Yahweh doesn't want you in Taanach *yet?* What do you mean?"

"I . . . I don't know, father. It just came out." Deborah's fingers bit into her robe.

Shamer's voice softened, puzzled. "You have turned away every man who has asked for you. What would you have me do?"

She could not answer.

"Let me go, father!" urged Gemalli. "Sisera can't object. I won't forget Yahweh! Two tanneries *is* a good idea. After all, you may marry again, and I will, certainly. This would not support us all."

Shamer, frowning at his daughter, barely heard Gemalli. Why had Sisera rebuked her? "Deborah?"

"Yes, father?"

"Has this man ever seen you before?"

"Only at the shore today."

"At the shore? Deborah, was he the soldier?"

"Yes, father. I was enjoying the water."

"Enjoying the water! Yahweh preserve us; you have shamed us with your body!" Shamer slapped his thigh in exasperation. Sisera's reputation was too well known. "Gemalli, do not allow Deborah from your sight until Sisera leaves Hammath!"

Seeing the worry on their faces, Deborah was contrite. "As Yahweh is my witness, father, I intended no evil. I shall stay indoors until he leaves."

Shamer's chin bulged like a sausage roll against his chest. Finally he said, "Tomorrow I will go to the priest and sacrifice to Yahweh. Perhaps he will give us a sign. Gemalli, take some coins from my pouch and go into town. Buy a pair of young goats from Nabal. He has a goodly herd. Make certain they are without blemish, now! We must not offend Yahweh with a sacrifice less than perfect!" Shamer covered Deborah's hands with his worn and stained ones. "Do not despair, Deborah, for surely you are close to Yahweh. If you feel you must not go to Taanach, then Yahweh must have the answer. Tomorrow, early, I will go to his tent."

3

AFTER SEEING THE MERCHANTS of the caravan safely inside the walls of Hammath, Lapidoth turned about and rode for the city gates. Hamid, the small, dark, energetic factor from Damascus traveling with him, was already busy drumming up additional trade from which he would extract commissions. The striking young woman in the simple, unbleached linen was nowhere to be seen. Well, right now he wanted to bathe.

Lapidoth rode north, past the camp being set up by his men, past a similar though smaller garrison which, he noted with surprise, was Canaanite. He had thought King Sisera's nearest garrison was a day's ride north. A little beyond, he turned into a verdant, steamy meadow, reeking of sulphur. Here mysterious hot springs broke through the surface of the earth.

The Naphtalites had curtained some of the springs so men might bathe and refresh. Tethering his horse, Lapidoth stooped to enter. He recognized several men of Hammath. With an exchange of greetings he stripped and immersed his muscular body in the nearly scalding water, soaking out the weariness of the long journey.

Later, sitting on a mat, pouring sweat, he talked and joked with the other men. Suddenly Lapidoth thought of the young woman standing like a cornered bird near Bithia. "I saw a maid today, with hair like flame, standing near the city gates. Who is she?"

"It was probably the daughter of Shamer the tanner," said Nabal, the oil and olive merchant. His soft, white belly glistened in the steamy tent.

"He should know."

There was a ripple of laughter.

Lapidoth looked from one to another.

"Nabal wanted to marry her last year. Didn't you, Nabal?"

"Why not? My precious wife, blessed be the name of Yahweh,

21

went to rest with her fathers. A house needs a woman."

"What happened? Was her dowry not pleasing?"

"Dowry!" another man said. "How much dowry could a tanner give?"

"Deborah did not wish to leave her family," said Buzi the wine merchant. Buzi had eight sons and daughters, and no sympathy with a man of Nabal's years coveting one at the mere bud of womanhood. "She is an only daughter, and as dear to Shamer as a son."

"She minds me of an eagle," said Lapidoth.

"Those sharp-looking ones sometimes have tongues to match," said another sourly.

The others laughed sympathetically, thinking of the man's shrewish wife.

Soon Lapidoth dressed and left for camp. In peacetime, it was customary for caravans to camp outside the walls of the cities and hamlets they touched, displaying their wares in broad, open fields where villagers might come to buy. Of recent years, only an extremely well-armed caravan would dare to do so. Raids by the desert peoples across the Jordan terrorized caravans and camps alike.

Lapidoth's caravan was garrisoned in a box canyon. He nodded to a guard as he entered. Inside the canyon, the caravan had already settled into a pattern. Dotting one section were cooking fires of families traveling under his protection. Camel and horse drivers and herders took up another corner, the flocks and herds yet another.

His aide had erected his tent on a slight bluff overlooking the encampment, and was preparing his supper.

In the cool violet of evening, after a solitary meal, Lapidoth rose and donned soft, fresh clothing. Bithia was expecting him. Unexpectedly, a vision rose before his eyes. *Deborah.* The merchant had called her Deborah.

4

THESE WORDS the Levitical priest recited to Shamer after the sacrifice of the pair of unblemished goats: "And when the Lord your God brings you into the land which he swore to your fathers—to Abram, to Isaac, and to Jacob—to give you great and goodly cities, which you did not build, and houses full of all good things, which you did not fill, and cisterns hewn out, which you did not hew, and vineyards and olive trees, which you did not plant, and when you eat and are full, then take heed, lest you forget the Lord."

As the priest's voice died, Shamer waited expectantly. But the priest said, "Come, my friend." A gnarled hand on Shamer's shoulder guided him out of Yahweh's Tent into the new morning. "Tell me, have you instructed your son in the laws and ordinances of the Lord?"

"You know I have instructed both my son and my daughter. We are a close family."

"Then you are not forbidden to sojourn in the city-state of Taanach. True, it is Canaanite, but in the days of Joshua, it was given over to the tribe of Manasseh. The Lord told Moses, 'Only little by little will I give these cities into your hands lest they be too much for you, and lest you be overtaken by wild beasts.'

"Therefore, Shamer," continued the old priest, "it may be that Yahweh grows restless. We are become too comfortable in our land. We forget that he has charged us to dwell in all of Canaan. Perhaps you are meant to dwell in the city of Taanach, as a sign to all other Israelites." Shamer matched the decorous stride of the priest as they paced the courtyard. The priest went on: "For who can doubt the power of Yahweh? If Sisera says you may safely worship Yahweh in Taanach, then may not Yahweh be working through Sisera? Is he not all-powerful? Would it not please him to bring Taanach unto him, even through a powerful enemy?"

23

Still Shamer hesitated. "But what of Deborah?"

"She is a woman. Exercise more control over her, or bring her before the elders."

For the first time, the edge of a smile crept to Shamer's lips. "Ah, you know we seldom deal with our daughters against their wills. The women of Israel are not chattel."

When Shamer left the priest, his spirit was not quite so troubled. Perhaps to migrate would not be a bad thing. Perhaps Yahweh meant it as a change for the good in his fortunes. He would ask the elders for their advice.

It was still early when Shamer reached the sun-washed benches by the gates. A freshness lingered in the cooling mists rising off Galilee, and over the murmur of his friends' voices he heard a bird chirping somewhere. Shamer took his accustomed place a little apart from the others, in order not to offend their sensibilities by any lingering odors. "Blessings upon you, my friends," he greeted them. "And thou, Lapidoth," he acknowledged the presence of the Philistine.

After that, Shamer lapsed politely into silence. It would not do for him to imply his business was more important than other matters.

" 'Tis Yahweh's own truth," said Buzi. "Lapidoth acted as my personal emissary on this trip, and never have I had better trades for my wines. In return he has brought me fine embroidered cloth for my four daughters. A good man, Lapidoth."

"That was but a favor," said Lapidoth. "I am a better soldier than trader. Now let Hamid be your factor; he is as wily as a fox and an honest man."

"On your word, I will."

The talk went on, sometimes in discreet tones, as Lapidoth filled their ears with stories of foreign cities.

Finally, Buzi turned curiously to Shamer. "My servant tells me King Sisera honored you with a visit last night."

"I need the elders' advice, if you have time," Shamer said. Lapidoth rose. "Stay, please, Lapidoth. You have been everywhere, perhaps you can lend some light to this." Shamer then told them of Sisera's thinly veiled demand that he go to Taanach and his curious remarks about the risks of caravan travel. "He knows I depend on the caravans to carry my leathers, else where would I trade?"

"Think you he was saying your goods will not be safe on caravans unless you agree to move?"

"I do not know. King Sisera is a devious man."

"It's rumored that some of the desert tribes are in his hire," Lapidoth said thoughtfully.

"Would Sisera rob his own merchants? Every caravan carries Canaanite goods, too," said Buzi.

"I think—" Shamer began with a frown of concentration, "but I am not certain—that he lusts for my daughter."

Lapidoth started.

"He suggested I take her to Taanach, to help set up the new tannery."

"A strange request indeed, to make a tanner of a daughter," said Nabal. "If ever she is wed, she would be no use to your tannery."

"That is so. Yet twice did he refer to her coming."

The elders sat in disturbed silence. "What can this mean?" Buzi pondered. "In our city, Yahwist and Canaanite have lived in peace for years."

"True, they do not worship the one God, but we have managed to get along."

"And our daughters have married their sons," said one elder slowly. "Is Yahweh warning us? Are some worshiping their gods?" Suddenly the morning did not seem so bright.

Privately, Nabal thought of the little wooden baal, fertility god for his orchards of olives, which he kept hidden. Certainly he worshiped only Yahweh, but after all, business was business. "I would not let a daughter of *mine* wed a heathen Canaanite," he declared.

"That is well, since you do not have daughters," replied Buzi.

"Friend Shamer," said Lapidoth. "What do you think will happen if you refuse to go?"

Shamer shrugged helplessly. "It would probably be good for business. Gemalli thinks so. But I fear for my daughter."

"Hold," said the chief magistrate of the elders. "We are free men! If he goes out of fear, none of us is free."

"Then I must not force Deborah to go to Taanach!" Shamer's voice was relieved.

"On principle, no Israelite should be forced," declared the magistrate. "But if you *want* to go, you must take her with you. If he has designs on her, it may not be safe either to go or to remain."

"You must strike your tent," said another. "It is the only way to protect your family."

"Leave Hammath?" Shamer's hand swept the neat square. "Leave the bones of my father's fathers? Whither shall I go?"

"Shamer."

"What, Lapidoth?"

The big man leaned forward. "Come with us. We move on in two days. Our way to the southern cities lies through Shechem. The Ark of the Covenant is there, in Yahweh's Tent. In Shechem you could dwell in peace."

"And the Feast of Ingathering is soon upon us," exclaimed Buzi.

Each year, Shamer knew, men of all the tribes journeyed to a tribal confederation in Shechem, to celebrate the ingathering of spring harvest. It was a time to settle tribal disputes and to bring tithes before Yahweh.

"Sisera could not touch you there!" urged Lapidoth.

"That is true," exclaimed Buzi. "I myself am going in but a few days. It is perfect!"

"And I," declared Nabal. "We will protect you."

"Many of us," agreed the chief magistrate. "We can bring King Sisera's action before the confederation. Free citizens of the Israelite tribes are not bound to Sisera!"

"So you say," said Buzi, "but I notice when his cutthroats come, you pay your share like the rest of us."

"Posh!" An ancient one, who had been listening with closed eyes, now opened them. "This is nothing but a dust storm in a cooking pot. I'll tell you what's bothering Sisera. And it has nothing to do with the tanner." He closed his eyes for a moment and felt the sun's warmth in his old bones. "Sisera spares no expense upon his army. And haven't we heard tales of the vast excesses at his palace? He spends huge sums of gold adorning his women and breeding fine horses. His halls are filled with treasures. Where does he get the money? Now, he is also general of all the armies, which he must use—"

"Yes, yes—to collect tribute for Egypt," said Nabal impatiently.

The ancient one nodded. "The facts are plain: Sisera has spent beyond his means. And now, when it is time to send the annual tribute, his coffers are bare, and he is preying upon all caravans to refill them."

"But why does he demand that Shamer move to Taanach?"

"Because he has something else in mind, too." The ancient one's lips cracked in a toothless smile. "Perhaps he sees himself becoming Pharaoh of all Canaan."

The elders burst into laughter. "What an amusing thought! And then what? War with Egypt? War upon the Israelites? Destruction of the Twelve Tribes?"

Suddenly they were all talking at once, until someone suggested, "Come, let us consult the priest." In a body, the elders departed, leaving the ancient to nod in the sun and Shamer appealing to Lapidoth with sad eyes.

"Everyone explains it so well. But no one has the answer. Do you have children, Lapidoth?"

"No." He laughed. "Although perchance I do."

"But you are not a young man."

"Thirty years."

"Have you no fear that the line of Lapidoth the Philistine may die?"

Lapidoth considered this momentarily, then chased it with a grin. "Shamer, I am a soldier. Let my seed strengthen other lines."

"Hah! You will not think so in your old age. Who will bring you wine when you are too old to see? Who will cook nice pots of goat meat, tender to your toothless gums? My son and my daughter are everything to me. In them and my children's children rests the hope of my old age." Shamer leaned forward. For some unaccountable reason, it seemed right to share his fears with Lapidoth. "My Deborah . . . she is a daughter of the wind. She knows things beyond herself, Lapidoth. I am growing more each day to cherish the thoughts she shares with me and to trust her counsel. If she says Yahweh does not want her in Taanach, then I believe her, no matter what the priest says, or the elders! Though I make plans, I fear she will never consent to be brought to the marriage bed. I . . . I sometimes feel that she sees too much." He sighed deeply. "Fortunate am I that the line of Shamer the Naphtalite does not rest with the loins of Deborah!"

5

ALL DAY, AS HE WORKED in the tannery, Shamer's mind churned. Among the familiar wooden vats and long tables and scrapers and scrubbers and leather bottles and various powders and bowls of fish oils, Shamer felt comforted. With him worked his children, amid tables piled high with hides in various stages of dress, in colors from pale milk to dusky brown—goat and sheepskin, cowhide and a rare white chamois, and a batch of horsehide destined for Sisera's military.

They heard nothing from Sisera that day. The following morning, an emissary appeared at the tannery. "By Baal, men of Hammath, how do you stand this odor? Sisera must be out of his mind," he said in an aside to the one with him. "My lord Sisera desires that you join him, Shamer. He is but a little north of town—upwind."

Gemalli stepped up beside his father. "Father, let me go for you."

"No, Gemalli. Stay with Deborah." Shamer shrugged out of his leather apron and washed his hands.

"Have you no horse?" demanded the soldier when he saw that Shamer was preparing to walk. "Nor ass?" His lip curled as Shamer shook his head. "Then you will ride behind Sem. Sem!"

Sem wrinkled his nose as Shamer struggled up behind. "Hold fast, tanner. I'll not wait for the wind to catch me."

Gemalli's eyes stung with dust and humiliation. He strode back into the shed. "Well, father's gone off with the soldiers. I'll wager Sisera means to have his way." He threw Deborah a glance. She was stroking the chamois, as if the soft leather offered comfort. "Taanach may be an evil city. But even there people are not forbidden their own gods," he reminded her gently.

"Yahweh would not permit. . . ." Deborah sounded lost.

"Yahweh would not permit *us* to have other gods, Deborah. We can still trade with those who do." He came to her and took her

hand. "Our father has the word of the priest on it. They are not
Yahweh's people. And though far, isn't Taanach still in Canaan?
And did not Yahweh, through Joshua, give all of Canaan to his
people?"

"Thou art dreaming, Gemalli. We are still strangers in the land."
The sorrow in her eyes began to burn away in indignation. "It's not
only Canaanites, it's the Philistines, the Phoenicians, the—"

"All right, all right! We are few. We are only twelve tribes. But
Yahweh promised us all the land. That includes Taanach, doesn't
it?"

"And would you put an altar to Yahweh in Baal's temple?"
shouted Deborah. "Blasphemy!"

"For a skinny female, you have a big mouth," said Gemalli. "Be
silent and listen. What choice do we have?"

"What choice if we go? Shall you marry me off to a Canaanite
who believes in fertilizing the land by lying with temple virgins?"

"Deborah!" Gemalli was shocked. "Where do you pick up that
language?"

"It's true, isn't it?"

Angrily, Gemalli whirled and stared out over the Sea of Galilee.
How could a man think, with Deborah around?

Sisera watched the two soldiers ride up the canyon with Shamer
clinging raggedly behind. Until yesterday, he had had no idea what
entrenched Yahwists the tanners were. The father and daughter in
Taanach could be hostage against defection by the son in Hammath.
What defection? Hammath was not controlled by Canaanites. For
the present. And the red-haired wench. He smiled, thinking how
utterly unsuitable Deborah was to be a temple virgin. No, better to
keep that passionate young thing for himself.

As he watched Shamer plod on foot up the stony hillside to his
tent, he wondered how such a squat toad could have sired Deborah.
What would Leah, his mother, ruler of his domestic household at
Taanach, think when he returned with another concubine? He
smiled. No matter.

When Shamer puffed up the last rise and presented himself to the
king, Sisera was in fine humor. "Sit, Shamer," he said graciously. "I
will pour you some wine, and we will discuss plans for your new
tannery."

Shamer shot him a worried glance, accepted the wine, and decided not to contradict him until he found his breath.

"Where did you learn your craft?"

"My fathers brought it out of Egypt, my lord Sisera."

Sisera nodded. "I myself have leathers from Pharaoh. Your work resembles it. It will be appreciated in Taanach."

Shamer made a futile gesture with his hand. "My home. . . ."

"You can be wealthy, Shamer! Chief of leather works for the army of Sisera! Making weapons and uniforms, fitting out horses and even my chariots. Wait till you see the city, Shamer! You will have finer tools and the rarest oils, as many workers as you need." Sisera refilled Shamer's cup, in the pause judging the effect of his words. "Here is all I ask. You come to Taanach yourself, and train my workers in your skill.

"At the end of a year's time, if you do not enjoy life in Taanach, you are free to go." He shot the man a calculating glance. "Leave your son here. Bring your daughter to assist you—that you may continue to see to her righteous upbringing. Or. . . ."

Shamer's beseeching expression reflected dread.

"If you fear for her safety, Shamer, I will buy her."

Horror registered on Shamer's face before he could mask it. Full well did he understand Sisera's meaning.

But Sisera had seen. His lips tightened. "It is an unusual honor, of course, for an Israelite maid to be chosen by King Sisera, but there is something uncommon about your daughter."

"My daughter is not for sale! I . . . I mean—that is—she is betrothed. Your lordship does her great honor, but in the manner of our people I have betrothed her. To an Israelite."

Sisera stared at him, amused though annoyed. "And who is the fortunate fellow?"

"It has not been announced yet. The final contract has not been signed."

"And can you give me no hint, Shamer the tanner? Is it Sopo the goatherd? Or the fat one who sits within your gate and perspires as freely as the oil of the olives he grows?"

Shamer shook his head, beginning to sweat himself. "No, no, none of these. Not a man from Hammath. He lives far away. Yes, that is why the negotiations are slow." At last came the inspiration for which Shamer had been praying. "That is why Deborah is leaving with the caravan led by Captain Lapidoth. Her betrothed is in Shechem. And of course I must accompany her, and naturally my son must see to the tannery while I am gone—"

"Shamer!"

"Wh-what?"

"How is it you did not have this information two short days ago?"

"As Yahweh is my judge, noble Sisera, Deborah will marry an Israelite!"

Sisera's face grew still.

Shamer rushed on. "And the house of Shamer will be honored to work for you in Taanach. Either I or my son will be there within the month, once my daughter is wed. Surely—"

"No! You must accompany me now. My need is greater. If Deborah must go, let your son accompany her."

"Yes. Anything." Shamer lumbered to his feet. "It is agreed. My word upon it. Now by your leave I must . . . I must . . . good day, noble Sisera." Shamer plunged downhill in a headlong rush, leaving Sisera cold with anger.

All right. One does not always win the battle in a single skirmish. *No one sells me or buys me!* Deborah without Shamer would not be so flippant.

6

WHAT HAD HE DONE? As Yahweh lived, how had this disaster happened? And what had he done to his treasured daughter? By all his forefathers, he knew not a man in Shechem. The name had come to him simply because Lapidoth had mentioned it. *Lapidoth!* He must talk to Lapidoth.

He found the big man poring over a stack of clay tablets spread on a low table in his tent. He looked up, smiled. "Blessings on thee, Shamer. Leathers to ship?"

Shamer shook his head. "No. Yes. I mean, yes. Lapidoth, may I speak to you in confidence?" He glanced uncertainly at the ruffians lounging outside the tent.

Lapidoth followed his gaze. "Do not concern yourself, Shamer." Lapidoth reached for his wineskin. Out of courtesy, Shamer took a small pull. Lapidoth considered the wheezing, distraught man sitting cross-legged before him. His hands were big and callused. The blunt fingers savaged the leather thongs of his purse into knots and then forced them apart.

"I have just come from Sisera. Lord Lapidoth, I am afraid for my daughter. It is hard to tell what that man is thinking. One moment he talks of his chariots and the next of my daughter." Words tumbled out as Shamer laid his woes before Lapidoth. *"Will* you take her? It's not a question of money."

"Of course, Shamer. But once she is in Shechem, then what?"

"I don't know. It is all too.... I will send Gemalli too, with silver for lodging and food. Beyond that.... A daughter should not be deprived of the protection of her family." The hands worked the leather thongs mercilessly.

Lapidoth got to his feet and straddled the doorway, his big frame blocking the sun. "It's well to get her out of here, Shamer." At length he added, "They could abide in my father's house. It's near

Shechem, in the village of Shiloh."

Shamer's hands stilled. "She would be safe with your parents. Oh, my lord Lapidoth! You are a good man—a good man! I will bring you all the money I have, to keep them in the bosom of your parents!"

Lapidoth laid a comforting hand on his shoulder. "No, Shamer. Deborah is a daughter of Yahweh. Did not Joshua charge us to be hospitable to our own people?" A quick smile kindled the bearded face. "And are we not fighting a pagan practice despised by our God?"

This was too much for the practical Shamer. Tears rushed to his eyes. "Not all Yahweh's people remember Joshua's charge so well. I confess I have not always treated men of the other tribes in the manner you treat me, O Lapidoth. Truly you are a lord among men."

"Good returneth for good, Shamer. Go and prepare for your children's journey. We leave at dawn. I'm sorry I cannot spare an ass for Deborah to ride."

"Yahweh bless thy future generations!"

Lapidoth watched thoughtfully as the bulky figure of the tanner receded. Sisera was becoming bolder by the season. How long before he openly attacked the hill cities of Yahweh? With all of Canaan brought under single headship, Egypt could whistle for its tribute. Perhaps the ancient one in the marketplace had not been far wrong.

Lapidoth could recall a time when Egyptian garrisons dominated passes and seaports days away from her capital, when long lines of slaves were driven into Egypt to work for Pharaoh. Now scarcely any of Pharaoh's arrogant armies were beyond Egypt's borders. And caravans which were strong, such as his, had wrested political immunity from the nations they crossed, without paying the onerous tribute demanded by petty kings of city-states.

Caravan routes were lifelines flung across a network of kingdoms. A country closed its borders to caravans at peril to its own trade.

But now Sisera was breaching the balance of power, though not openly. Lapidoth lifted his eyes across the scarfed slope to the Sea of Galilee. Brigands who had harassed his caravan between Astaroth and Damascus had been in the pay of Sisera; he was almost certain of that now. But that was the land of the Arabian tribes.

Sisera had never reached beyond the Jordan. Why harass caravans there, unless to allay suspicion while filling his coffers for a major offensive?

Lapidoth did not dismiss Shamer's strange tale that Sisera needed his unique talents at his capital city of Taanach. Likely he was gathering top craftsmen from all cities, creating a stronghold at Taanach, which would then be completely self-sustaining. What really mystified him, although he wouldn't have embarrassed Shamer by bringing his attention to it, was why Sisera coveted a simple tanner's daughter.

When Shamer returned, his children were waiting. "Gather your things," he told them.

"But why must we go away, father? It isn't fair!"

"We must seek the hand of Yahweh in this, Deborah. It doesn't please me to send the flower of my heart away! But if it brings you to safety, then I must be content."

After a night in which her heart seemed to weigh like a stone within her breast, Deborah arose and awakened her father and brother. Gemalli slipped outside to feed the ass that Lapidoth had sent over for their possessions.

In silence Deborah and Shamer munched cold biscuits and dried strips of mutton, and washed them down with goat's milk. She mustered a smile. "I feel as if we were eating a Passover meal."

Shamer nodded morosely. "This morning Yahweh is not leading us out of bondage but away from our home."

"Oh, father, as thou hast said, surely we must seek the hand of Yahweh in this. If he takes us from our home, he is leading us somewhere." Shamer's great arm wrapped around his daughter.

Gemalli returned. "The ass is loaded. I grained her too. She'll be ready when we are." He took the food offered by his sister and smiled at her. "It reminds me of—"

"Passover. Yes. All of us," answered Shamer. "Are you sure the pack is secure, son?"

"Nothing to it."

"Then come."

Deborah cast a final glance around the room where she had grown up. The dear familiar hearth, the walls hung with leathers, the loft ladder, which she herself had repaired so many times. She stepped outside into the grayness. Dew clung to the prickly bushes beside the path. The little ass had finished the grain and was cropping on sparse grasses within reach. It was harvest season, and no rains were due for weeks. Deborah untethered the ass and fell into step beside her brother.

The question in her mind was when she would ever see her father again. She reached for Gemalli's hand.

Sounds of the caravan greeted them before they could see it: coarse shouts of drivers as they hoisted huge packs on unwilling beasts, squeals of outrage from camels who lacked the gentle forbearance of the donkeys, sounds of scuffle between man and beast, and the clip-clop of a soldier on horseback urging groups into line.

Shamer and his family pressed toward the head of the caravan. Suddenly a man swung down from a huge roan. Deborah could not keep her eyes off the soldier. He was a head taller than her menfolk, as big as one of the Philistines in the tales Shamer used to tell.

Gemalli poked her with an elbow. "Put your eyes back in your head."

"I saw him when the caravan came in," she whispered.

Brusquely Lapidoth acknowledged introductions. With a flash of recognition, he realized that the daughter of Shamer the tanner was indeed the tall young woman with the hair like fireweed he had noticed in the marketplace. She had the fierce, deep-set eyes of the hunter. At once he understood the passion of Sisera. What kind of woman gazed out at the world from within such a face? His glance flicked to Shamer. This feast of fire the issue of his loins?

If she was fearful at undertaking sudden flight, she did not show it. With a slight lift of her chin, she said, "My father is pleased that you have extended your protection to us. We will not be an encumbrance."

Lapidoth looked down at her with amusement. "That's good to know. You will be traveling with the metalsmith and his family. Shamer, you know them—the Kenites, Heber and Jael."

She saw his eyes go over their packing job.

"By your leave, one of my men will readjust your pack. We don't halt for lost stores."

As Lapidoth left, Deborah stole a sly glance at her brother. Gemalli looked away. Much to his chagrin, the soldier dumped the entire load on the ground and proceeded to repack it. In a matter of minutes the job was done. The soldier slapped the ass's rump and moved it down the line.

Wordlessly Shamer opened his arms to his children. They clung together. In a choked voice Shamer pronounced a blessing.

Deborah felt an overwhelming sense of being torn asunder. Without looking back she broke away and followed the soldier and her brother.

There were merchants or their factors from Damascus and Babylon and beyond; men with skins as dark as dung chips, or as pale as sour milk; men in fine silks, with strangely curved weapons in their girdles; Nubian slaves lounging among the pack animals; wealthy family clans, able to afford the protection of a commercial caravan. And everywhere, as distinct from the others as they were among themselves, roamed the band of mercenaries who served the lord Lapidoth.

Deborah had heard it whispered by some that they knew ways to kill a man that left not a mark, that they were fierce fighters who would as soon kill a babe in a mother's arms as a soldier on the field.

Ahead, the soldier leading their ass stopped. Deborah caught a glimpse of bright, patterned robes. That must be the Kenites. Her father had said only that they should not fear the Kenites. Though they had strange ways, they served Yahweh.

Despite her sorrow, Deborah's heart quickened. Yahweh would protect her, Gemalli was at her side, and they were beginning a journey through strange new lands. Eagerly she sought a glimpse of Lapidoth, anxious to begin.

7

By MIDMORNING the dew on the brush had dried and the freshness of the wind blew hot. There was no shade. The caravan followed the shore of Galilee south to the river, where a fringe of green followed the oxbow course of the Jordan. An occasional spearhead of green darted up a canyon.

For the most part, Lapidoth led the caravan above the belt of green. Everywhere Deborah looked, she saw one of his men on horseback, on the hills to the west or jogging near the riverbank, working the fringes of the caravan back and forth, back and forth.

Walking beside Jael, Deborah noticed the spring in Gemalli's step and in his speech, as he kept pace ahead of them with Heber the metalsmith. Since leaving Hammath, his spirits had brightened steadily.

"How is it you worship Yahweh? You are not Israelites," she heard her brother say.

"True," agreed Heber. "The Kenites live far to the south, in the Sinai. But metalworkers must follow their trade. Even as in your tannery, Gemalli, there is little enough work in one small town. We met Lapidoth, and since then found a steady business. We labor at every town, and are as free as birds the rest of the time."

"Free to get into mischief, you mean," Jael threw in. "Were it not for Lapidoth, husband, I would have chased thee out years ago!"

Heber turned and smiled back indulgently at his wife. "Lapidoth shared his god, Yahweh, with us. And now. . . ."

"And now we are children of Yahweh, too," Jael said. The linen robe she wore matched her husband's. The weaving was of an intricate geometric pattern of black on natural, alternating with broad bands of bright blue and burnt brick.

"It is a shame your father could not attend the Feast of Ingathering this year," remarked Heber.

"It is our first," said Gemalli. "What do tanners want with such meetings? Our father gives Yahweh's tithe to the priest in Hammath. He must live too, father says."

"I would not miss it!" said Heber with relish.

"He is like all men," Jael said to Deborah, loud enough for Heber's ears. "He pretends it is Yahweh he celebrates. Actually it is less in the words than in the wine that he doth rejoice."

"Hush, woman, or I will tether you with the goats."

"Sleeping with the goats might be a nice change. They smell sweeter."

Deborah burst into laughter. She looked anew, and saw a small, muscular person whose plain, rugged face verged on being homely. Jael's lively, expressive eyes seemed to say that if she thought at all about her looks, they certainly were too unimportant to bother about. She was perhaps a dozen years older then Deborah—nearly middle-aged. The swarthy skin and full, rounded cheeks against her boldly patterned caftan suggested a barely tamed primitiveness that tied Deborah's tongue.

Jael surprised her with a swift glance. "What is the matter? Fear you my bite?"

"Oh, no. You're just not like anybody I know in Hammath."

Jael grinned, exposing brilliantly white teeth. "Good." She erupted into laughter at Deborah's dismay. "Don't be afraid. You get used to this life."

"But where do you live?" Deborah stammered.

"Here."

"On a caravan? Your whole life?"

Jael laughed again. "Yes."

"Where do you go?"

Her face set squarely forward, Jael answered, "Beth-shan, Jericho, Shechem, Japho, Gaza, Raphia, Pelusium, across the river of Egypt."

The foreign names rolled off her tongue—names Deborah had never heard of. "Which city is yours?"

"All of them. Every city needs metalworkers. Our home is wherever we pitch our tent."

"Do you go to Canaanite cities?"

It was Jael's turn to be surprised. "Of course!"

"But they worship false gods. They still sacrifice human beings! Yahweh cannot abide them."

"We do not *love* them, Deborah, daughter of Shamer. We mend their pots. In the city of Pharaoh, where we buy our copper and tin, they don't ask if we worship the unknown god before they sell to us. Why should we ask them if they worship Baal or Ashtoreth before we mend their tools?"

Deborah caught her breath. "This is blasphemy!"

"How so?" Jael's bold eyes challenged her. "Yahweh protects us. We follow Moses' laws. We cheat no one."

"How can you speak of Yahweh when you are not even Israelite?"

"You Naphtalites are not exactly open-minded, are you? I speak of Yahweh because he is our God. He is a nomad, just as we."

Deborah's mind was a welter of confusion. This pagan, daring to speak so freely of her Yahweh! Yahweh, who dwelt in the winds of the mountaintops and spoke to her. She felt a stab of jealousy.

Jael seemed amused. "How old are you, Deborah?"

"Almost sixteen."

"Huh! Why did your father not get you married?"

"I'm not—I mean, I did not wish to marry."

"Oh."

"I—I do not feel ready to marry."

Jael shrugged. "What else is there? A woman's purpose is to bear sons to extend the line of her husband's forebears." Her eyes rested on the thin shoulders of her son, whose arm lay around the neck of one of the donkeys ahead. "Yahweh has given us only one son, Ehi. I bore two daughters, but they did not live." Jael looked away.

Deborah caught the glint of sunlight on a bronze-tipped spear carried by a soldier on horseback on a promontory ahead of them. Jael's words broke in.

"This is a good life, Deborah. We are received everywhere. Metalworkers are people of peace, welcomed by all. And for this, we do not fail to give blessings to Yahweh and to share our good fortune in our offerings."

Deborah found it hard to dislike Jael, pagan though she was. Her forthrightness was refreshing. She passionately hoped Yahweh would forgive her for mingling with heathens. Perhaps she would ask him not to be angry with these pagans for daring to claim him, the God of the Twelve Tribes, as their God too. She would remember to speak of it in her prayers.

Suddenly Jael called out sharply, "Ehi!"

"Hum?"

"Attend the animals. They'll be off the path snatching grass if you don't watch."

Ehi yawned and scooped up a handful of stones, which he delivered with unerring accuracy at the straying goats and sheep. The pack animals plodded on, heads bobbing up and down beneath the heavy loads.

Finally, ahead, Deborah saw tall palms signaling an oasis. Soon they were within the cooling lattice of its shade. Animals were bellowing for water while travelers unloaded food from easily accessible pouches in their packs. The animals were not unpacked, but were loosely tethered near a spring rising through the sand. In the center of the oasis was a well so ancient none remembered a time when it had not been there. The rocks around it appeared hewn from bedrock. Deborah fetched the packet of food she had assembled yesterday. Their meal consisted of dates, olives, fig cakes, and goat cheese. Jael insisted on adding bowls of clabbered milk to their fare.

The well water was deliciously sweet, better tasting to Deborah than the water of Hammath. As she refilled her waterskins, she spied Ehi squatting near the packs of his father's asses. "Hello, Ehi," she called.

He started, then returned her greeting. She saw that he was casting stones at a lizard. It appeared the lizard was injured and could not run away. "Aren't you going to eat?"

"Just going," he muttered. As he walked away from her, a dozen men on horseback passed by, riding out, and another contingent came in. Though it was the height of day, they still wore the heavy burnooses that helped their bodies retain moisture.

Gradually the noises of the caravan settled down and life became measurably slower. A gentle hum hovered in the air, as if bees and other insects had overtaken the slumbering universe to remind them of the pungent aliveness of Yahweh's land. Animals and men rested, and the earth throbbed in the sun.

When shadows began to inch out again, Lapidoth recalled them to line. Refreshed and cooled, Deborah and Gemalli took their places with Heber, Jael, and Ehi. The afternoon was long, but Deborah found each new horizon endlessly fascinating. She examined the faces of the soldiers who passed them. Some were thin faced and olive complexioned. Some were full lipped and dark as the lowly drivers. They rode their horses with conscious pride. Suddenly she realized she was hoping for a glimpse of Lapidoth. The broad-shouldered form, the burnt-wheat hair curling out from under his helmet, was unmistakable. But Lapidoth remained at a distance all afternoon.

Finally, when shadows from the western hills sent long fingers across the Jordan, the weary caravan turned away from the river into a steep-walled canyon, and followed a nearly dry wadi westward.

"Where are we now?" Deborah asked Jael.

"Coming to Beth-shan."

The streambed looked as if it spewed rocks instead of water—rocks so sharp the animals must be watched carefully lest they stumble and cut their feet. Occasionally, as a soldier galloped along the crest of the hill, a rock came bounding down the shallow foothills, ringing with a hollow *thock* as it fell.

The village of Beth-shan lay in a fertile, tropical valley watered by an outcropping of springs. The houses clustered like a string of beads around the edges of a broad, marshy clearing. Here the grasses were tall and sweet, and mighty oaks offered cool shade.

Lapidoth galloped to the crest of a knoll as the caravan filed into the field beside the city where they would camp for the night. As he contemplated a mountain pass beyond Beth-shan, worry traced a sweaty ridge on his brow. They had seen nothing of Canaanite soldiers on the journey from Hammath. He was confident his desert-wise scouts would have picked them up. But how many brigands were hiding in that tangle to the west?

Below him passed the Kenite family. His thoughts centered on the slender, striding form of Deborah. He felt a stirring in his loins. What sons she would bear! For the first time, Lapidoth thought of marriage. He would speak to her brother.

8

WHILE EHI AND GEMALLI tended the animals, Jael swiftly unrolled her tent. She had it up so quickly Deborah was astonished. Hands on hips, Jael cocked a look at Deborah. "Well? Waiting for Yahweh to do it?"

Deborah glanced down at the tent peg and mallet in her hands and the neat roll of tenting on the ground before her. Then she giggled. "I don't know what to do first."

"Foolish girl," said Jael, taking the mallet and peg from her. "That is what living in walled houses does for you."

Deborah stood by as, with a practiced toss, Jael began to lay out her tent. Timidly, she asked if she might prepare the meal for the five of them.

"Of course," said Jael promptly. "It will keep your eyes away from those runagates who have been parading before you all afternoon."

Swiftly, Deborah's tent rose beside the Kenites'. Deborah would sleep within, and Gemalli outside with Ehi. As Jael finished, townspeople from Beth-shan surged across the field.

Soon Heber and Jael were swamped with broken pots and plowshares, enough to busy them till light failed. Ehi had a fire going, and Heber was setting out iron ladles in which to heat metal, when Jael called to him. "Husband, look at this."

"What is it?"

"This woman is selling a lovely pendant. Buy it for me!"

Good-naturedly, Heber dropped his tools to inspect the pendant his wife fancied. It was a pretty one, inlaid with turquoise. Heber glanced at the vendor in apparent distaste. "It's poorly wrought. I can see why you want to rid yourself of it."

"What?" the seller shrieked.

Deborah watched with delight as Heber and the woman haggled

45

and finally agreed. Heber disappeared into the tent. Minutes passed. The seller moved from one foot to the other. Jael glanced from the woman to the tent. An uneasy frown creased her face. At last Heber returned, his face a peculiar gray. He croaked, "Our silver is gone."

Jael uttered a cry. "You must be mistaken, husband. Here." Shoving the pendant at the woman, she followed him inside. They returned empty-handed, frightened looks on their faces. It must have been all the money they carried, Deborah realized. She glanced at Ehi. The boy was engrossed in his work. Thieves on the caravan! Deborah's heart filled with outrage. Captain Lapidoth should be told right away.

Suiting action to thought, she whirled off in search of him. She found him sitting cross-legged with his men before a common trencher of food. At the sound of hearty laughter, her courage left, and she returned to the oak grove, to wait inconspicuously until he should finish.

Soon he came to her, halting a man's length away. "Did you wish something, daughter of Shamer?"

Deborah felt she could not have enough of looking at him. His skin was as tanned and smooth as oiled leather. His tunic bore sweat stains from a leather jerkin recently removed. Deborah's heart beat furiously.

"Well?"

"Well—well—I. . . ." she stammered. "Some silver is gone from the pack of Heber and Jael, they are even now looking for it. I thought you should know."

"Did Heber send you?"

"No, but I thought—"

"Don't you think I should wait for Heber to speak?"

"But some evil person has pilfered their silver!"

"It is not your affair, Deborah."

"But those men of yours. . . ."

Lapidoth scowled. It seemed to her that he was leaning over her, though in fact he had not moved.

Deborah's chin thrust up. "I mean, how *well* do you know them? They look like a pack of brigands!"

"That is exactly how I mean them to look. Wouldst rather be guarded by eunuchs?"

Deborah's face flamed. "I beg pardon, lord. You are right. It is none of my affair." Off she stalked, fuming. *Yahweh deliver me from the obnoxious boors thou hast put in my path!*

Lapidoth watched her eloquent retreat with amusement. Suddenly his attention was diverted by a loud exclamation from Ira, his lieutenant.

"Hah, you're like a cat! Here's a young hellion for you, Lapidoth. Be careful, he's stronger than he looks." Ira placed a boot on the young man's rear and shoved him in the dirt before Lapidoth. "I caught him sneaking around the horse lines."

The young man picked himself up and beat at the dust on his tunic. He was of medium height and slight build, as though he had not eaten too regularly of recent. His hair was the color of ripe dates and clustered in haphazard curls around his face and on the nape of his neck. His light olive skin was peppered with freckles. He was smooth shaven, in the manner of wealthy Canaanites.

"I beg to differ with your slave. I seek Lapidoth the Philistine, and if you are he, I will present myself. My name is Joash."

"Slave?" Ira cocked an eyebrow.

Hamid and a score of Lapidoth's men looked Joash over curiously. "By his accent, he's Canaanite, lord," Hamid said in a low voice. "A spy for King Sisera, I'll wager." Hamid had been everywhere in the world, had done many things, and had known women of every hue. He spoke several languages, and could distinguish between dialects of a score more.

Lapidoth glanced around the encampment. Twilight was nearly gone. Shadows under the oaks were dark enough to hide a dozen brigands. He motioned to Ira. His soldiers disappeared into the darkness.

Finally Lapidoth spoke to Joash, whose wary expression had not changed. "You are well-spoken, for a peasant. Peace be unto you," he added, noting the strain of the other.

Joash glanced at Ira and fingered his empty scabbard. "I want to speak to you."

"You're safe. Sit down." Lapidoth reached for his wineskin. He waited while his guest took a deep draught. Joash passed the skin to Hamid, seeming scarcely aware of what he was doing. "What's a Canaanite doing here?"

"I am Habiru!"

Lapidoth glanced at Hamid.

Hamid shrugged.

"A host of pardons, Joash, but who are the Habiru?"

"Just the poorest scum of the earth. Just those Sisera hates above all. We are Canaanites, but no better than slaves! My family owned lands from the time of Abram. Other kings demand a tenth. Not Sisera! Those who till must give all their harvest to Sisera. When he is pleased, which is not often, he returns enough for families to live on. To stay alive, we steal. For this we are his enemies."

"From whom do you steal?"

"Caravans," Hamid suggested. "Everybody has a reason to steal from caravans."

Joash turned on Hamid. "We have never stolen from Lapidoth's caravans!"

"Naturally," said Ira. "You wouldn't be alive to tell about it."

Lapidoth found himself admiring the young man's audacity. "Why have you come?" he repeated.

Joash seemed to hesitate. Then he blurted, "I am hunted in Canaan." In a sudden movement, he pulled at his right ear. "See you this bolt, Captain Lapidoth?" Joash fingered a large piece of metal riveted through his ear. It had been flattened on each side of the flesh and stamped with a design.

Hamid leaned in for a close look. "You're a royal slave, by the baals! I've seen that stamp before, Lapidoth. It's Sisera's."

"I escaped from Sisera a year ago. For a while I was safe. Then last week in Beth-shan two men recognized me." Now on his feet, Joash paced back and forth. The watchful Ira traced his movements with the tip of his spear. Joash seemed not to notice.

Lapidoth's eyes narrowed. "Interesting." *And rehearsed?* "And how did you become Sisera's slave?"

"That is my business."

"You are here. That makes it our business." The young man had a certain aristocratic bearing. "This is a merchant caravan. We are not at war with Sisera or anyone else."

"You pay for your men's services with silver. And you give protection. I have heard it. I would work for you as a free man!"

"What do you propose to do?"

Joash glanced at him in surprise. "Why, be a soldier, of course."

"Soldier!" Lapidoth grinned at Ira. "What do you think?"

"I think a soldier needs more meat on his bones."

"I can kill a man as well as the next!"

Lapidoth waved his hand. "No, no. I have plenty of soldiers. Do you have any other trade?"

Joash sighed. "Yes," he muttered.

"Well?"

"I was a scribe at court."

"A *scribe?*" roared Ira. "And now you want to play soldier?"

"I've lived a year by my wits!"

"A scribe?" Hamid's ears perked up. "I can use a scribe, Lapidoth."

Suddenly Ira rose and seized Joash's hands. "Tell me, scribe. How came you by these calluses?"

Joash wrenched his hands away. Lapidoth reached up for his hand. Reluctantly, Joash submitted. A heavy layer of calluses covered the man's palms.

"You were a scribe," he looked intently into the other's face. "Then Sisera put you at manual labor."

"Stone fitter."

"What?"

"Stone fitter!"

"And that is when he bored your ear?"

"Yes."

"What we have here, lord, is a jack-of-all-trades," joked Ira.

Joash threw Ira a murderous look. "I will say no more."

Lapidoth leaned back on his elbows and studied him. A scribe was a very valuable person. What had happened, that a scribe was thrown into slavery and reduced to the level of stone fitter?

"We will grant you protection to Shechem. A scribe can live well there."

Joash looked desperately at him. "But I—"

"You are not a soldier, Joash," said Lapidoth gently. "And the Israelites have no armies."

"I have heard of your armies."

"When Yahweh calls us, we go. After his battle, we go home. Yahweh does not need to surround himself with soldiers to be king." His words seemed to puzzle Joash. No matter. Lapidoth yawned. "Who knows? Maybe you will get a chance to fight before Shechem."

Joash's chest heaved. "It is well. Thank you for taking me in. I will not forget."

"Ira, find him a place to sleep."

"Do you think it's safe?" Ira grinned. At Lapidoth's scowl, he added hastily, "Yes, sir—come along, Habiru."

Lapidoth waited until the men left, then glanced at Hamid. "Well?"

"It is true there are tribes of Canaanites who call themselves Habiru. It is true they have a particularly violent hatred for the Canaanite kings. Some say they are merely brigands." Hamid paused to search his memory. "In the days before I met you, Lapidoth, I cannot say whether any of the men who raided caravans I traveled were Habiru. But then, brigands do not usually stop to pay their courtesies."

Lapidoth barked a mirthless laugh.

Hamid lingered by the fire. "Would it not be a huge joke on us, if we had invited the wolf to dine among the sheep? Good night, Lapidoth."

Alone, Lapidoth mused to himself: *Now what? Is he a spy for Sisera? A slave winning back his freedom, perhaps?* He grunted. Intrigue did not interest him. Still. . . . He would have Ira keep an eye on him.

The night was warm. Lapidoth was seized by an unfamiliar restlessness. When he realized why, he set off through the camp. At the banked fire of the Kenites, he found Deborah alone, staring into the embers.

"Good evening, mistress Deborah."

"Good evening, my lord." Deborah smiled, her earlier pique forgotten. "Is it not a beautiful night? On a night like this, I could run among the stars and never tire."

Lapidoth smiled. "So you are an adventuress at heart, mistress. I have need to speak with Gemalli."

"He has gone to speak to the stranger who came into camp this evening."

"Then I would speak with you."

Quickly Deborah rose and returned with a rug for him to sit upon. Lapidoth dropped to his haunches. She could smell the good odor of his body, feel the warmth of his presence. The brush of his beard threw off glints of copper and bright gold in the firelight.

"Deborah," he said gently, "you must tell me the whole story of your father's move to Taanach. Obviously, he believed it was the only way to protect you."

A delicate sliver of fear pierced her. "Is my father in danger?"
He scowled. "Do not answer a question with a question, woman!"
"I always question my father!"
"Before you answer his?"
Deborah's gaze dropped. "No, my lord. I will answer your question, though it shames me. Father is sending me away because I refused to accompany him to Taanach. It . . . it's a pagan city."
"Why go to Taanach at all?"
"I wish I knew! For years, things were the same. Now they are different. Perhaps Sisera's wrath is upon us because I spoke rudely to him."
"You spoke with Sisera? Was this before he ordered your family to Taanach?"
"Yes, lord. When I was wading in the Sea of Galilee."
Lapidoth had the sudden image of glistening wet calves before a man of Sisera's reputed appetites.
"He was seeking my father. Two days later, he sent word that father must go to Taanach."
"*Was* it an order?" Lapidoth persisted.
"Not exactly. But my father doesn't frighten easily, and I believe he was frightened—not for himself, but for us."
"Then what?"
Her hands flew together in a tight clasp. "I knew I must not go."
"Why?"
Deborah's tone grew agitated. "Yahweh told me."
Lapidoth felt laughter rising in him, but he cleared his throat to disguise it. "Did he tell you why?"
"He didn't *tell* me anything," she flared. "I just knew it. I do not know why. What is the matter? Now *you* must tell me!"
Lapidoth appeared to take her measure before answering. In a detached voice, he said, "I have heard that Sisera frequently covets young maidens. It is possible that he desires. . . ."
Her breath came in a sharp gasp. "Then my father *is* in danger!"
"Not necessarily. But Sisera might try threats upon him, to persuade you to join him."
"But my father is a free citizen!"
Not anymore, thought Lapidoth. His eyes lingered on the sharp planes of her face, softened by the fire. Her concern seemed only for her father. No matter. He, Lapidoth, would care for her. "Do not

fear for Shamer, Deborah. Men of skill and craftsmanship such as he are too valuable to toss away. Sisera will not destroy him for a woman, even a jewel such as you."

Deborah lowered her lashes, suddenly overcome with an unfamiliar shyness. "I . . . I praise Yahweh that I am here."

Lapidoth felt his blood sing. He would seek out Gemalli without delay.

9

THAT NIGHT, DEBORAH had a strange dream. She could not breathe without feeling the weight of Jael's silver upon her breast. In the morning she spoke to no one about it, but prepared the morning meal for Gemalli and Heber's family. She herself did not break the fast.

When everything was done, Deborah climbed a low hill above the campground. Through the oaks, she could see the fragile ribbon of the Jordan an hour's walk away. In the tall, brown grasses, she extended her arms and prayed to Yahweh about the meaning of the burden of silver upon her heart. She felt the fresh breeze tilt the cloak away from her hair. The odor of dried weeds rose in her nostrils. She heard the comforting thrum of insects.

Was this also the voice of Yahweh? Deborah felt the sun warm her back. Suddenly a total peace filled her. Yahweh had taken the burden.

After a while, she lifted her voice and sang a song often sung by the young villagers of Hammath, a song full of enthusiasm and life and praise to Yahweh. Then she turned and ran down the hill, springing over the rocks like a young roe.

"Jael!" she cried. "Jael!" She ran through the scattered tents. She found Jael, maul in hand, beating a lump of copper into a fine, thin sheet over a wooden block. Jael ceased pounding. Sweat shone on her brow. Her face was haggard. Deborah knew Jael had not slept last night.

Deborah plumped herself before the woman and announced, "This is what you must do to get your silver back. First, you must dedicate it to Yahweh. Then, when everyone has returned to camp this afternoon, you must heap ashes on your head and, in a loud voice, curse the thief. You must say that the silver was dedicated to Yahweh, and now the thief must share the curse with you because you cannot honor your dedication."

Jael stared at Deborah, the tools in her hands forgotten. "Art thou a prophetess, Deborah?"

"Who, me?" Deborah laughed. "Yahweh does not thunder at me from Sinai, but he speaks to my heart."

"Not to me he doesn't." Jael raised the maul to strike the copper again and paused. "I will do as you say, Deborah." She brought the maul down with such a blow it rent the thin plate. She swore at it. "I don't know why, but I will do it."

Meanwhile, in the marketplace of Beth-shan, Lapidoth found Gemalli examining the work of the resident tanner. Gemalli smiled at him. "Ho, Lapidoth. Perhaps Sisera knows best, after all, requiring my father in Taanach. Have you seen the quality of this tanning? Even the dye runs. See how pale the color is here, where somebody fell asleep on the job!" He grinned at Lapidoth. His words had been low, not meant for the ears of the tanner selling his wares.

"I wouldn't have known the difference, had you not pointed it out," confessed Lapidoth. "Gemalli, I must speak with you. Will you walk?"

"Certainly, captain."

Joash, Lapidoth noted, had already drummed up some business. Seated by the city gates, he was busily inscribing records of transport on tablets of wet clay. And the wiry form of Hamid, cloak flying (a bright Phoenician blue, of which he was very proud, since by the color one would know how expensive it was), seemed to be in many places at once, completing transactions for the goods of his masters in other cities.

When they had strolled out of earshot, Lapidoth said, "Gemalli, I wish to court Deborah. I will protect her with my life, if you grant my petition."

"But you are a Philistine! Our father would never marry her to a Philistine!"

"I am an Ephraimite."

"But I have heard you called—"

Lapidoth nodded. "Yes. My father married a Philistine, but I was circumcised by my father. My sons shall know no god but Yahweh!"

Gemalli laughed ruefully. "How I wish my father were here! How he has tried these past five years to betroth Deborah. She would have none of it. In my father's name, I accept you as a suitor for my sister; but even so, I doubt I can persuade Deborah of it!"

"Then I will," said Lapidoth.

"You would speak to her yourself?"

"Aye. Then I will know, before she speaks, how she regards me."

Gemalli sighed. "Yahweh be praised; but sometimes I wish he had seen fit to keep women at men's obedience, rather than allowing that they should marry whom they wished!"

Lapidoth bellowed a laugh. "That would take the spice from the dish, brother Gemalli."

An hour later, humming to himself, Lapidoth was bathing in a spring near the camp. Fresh clothes were laid nearby in the grass.

"Hah, Lapidoth! Here you are," called Hamid. "Why art thou bathing at this hour? Is there a heat in your head?"

Lapidoth only grinned as he climbed from the spring and with quick strokes brushed the water from his hard body.

Hamid unfastened his cloak and spread it carefully upon the ground. "Joash the Habiru is a fine scribe," he began as he sat down. "I had occasion to use his services today. More, he has the head for it. I would like to hire him, if you're willing to have a Canaanite of unknown background among us."

Lapidoth shrugged into a fresh tunic. He adjusted the girdle and dagger at his waist and picked up his cloak. "Do you think he is honest, Hamid?"

"I think he has had some sad experiences. I will learn more."

Lapidoth combed his beard with his fingers. "I have no objection, as long as you keep an eye on him."

"Good. Then I will speak to him." Hamid eyed the captain slyly. "I have some perfumed oil in my tent, lord Lapidoth. By all the gods of Babylon, a few drops on your face will draw women as honey does bees!"

Lapidoth's teeth flashed in a grin. "Am I so badly struck that it shows?"

"Aye. And I have a good idea who draws the fever that forces you to bathe in a cold spring in midafternoon."

Lapidoth burst into laughter.

"Captain Lapidoth!"

"Here!" His hand went casually to his dagger.

Through the shrubbery screening the spring came Joash. "I was looking all over camp for you."

"Well, you have found me. What is it?"

"Sisera's men, captain."

"I knew it!" Hamid interrupted. "The accursed dog has discovered I carry Sorgan's jewels!" It was out before he realized it. Now the fat was in the fire.

Lapidoth ignored the outburst. "Sisera's men, in Beth-shan?"

"They are not wearing his leathers, and they aren't the ones who were following me, but I'm sure I've seen them in Taanach," insisted Joash.

"How are they dressed?"

"As peasants. But by El Baal, they are too well fed to be peasants!"

"And their voices?"

"The three of them are in the marketplace. Not one has opened his mouth."

"Hmm. Hamid, do you carry any luxuries that would appeal to three peasants? Say, more of that oil that draws women like bees to honey?"

"What?" asked Joash, looking from one to the other.

"It might make them open their mouths." Hamid looked grim. "My lord, I will go for myself as well as for you. Within the hour I will know the ancestors for the last thousand years of every one of the pigs!"

As Hamid left in a flash of blue, Joash's eyes widened eagerly. "An oil that draws women?"

Lapidoth clapped his shoulder and gave him a shove. "Joash, aren't you tired enough from your day's labor?"

"Not too tired for that sort of labor!" Off he went with a jaunty swing.

Lapidoth found himself liking Joash the Habiru. Slowly he strolled back to the campground. And what if men of Taanach were in Beth-shan? What would it mean? He would hold judgment until he heard from Hamid.

10

In MIDAFTERNOON, as Heber was returning from Beth-shan, Jael put away the tools of her trade. As Heber drew near, her appearance struck him. "What are you doing in *that?*" Jael had donned the meanest of rags. Around her waist was tied a cord of rope. Ignoring her husband, Jael continued to smear her face and bare arms with cold ashes. Heber glanced uneasily at his son. Suddenly Jael planted herself before their tent. She began to beat upon her breast and wail loudly.

"Shush!" cried Heber. "You sound like a ewe in mating season!"

Jael only wailed louder. Her voice rang throughout camp. In round tones, she declared the history of the Kenite tribe and the genealogy which had brought her, wife of Heber, to declare herself of the people of Yahweh. And now her voice grew strident with sorrow. Someone had desecrated Yahweh's covenant by stealing all their silver, which had already been dedicated to Yahweh.

Murmurs of shock rippled through the community. For truly, to steal from one another was expressly forbidden since the time of Moses. And to steal dedicated silver! Gathering before the tent of the unfortunate, the people cast sidelong glances at fellows among them who had always looked sly and who probably were the culprits.

Jael's cries rose to Deborah, who had retreated upon the hill. Were it not so serious, she would have burst out laughing. Jael was throwing heart and soul into her role. Deborah felt someone at her elbow. She turned, and her heart gave a joyful lurch. Lapidoth smiled at her, and to her it seemed the sun was rising instead of setting.

He smelled as fragrant as a spice merchant. "So Jael has taken her problem to a higher authority," he said lightly.

"Truly," Deborah agreed, fascinated by the drama below.

Abruptly, Jael ceased wailing and disappeared within her tent, flinging the flap down behind. The crowd of the curious began to disperse. Heber tended to the ass, and Ehi went off with other lads to gather firewood.

Finally, Deborah spoke again. "By this will her silver be returned."

"Are you sure, now?" Lapidoth's voice held a gentle mockery, as if speaking to a child caught up in a spirit tale.

Deborah's eyes flashed imperiously. "Thus saith Yahweh!"

Lapidoth was stunned into silence. Shaking it off, he said in a low, intense tone, "Deborah, daughter of Shamer, I have asked Gemalli for permission to court thee."

Deborah whirled to face him. "You say this to me? Gemalli has not spoken to me!"

Lapidoth's big hands reached toward her in a placating gesture. "I know, I know. But thou art a strange one, Deborah. Maybe it is thy flame-colored hair. Things which are said are not heard by thee in the same manner as with others. I feared that if Gemalli spoke to you, you would discuss it in the manner of business among tanners. I would not enjoy being bandied about like the hide of a horse!"

Deborah broke into laughter. "Why, my lord Lapidoth! Is there a tiny crack in thy warrior's armor?"

He grinned. "I would know from you personally whether you will be my wife."

Tears rushed to her eyes. "In truth, no other man has filled my heart. I have seen thy face before me since I stood beside the woman of the street of Hammath and feared that you both mocked me."

Lapidoth seized her hands. "Mocked thee! If Bithia mocked thee, it was the mocking of a sparrow at an eagle! Be mine, Deborah."

"I am, Lapidoth."

He longed to kiss her, to crush her to him here on the hill, in view of all who cared to see. He dropped her hands. "I will try to reach your father for his blessing, so we may be married soon."

"I would take thee here and now, Lapidoth." Her voice trembled.

He laughed. "So would I, my Deborah, so would I!"

She reached for his hand. How big and firm, clasped between hers!

The hillside flamed in the last sunset and caught fire in her hair. Lapidoth's heart swelled with praise for Yahweh, who had entrusted to him this light among women!

Their rapture was rent by shrieks of joy from Jael. She had seen them and now ran up the rocky hill, elbows out, both hands holding her apron, as if carrying a weight therein.

She stood before them, tears streaking through the white ashes on her face. "My silver! Deborah, just as thou hast said!" She opened her apron, and several heavy lumps of silver rolled upon the ground. "To the glory of Yahweh shall a full tithe go! In Shechem, at the Feast of Ingathering, shall Yahweh be glorified by his servant Jael!"

Deborah and Lapidoth rejoiced with her. It was Lapidoth who finally asked, "Who has done this, Jael?"

Her joy blighted. "It was the son of mine own loins."

"Oh. . . ." Deborah's hand went out to her.

"So affrighted he became that he immediately repented."

Lapidoth was not surprised. Ehi was a lad of no ambition, who had sought out ass and camel drivers of unwholesome reputation, even as water seeks its own level. His heart filled with pity for the parents. Of one thing he was certain: sons of Lapidoth and Deborah would never be thieves!

Jael continued. "Perhaps this is a good thing. Perhaps Ehi has been brought to the branching of the way in order that the withered vine might be cut off. Deborah, will you come and speak with Ehi? Yahweh blesses you."

"Jael, you give too little credit to yourself. You have taken the words of Yahweh to heart; therefore, it is thou who art blessed, even though thou art a pagan."

As Jael retrieved her silver, Deborah turned for a last glimpse of Lapidoth's face. A spirit of wonder passed between them. Deborah followed Jael back to camp.

In the dead of night, Lapidoth was awakened by very loud and drunken singing. He raised to an elbow, recognizing Hamid's nasal voice. His bellowing was enough to waken the spirits beneath the ground. Lapidoth reached over by the fire and tossed a dung chip at Hamid. "Hamid, you fool! Quiet down, before someone quiets you permanently!"

Hamid labored through another chorus, his voice dying as he navigated a path to Lapidoth's side. "Dear Captain Lapidoth!" he bellowed.

Lapidoth reached and gave Hamid's cloak a yank. Hamid fell at his side. Lapidoth waited for a report, but he heard only a snore. He gave Hamid a not-too-gentle cuff.

"Eh!"

"What happened? Did you find the Canaanites?"

Hamid groaned softly. "I am not cut out to . . ." he struggled to a sitting position, ". . . be a spy, Lapidoth. Factors drink after business, not before. What can I say? They are Canaanites." His chin thumped against his chest. His teeth clacked. Lapidoth sprang up and hauled him to his feet. "Wherer-r-r-r?"

Lapidoth's powerful arm had him around the waist; his feet were dragging the ground. Before his addled brain knew it, Hamid found himself sailing into the middle of a spring. "Oh! Oh!" he howled. "You didn't have to do that! My cloak! My beautiful cloak!" He crawled out of the spring, glaring at Lapidoth in fogged sobriety.

"Now can you talk?"

Hamid groaned. "I went into the square just before dusk. I did not find them until after the gates were locked. You don't know what trouble I had getting out again!"

"Yes, yes. . . ."

"They claimed to be escaped slaves, like Joash. But they had no rings in their ears. We traded insults about the Canaanites and the Philistines—begging your pardon on your beloved mother's ancestors, lord."

Lapidoth nodded impatiently.

"They said they had never seen such a well-armed caravan. They joked about our carrying Pharaoh's crown jewels."

"Were they alone?"

"Yes, lord. But they seemed to know many of those drinking nearby. They wanted to know if a tanner traveled with us."

"How did you answer?"

"Most eagerly, my lord. Anything to escape talk of jewels! Can you imagine what would happen to me if I were to lose the jewels being sent to Pharaoh?"

"Get on."

Hamid wiped his face with his sodden cloak. "They said they had need of a tanner, and they had heard a good one traveled with us. They wanted to know if the red-haired woman still traveled with him. I told them yes. Oh!" With a howl, Hamid flung himself away from Lapidoth. "Oh! I am as foolish as a goat. I have the brain of an ass!"

Lapidoth clasped his friend's shoulder and shook him firmly. "Do not berate yourself. To know is to be warned. Go and sleep. It will be dawn in a few hours."

Mumbling sorrowfully to himself, and with elaborate shaking of his head, Hamid retreated to his sleeping mat, leaving Lapidoth with an entirely new feeling: a chilling, prickling fear. So Deborah's premonition, instinct—call it what you will—had been right. Something had warned her not to go to Taanach.

Clearly, Sisera had other ideas.

11

EHI GRUMBLED TO HIMSELF as he watered the pack animals. Since he had taken that cursed silver, his mother would not trust him with anything. Before, they shared every secret. He would not even have known his mother changed the color of Deborah's hair if he hadn't wondered about the light inside the tent that last morning at Beth-shan. Who cared whether or not she had red hair? He hated her. If she hadn't spied on him, she wouldn't have known about the silver. Now his mother didn't trust him. And that wasn't right. Sons were to be respected. They were worth a dozen girls. Didn't the men say, upon arising each morning, "Praise Yahweh for not making me a woman"? Pah! Probably the silver wasn't even for Yahweh! Probably Deborah had made that up, too.

Ehi's head sank against the ass's flank, his arms flung over its back. Suddenly he felt his wrists seized in a strong grip. An arm went about his neck, and a hand clapped roughly over his mouth.

"Not a peep, or I'll slit your throat," said a cold voice. The man holding his wrists released them. The man behind still gripped his neck. The one on the other side of the ass spoke. Though dressed like a peasant, his manner was commanding.

"We are looking for the red-haired woman. Tell us which one she is and you live."

Ehi's eyes shot around in terror. Lapidoth himself had brought Deborah to travel with his parents. If he told and Lapidoth found out, he would surely be killed.

The soldier seemed to read his thoughts. "They won't find out."

Ehi made up his mind. He nodded.

"Smart lad. Quick, now. Which one?"

"She dyed her hair brown."

The men exchanged looks. One of them nodded. "I knew that slimy little factor was a spy! But is she the one called Deborah, daughter of Shamer, tanner of Naphtali?"

"Yes. We got her at Hammath."

"What else? Quick!"

"She is traveling with my father."

"Good. Finish watering the animals, then find the woman Deborah. Tell her you want to see her alone."

Ehi was beginning to enjoy himself. "That will be easy."

"Take her out of camp. Not here. There." He pointed to some outcroppings of huge boulders.

"Is that all?"

"That is all you have to do."

"But I want to help, too."

The man snickered. "Don't like her much, do you?"

"I hate her!" Ehi cocked his head and looked from one man to the other. "What will you pay me?"

One of them reached for his knife.

Ehi stepped back. "No, I will do it. But let me go with you! I hate this caravan. I hate these old animals. I am quick—honest."

"You may be quick, but honest you are not. Now off!"

The other soldier stared after him. "He is a comely lad. There has not been a new young boy at Ashtoreth's temple for an age."

The first soldier threw his companion a look of disgust. "And who would be first at the temple, I wonder? Let's go."

When Ehi returned to camp, Deborah was plaiting leather, while Gemalli held the end. Two soldiers lounged near.

"What kept you?" snapped Jael.

Ehi threw his mother a smile of cool contempt. "I was thinking." He glanced over his shoulder. He wondered where the bandits were. He wouldn't tell on them, even if he could!

"Well, it is finished." Deborah worked the ends of the strands back into the rope.

Gemalli nodded. He took the leather rope and tested it. "No horse will slip that hobble. I'll give Lapidoth a look at it."

As Gemalli left, Ehi seized his chance. In a voice both hopeful and tremulous, he said, "Deborah?"

She smiled up at him.

"Can we take a walk?"

"Ehi, we have been walking all morning! Let Deborah rest."

"That's all right, Jael." She scrambled to her feet and adjusted her cloak. The soldiers also rose. Ehi glanced at them in dismay. He appealed mutely to Deborah. She threw an arm around his thin shoulders. "We won't go far," she promised the men. She smiled at the ridiculousness of it. What had made Lapidoth so suddenly cautious? They had left the vulnerable Plain of Jordan behind. The tribes of Israel dominated these hills. And soon they would be on the highland route, where, Lapidoth had explained, the seasonal streams flowed west instead of east, toward the Great Sea.

Ehi shrugged off Deborah's arm and plunged ahead.

She hurried after him. "This is far enough, Ehi. What did you want to talk about?"

Ehi glanced about. He pointed ahead. "Just to those rocks." Before Deborah could object, he headed toward boulders ringing a sandstone plateau. The plateau formed a natural corral that was hidden from camp.

Deborah paused at the edge of the corral. "I promised Captain Lapidoth to remain in sight."

"But you're with me. Don't be afraid." Calmly, Ehi walked to the center of the bald rock face and sat, extending his legs and crossing them. He leaned back, eyeing her.

Deborah studied the petulant face. Her eyes roamed the rocks, heard the hum of noonday noises behind her. She felt the hairs prickle at the back of her neck. "Oh, Ehi, let's go back!"

"First I've something to show you."

As Joash and Ira moved slowly up a rocky streambed, the clatter of their horses seemed unnaturally loud. They were riding one of the trails which paralleled the caravan road, a tiny goat path upon which a few men could keep abreast of a caravan and yet remain unseen. When they reached the ridge, Joash looked back upon the peaceful camp. Thoughts of the three Canaanites he had seen in Beth-shan preyed upon him. He would stake his life they were not far away.

He could see the captain gesturing to men coming off duty. Their voices and occasional laughter floated upward. And there was the family of the Kenites. Joash couldn't see Deborah. The two soldiers were on their feet, staring off to the north, a quarter turn ahead of where he and Ira sat the ridge.

Joash scanned the silent hills. "What are they looking at?"

Ira nudged his horse. "Let's take a look." Joash followed. He heard a low curse from Ira. Then he, too, spotted the three horses tethered beneath a jutting slab of sandstone.

"How did they get past us? We've got men all around the camp!"

"No matter. Get to Lapidoth. Quickly!"

Joash wheeled and clattered back the way they had come. *Why out here?* Raiders wouldn't strike a fully armed camp. Strike and run was their pattern. Unless—what had he overheard Ira tell his men? Something about Lapidoth's woman, Deborah, and he had also heard Sisera's name.

"Go!" Joash kicked the beast, nearly falling off as the horse plunged down the trail.

"Ehi, are you playing games with me?" Deborah laughed nervously.

Ehi's face seemed frozen in an idiotic smile. Suddenly two men stepped out from behind the rocks. Deborah backed a step and found another man behind her. Ehi hadn't moved.

"Do not worry, Deborah. We're just going to take you somewhere."

Suddenly one of the men brought Ehi to his feet with an arm-wrenching hold. A hand clapped over his mouth stifled his cry. "One sound, woman, and he dies."

"Ehi!" Despite her fear, Deborah turned on her attackers. "You are from Sisera! I shall not go with you."

"Think otherwise, peasant whore!" The man behind her reached around her waist.

Deborah whirled free. "No! Your blood will be upon these rocks if you do this. Go! Now!"

The man threw a frightened glance at the others. "Something's wrong. Something's here. Let's get out."

"Goat! You know what will happen if we go back without her." Roughly, the man pulled Ehi around and headed through the rocks in an oblique line away from camp. "Let's get to the horses."

"Captain Lapidoth! There are three horses. . . ." Joash sawed on the reins. The horse tucked his head and kicked out behind, and Joash sailed through the air.

Lapidoth sprang to his feet.

Suddenly shouts and war whoops split the air. "It's a raid! It's the Midianites!" At breakneck speed, raiders on camels whipped through the camp, brandishing long, curved swords. In an instant, the camp was a confusion of soldiers running for horses; factors trying to protect goods; goats and children and families zigzagging out of the way.

"To your horses!" Lapidoth roared. "Raid!" Within seconds they had joined the attack.

Joash scrambled to his feet. He saw Heber and Jael with their arms around each other. "Where's Deborah?"

Jael pointed off toward the rocks. "She's with Ehi."

"Gemalli just went after them!" said Heber. "There he is. Look, he's seen the raiders. He's coming back!"

"No!" cried Joash. "The other way!" He caught a horse and spurred toward Gemalli.

As they were being pushed along by their captors, Deborah heard the sounds of battle. Suddenly she broke away and raced for the rocks.

"No you don't!"

Hands pulled at her clothing. With one hand, she unclasped her heavy girdle and pivoted to whip it across the face of the man clutching her garments. His answer was a vicious yank. Deborah screamed as she fell into his arms. He stuffed her mouth with cloth.

"Don't hurt her!"

"She is possessed of devils. Give me a hand!"

Ehi's captor pushed him roughly aside and ran to pinion her arms. Ehi backed against a rock, forgotten, watching the struggle.

"Come on!"

Deborah went rigid. Cursing her, the man slapped her so hard she fell, semiconscious. As he dragged her past the boy, Deborah heard Ehi's frightened voice. "I'm coming too, Deborah." She opened her eyes.

"Is that what you thought?" said a raider. "A traitorous brat, spawning trouble in our midst?" He drove a knife through the boy's windpipe. With a soft hissing noise, Ehi fell slowly to earth. The three men raced toward the horses.

Each time Deborah stumbled, she was lifted bodily and pushed along. *Ehi. Ehi.* Her mind reeled. *Must Yahweh's punishment be so terrible?*

She did not know this Yahweh, who allowed evil to sprout in the mind of a child only to strike down the child, even as he repented. For surely Ehi had! Why had Ehi delivered her to the enemy?

Suddenly a shadow fell upon them. Deborah looked up. Ira was poised on an outcrop above them, his spear raised. With a tremendous thrust, he skewered the soldier behind Deborah. He dropped without a sound, driven through the breastbone. In the same instant, Gemalli and Joash came from behind. The soldier ahead of her drew his knife.

"Get back!" shouted Gemalli, careening up a slanting ledge above them. As he jumped, the Canaanite turned, blade held upward like a salute. It caught Gemalli in midair. Gemalli screamed and clutched his belly, crashing at Deborah's feet.

"No! No!" screamed Deborah. Joash leaped to the back of the third man, dagger in hand, an arm around his neck. The powerful raider caught Joash's arm and threw him against a boulder. Ira was on him in seconds. When the dust settled, the three raiders were dead.

In the sudden silence, they could hear the cries of Heber and Jael, who had reached the corral.

Slowly Joash got to his feet, holding his head. He looked around. "I guess I'm not a soldier."

Ira smiled grimly. "You'll do. Where's Lapidoth?"

"They struck the other side of the camp at the same time."

Ira turned his attention to the tableau at his feet. "Deborah."

Crouched in the dust, cradling her brother's head in her lap, Deborah looked up at Ira. Her hand moved protectively down Gemalli's belly. "There's not much blood, Ira." Tears streaked her face. "Maybe it didn't go in very far."

Ira knelt beside her. He had seen so many mortally wounded. Gemalli was dying.

Deborah read the truth in his eyes and wept.

Gemalli's eyes opened. He reached up and stroked her hair. "Deborah. Deborah. Lapidoth will care for thee. . . ."

"Oh, Gemalli, don't die! Yahweh! Yahweh!" She rocked back and forth.

Gemalli sighed with great effort. "It is . . . Yahweh's will. Praise . . . be to Yahweh."

In the other part of the camp, the raid was over as quickly as it began. To Lapidoth there was little doubt, once the men gathered together after the wounded had been cared for, that it had been a diversionary tactic for the three on horseback. With the exception of one, the camel raiders had escaped without any goods.

"Praised be the gods," said Hamid jubilantly, "for saving this worthless hide and my precious stores!"

Is life no more than stores on a camel's back? wondered Lapidoth. Before he had died, the raider had uttered a few words. By his accent, he was not Midianite. More, under his robe had been a leather tunic such as worn by Sisera's men. Fortunately, the man had died quickly of his wounds.

Gemalli lived through the night and into the morning. The bodies of the four dead soldiers were stripped and left where they had fallen, to be devoured by carrion, so their souls might never rest in peace. The body of young Ehi was embalmed with what spices and oils the caravan could muster and laid to rest under the rocks. Donning sackcloth, Heber and Jael went into mourning. Deborah remained beside Gemalli until the end. Bruised, aching, and exhausted, she refused to allow anyone but herself to prepare his body for burial.

When the thing had been accomplished, when the songs and prayers were done, when the incense had carried their prayers to heaven and only cold ashes remained, Deborah allowed Jael to lead her to rest. "Oh, the cruelty of Yahweh," mourned Jael. "To cut off the line of Heber, the only fruit of my loins."

"To some purpose have the lives of Ehi and Gemalli been taken," Deborah responded dully.

Of no purpose would it be to reveal the terrible truth of Ehi's treachery.

Oh, Yahweh, she said bitterly in her heart, *why hast thou also taken my sweet brother?*

It was a sad caravan that left the bloody watering hole and rejoined the caravan route. Slowly and watchfully, they wound through the rocky hills toward Shechem. The second morning out, Joash made his way to Deborah's side. Lapidoth had insisted that she now ride, and had given her a gentle ass. Joash had not observed her closely before. In spite of a bluish green bruise on her cheekbone, she was quite lovely, though in a sharp-featured way. It was the hollowness of her cheeks, he decided, that made her look more like a woman than a maid.

Deborah managed a smile at the slight figure on horseback. "I have not thanked thee for saving me, Joash. Thou art very brave. It was a battle that did not concern thee."

"I am sorry about your brother." He cast a sidelong glance at her. "What is it about you that makes everyone so. . . ." A red flush crept up his neck to his cheeks. "I don't mean that any maiden wouldn't . . . that the men wouldn't . . . that Sisera. . . ."

Deborah's face was unreadable, her body swaying in rhythm to the ass's steps. Joash quickly changed the subject. "Tell me about Shechem. Have you been there?"

"No. But it is a city of refuge."

"A what?"

"When our God gave us laws to guide our lives, he told Moses to set aside cities of refuge throughout our land. In these cities, it is forbidden to give up an escaped slave to his former master."

"Forbidden!" Joash's voice went up a notch, then grew lightly cynical. "But what is the fate of a Habiru slave to an Israelite?"

Deborah searched his face. "Thou art a man like other men, Joash. Thou shalt be free to dwell in our midst, where it pleases thee."

"There is a price on my head."

"Under the law, thou art a free man in Shechem," Deborah answered firmly.

"Then on to Shechem! Yahweh is *not* like other gods!"

"There is no other God," Deborah sniffed.

Joash smiled at the girl. "Come, Deborah. Even Sisera doesn't deny there are other gods!" Playfully, he slapped the ass's rump and moved on to engage Heber's attention.

In a moment, Lapidoth rode up beside her. "Art thou tired, Deborah?"

"Nay, my lord. Not as tired as thou must be."

He brushed aside her concern, as though such tenderness embarrassed him. "What did the Habiru want?"

"We spoke of Yahweh, of Shechem. Now that he understands he will be safe there, he is eager to go."

Lapidoth's eyes narrowed. "Do you trust him?"

Deborah glanced up at him in surprise. "Why, I never thought not to. Don't you?"

12

TRUST JOASH? PERHAPS. Nevertheless, Lapidoth knew he would feel easier if Joash's path did not cross Deborah's again until they were safely in Shechem. Thus, as the following day dawned, Joash and five soldiers headed for the village of Shiloh. They led two asses carrying a cart that Lapidoth had had made for his father in Babylon, and gifts for his mother.

Lapidoth's bearded face creased in a grim smile as he watched them go.

Ira glanced curiously at him. "You look like a desert rat at a watering hole full of honey."

With a laugh, Lapidoth clapped Ira's shoulder. "Let's get moving."

An hour later, he noticed Deborah walking with Jael behind their stock. Jael carried a long stick with which she occasionally prodded the beasts. Lapidoth trotted up beside them.

"Methinks I like thee not with brown hair, Deborah," he said by way of greeting. The faces turned up to his wore identical patterns of sorrow.

Deborah smiled slightly. "Hair is of no import."

He said in a low voice, "When it crowns thee like a torch of fire?"

"Thou should have been a poet, Lapidoth."

"Hah! Can you ride, Deborah?"

"A horse? I have never been upon a horse."

" 'Tis time you learned, then." Signaling one of his men, Lapidoth requisitioned his horse and helped her mount. "Keep a tight rein, thus, hold it thus in your fingers, grip tightly with your knees, and you will be fine."

In spite of her grief, the feel of the huge beast under her, the gentle forward-rocking motion, so unlike the jouncing of the ass, pleased her. She leaned forward and stroked the arching neck.

"Truly they are noble beasts, Lapidoth!"

"Aye. Perhaps that is why Joshua warned against them."

"He did?"

"He feared the love of horses could prove so strong it would wean men's affections from Yahweh."

"How silly!"

"Nay. Any possession which becomes dearer than Yahweh is dangerous. He will have no one and nothing before him." Lapidoth threw her a passionate glance. "That is why I am so afraid for thee, Deborah. I love thee more than life itself!"

They reined in a little out of earshot. "Oh, Lapidoth, I have no one but thee, now. I long to lie in thine arms, to tell thee the things in the night that frighten me. Dreams . . . to know thee, Lapidoth."

Lapidoth marveled at the boldness of her words, for the eyes meeting his were without cunning. He felt the heat of his body swirl up and create a buzzing in his ears. He glanced around the hills, settled on a spot not too far away, which appeared to offer discreet shade, a cooling spring, perhaps. . . . No! Could he take Deborah like a harlot? Could he dishonor the woman he loved? *There is no dishonor in love,* he told himself. The decision was not his, for Ira rode up with a stranger in his wake.

With a respectful nod to Deborah, Ira said, "There are some travelers ahead who want to join us until—"

"Are you the master of this caravan?" the stranger interrupted. "Here, I will talk for myself."

Ahead, Lapidoth could see a forlorn little band of women, men, and children waiting, plus a few sheep and goats and a string of five heavily laden asses.

"I am Mamre, chief elder of Not. Our village is an hour away." Mamre waved a fat finger at a remote path to the west. Deborah noticed several rings sparkling on his pudgy fingers.

"By your gracious leave, kind lord, we will travel with you to Shechem." His eyes flickered over Deborah and her horse. "My servant made the trip on foot many days ago to hire bodyguards for the journey." Mamre patted his sweating face with a corner of his headcloth. "But the imbecile paid the wretches in advance, and they never showed up. And you know about the raids. I can't risk my fairest jewels to their mercies." His voice rising at the end of his speech, he bestowed smiles on the two women, apparently his wives, whom they were now approaching. "I told them Yahweh would be just as satisfied if I attended Ingathering myself. But no. They insist upon putting me out. Between you and me," Mamre poked an elbow toward Lapidoth in a gesture of camaraderie that repelled Lapidoth, "they only want to visit the marketplace and finger the wares brought by the caravans."

Mamre stopped to catch his breath, and Lapidoth took the breach. "You are welcome to join us, Mamre, elder of Not. By your leave."

But this time the fat hand reached up and engaged his arm. Mamre gouged his heels into the poor beast under him, to keep him in step with the horses. His family aligned themselves behind as best they could, fitting into the caravan as it passed them.

Deborah, on Lapidoth's other side, listened in fascination as the elder of Not went on. "I say this business of gathering the tribes together every year is a bunch of poppycock. After all, do not we each, in our own cities and towns, have a shrine to Yahweh? We could just as well celebrate Ingathering at home."

"There is only one Ark of the Covenant," Lapidoth responded. "At Shechem."

Mamre shrugged. "Can't have everything. Travel is becoming nearly impossible. You fellows, of course, don't have to worry. If the tribal confederation really wants to do something, it should make travel safe between towns. A decent man can't walk about in safety anymore! Where is Yahweh's help today, I wonder?"

"He brought us to our land."

"This land! It's useless even to plant. It isn't enough that we plow up nothing but stones, but one must be a mountain goat to farm. Surely Yahweh meant us to dwell on the plains by the Great Sea. Anything will grow there."

"I doubt the Canaanites would be willing to give up their fields so you may plant them," said Lapidoth dryly.

"Answer me this, caravan master: Why do the Canaanites still dwell in the cities of the plains while Yahweh's chosen grub in the hills? Why do we eat only barley, which is fit fodder for beasts, while the pagans feast on wheat?"

That's blasphemy! thought Deborah furiously. *Yahweh will surely strike him dead!*

"Why, already this year, my servants, the clumsy fools," he flicked a ringed finger at the hapless fellow trotting beside his ass's head, "have broken three plows in the stony fields. It wouldn't surprise me if what I heard was true," he finished.

"What is that?" asked Lapidoth, with a glance at Deborah.

"Yahweh has no power in the land of Canaan."

"Oooh!" said Deborah. "Thou art a fool! Yahweh can blow thee away like dust for such talk!"

"Deborah!" Lapidoth scowled at her.

Mamre appeared indignant, as if to say, Who is this female? Glancing at Lapidoth, he changed his expression. "I still say he's only a wilderness god. Look who has the best land. We would do well to remember *that* when we are sacrificing our wealth to the gods."

Lapidoth halted, forcing those behind to make a path around him. "Mamre," he said softly, "I would be happy to deliver you and all your household to the Canaanites at Taanach, so that you may sacrifice to El Baal in person."

Mamre blanched. "I—I was just telling you what they all say these days!"

"Get hence from my sight." Lapidoth led Deborah away from the astonished elder of Not.

"Watch where you are going, fool!" they heard him say, and then they heard a yelp as he struck his servant. "Know you not this is a holy pilgrimage, dung gatherer? So make haste, before I peel the hide off you!"

As the elder of Not was joining Lapidoth's caravan, a similar caravan from Judah was moving north through the tribal lands of Ephraim. On it were Elimelech and Naomi and their two half-grown boys, who had a comfortable home in Bethlehem. There had been a drought in the south country, and Elimelech was worried that the tithe which he planned for Yahweh at Ingathering was not enough. He and Naomi had been arguing about it since they started.

"What do you mean, not enough, my lord?" she had demanded. "Everyone knows there has been a drought, and we've got to save something for our boys. We are only lucky that the raiders have spared our fields this year."

As if the drought had left anything worth raiding, thought Elimelech. *Still, the others might wonder that we are giving so little.* He glanced behind them at Boaz the grain dealer, reputed to have shared his fortunes equally with Yahweh for years.

"That's all right for him, he's rich," muttered Naomi, seeing the direction of her husband's gaze.

As they passed Shiloh, other pilgrims added their numbers to the caravan, for from every tribe they were coming forth to honor Yahweh. Among the newcomers was a strong-looking woman, with the mien of a Philistine warrior, striding at the head of a creaking new oxcart, wherein sat a man on cushions. Around him in the cart were many pottery vessels laid in straw, with decorations painted and etched upon them, the like of which Naomi had never seen.

At the noon rest stop, Naomi nagged Elimelech to seek them out. In the shade of a goat-hair curtain tied back to poles, they found the couple settled on cushions. Nearby lounged several soldiers, who appeared to be an escort.

"Peace be with you," Elimelech said.

"Yahweh be with you," responded the man.

"I am Elimelech, a farmer. We are from Bethlehem, in Judah."

"I am Dimon the Ephraimite," responded the man, who Elimelech could see was crippled.

"I see you have brought along your own soldiers for protection."

"My son sent them from Shechem to escort us to Ingathering," Dimon acknowledged proudly.

"Who is your son?" Elimelech inquired courteously.

"Captain Lapidoth, the caravan master."

Elimelech felt Naomi's fingers pinch the flesh over his back ribs. "My wife, Naomi, begs to be presented," he apologized. "She has been admiring your wares."

"My wife makes them. This is she, Dorcas." The warriorlike woman smiled—a hearty smile with a direct gaze that took Naomi aback.

Naomi stammered something about the pottery, and the woman answered in a strong accent which confirmed for Naomi that she was a foreigner.

"My husband is the artisan. Without his skill, my pots would be nothing."

Dimon gave Dorcas' hand an affectionate squeeze. "All the decorating in the world can't disguise a poorly made pot."

Naomi agreed. "Do you sell your pots on caravan?"

"Oh, no. Travel is hard on my husband."

"Pah! 'Tis not, woman. I at least am going to Shechem for the Feast of Ingathering. And, if my wife sells a few pots while we are there, Yahweh be praised!"

This time Naomi laughed aloud. She liked this mismated pair, who so obviously cared for each other. When the caravan began to move again, the families of Elimelech and Dimon traveled together. Although, Naomi didn't think much of a son who would go off and leave a crippled father. Her sons, she was sure, would never leave her. "It must be terrible to be without children in old age," she said slowly to Dorcas. Then quickly she realized the import of her words and apologized. "I was not thinking of you, but of myself. I confess I have always had a fear of being left alone when I am too ancient to care for myself."

"What you fear is having no one around to boss," said Elimelech, only partly in jest.

"But we are not alone," said Dimon. "Yahweh fills our days. We have no time for such worry."

"Well, I worry," declared Naomi. "I worry about my sons. What if the women my husband chooses for them should prove base?"

Dorcas laughed. "That is in the hands of the gods."

"Of Yahweh," corrected Dimon. The look of irritation that passed between them was not lost on Naomi.

"Yahweh takes care of those who take care of themselves," Naomi said slyly.

13

NEAR THE END OF DAY, Lapidoth's caravan emerged from the depths of Wadi al Fariah into a fine, sweeping valley of harvested fields marked with outcroppings of limestone. Limestone caves overlooked the valley. At the center rose the imposing walls of Shechem.

Lapidoth left Deborah's side only to issue instructions about the quartering of the caravan. In a city the size of Shechem, they would all rest within protective walls that night.

Nestled near the southern border of Manasseh in the hill country of Canaan, Shechem was a crossroads of culture. It possessed a thriving Israelite population though the Israelites had never conquered it. Long before the Israelites, Shechem had been occupied by the Philistines. They in turn were driven out by the Canaanites, but left their remnant. Shechem remained on the fringe of Canaanite strength, far from the centers of power located along the better and faster caravan route that followed the coast of the Great Sea.

Left in isolated peace, the motley peoples of Shechem had flourished. Not in all the generations before them had the Israelites sunk roots and called a land their own. But as they came to regard Shechem as theirs, numbers of them gradually left their flocks to abide in the city.

As the years passed and the community of Israelites grew strong, the Ark of the Covenant was carried there, a temple built, and a host of Levitical priests came to serve.

Of all the tribes, only the Levites were landless. Moses had decreed they should forever be keepers of the Ark and so keepers of the faith. Wherever they dwelled, all other tribes would supply their wants.

As the caravan drew close to the city, Lapidoth pointed out to Deborah the twin peaks of Mount Ebal and Mount Gerizim. Ancient cylindrical watchtowers dotted their heights, manned through

the centuries by Philistines, Canaanites, and now Israelites. "Here
the Samaritans claim Yahweh put Adam and Eve in the Garden of
Eden. But Hamid swears Eden is in Damascus," he added with a
laugh.

"And over there—up on Mount Gerizim—is where Abram
brought Isaac to sacrifice to Yahweh. Then Yahweh himself, knowing that Abram was his servant in all things, provided a young ram
for the sacrifice and blessed Abram and Isaac."

"How many times my father has told me the story," exclaimed
Deborah. "Now to think I am actually here! And did Abram raise
the stone altar that I see?"

"No, it was Joshua. And in a few days, you will see both of these
mounts covered with people."

Deborah had heard of the tribal confederation, but never heeded.
She knew that each year at harvest, cities of every tribe sent repre-
sentatives—all who wanted to go—to meet at the central shrine of
Yahweh to worship and receive his blessing. Though her father had
never gone, the elders and priest of Hammath attended faithfully.

"To be at the tent of meeting! To be in the presence of the Ark
of the Covenant!" A new excitement filled Deborah's heart, as
though Yahweh himself awaited her. "I shall go, Lapidoth!"

He laughed. "Only the priests are allowed into the sacred presence, dearest."

"Why?" she demanded. "Does not Yahweh speak to us all?"

Lapidoth grew suddenly serious. "Then he speaks to thee still,
Deborah?"

"Yes."

"Of what?"

"Everything he wishes to be on my heart."

"Just as he told thee not to go to Taanach?"

"Yes."

"And who had Jael's silver."

"Not who had it: how to get it back."

Lapidoth said nothing, but he reached across for her hand and
held it a moment before urging his horse forward.

The wooden gates of the city loomed before them. As they passed
through the immense portal, Lapidoth stole a glance at Deborah. A
far cry from the sleepy market of Hammath! Though not so large
and varied as the marketplaces of Babylon, it compared well to

other markets in Canaan. Deborah seemed entranced.

Street vendors jostled one another in attempts to call attention to their wares, stray dogs barked while herders hustled small flocks through the crush crying, "Blemish free! Blemish free!"

As factors took over responsibility for goods of merchants they represented, Hamid was once more very vocal, flying about in his robe of Phoenician blue, giving orders, hailing acquaintances not seen for several months.

Lapidoth lifted Deborah down and gave the horses into Ira's care. "Come, let's walk." They followed the delicious aroma of freshly baked bread to a stall. He purchased a loaf to munch as they roamed among rows of palmetto baskets filled with barley and a small, hard, red grain the vendor called emmer. There were dried beans, clay jars filled with spicy olives packed in oil, tantalizing grapes, bound bundles of raw flax, textiles, fine woolens, and woven goat-hair mats. In wonder, Deborah ran her fingertips over a lyre with a sounding box of lapis lazuli inlaid with mosaics of shell, gold, and silver.

The marketplace was filled with Israelites from every tribe, whose tongues sounded strangely disparate. Deborah paused and cocked her head. One man's speech reminded her of Sisera. She questioned Lapidoth.

"Shechem has many Canaanite citizens," he told her. "Many are now Israelite, just as Jael and Heber are Israelite because they have accepted Yahweh and have become one with his chosen people."

"You cannot believe that!" said Deborah.

Lapidoth glanced at her in surprise. This was not the place to discuss it. Suddenly he heard a high, musical voice calling his name. Its owner was a dark-skinned girl with eyes like ripe olives. They gleamed in soft playfulness. She wore fine golden bracelets, and on the hem of her skirt jingled coins.

"Who is she," asked Deborah, "a princess?"

But Lapidoth had a sudden fit of coughing, which lasted until they were well past the woman.

From a wine shop two men watched the incoming caravan. Suddenly one leaned forward. "Did you see that?"

"What?"

"A horse with the trappings of Sisera. Look, there goes another

. . . and another. And look who's riding the last—Joash! El Baal strike me, if it isn't! Hail, Joash!"

Joash turned on the saddle rug and appeared to scan the throngs beside the square. Suddenly he started. He had seen them. They saw him speak to others—soldiers and a tall woman and a man reclining in a cart. Joash dismounted, leading his horse to the wine shop.

"Well! You left Taanach without a fare-thee-well! The rock quarry not to your liking?"

Joash eyed the pair warily. Shechem was a city of refuge, he reminded himself, keeping at bay a sudden well of fear. What if these two had added bounty hunter to their list of unsavory occupations? Even at Taanach, in the days before his fall from favor at the palace, he had distrusted Gaius and Sacar as men too much in their own company, too little occupied, and too full of gossip. He knew beyond doubt that his whereabouts would soon be known to Sisera, plus the fact that he was in possession of three of the royal horses.

When Joash did not answer, Gaius added, "Is that your horse?"

"He is now."

"Fine stud."

"Sisera always did have an eye for the best," Sacar put in, eyeing Joash slyly. "I saw two more horses that looked like Sisera's. Didn't you, Gaius?"

Gaius smiled. "Are you now in the horse-trading business?"

"I work for Captain Lapidoth, master of a caravan."

"My, my, *my!*" Gaius nudged Sacar. "And is it a—ah—rich train?"

"Like others."

"Then worth plundering, hah?"

"I have people in my charge. Baal be with you."

Gaius scowled as Joash slipped once more into the stream of traffic. "I smell something afoot. Who hits caravans in the hills?"

"The Midianites," replied Sacar.

"Right. Now, would Sisera have sent men on his best horses, far from his realm of protection, merely to raid a caravan?"

"No?"

"I doubt it. Sacar, think you there is something here Sisera would buy?"

Sacar exposed a mouthful of bad teeth. A soft, greedy gleam entered his eyes.

A short distance away, Kanah, from his shop, was also observing the most recent arrivals. Kanah was a respected elder of Manasseh. He had been among the first to bring his clan to settle permanently in Shechem. A worthy patriarch, he saw wisdom in Joshua's words that Israelites might dwell among pagans in peace, be they watchful that their sons and daughters did not yoke themselves to the Baal by intermarrying with believers of the false gods.

Kanah practiced Moses' teachings of honesty and truth to all. Those who petitioned the elders at the north gate were eager for Kanah's ear, for he listened well, with no impatience, until the tale was done. Kanah did not intentionally sway other elders in the disposition of a case, but it was known that where Kanah sided, there usually went the decision. He was a man of few enemies, and in the course of years as a seller of woven goods made by his womenfolk, numbered among his friends Canaanites and Philistines too.

Moses had decreed that every year a tithe of all a man's earnings should go to Yahweh. Kanah had a love for human nature that did not cloud his judgment. Thus, when it came time for the tithing, he was careful to select the very best goods his shop had to offer and to carry them to the temple in sight of the Israelite elders and citizens. How easy it would be, he reasoned, to slip in imperfect goods. Seeing this, his friends might then also be tempted to hand off to Yahweh less than their best. So Kanah gave his best and rejoiced in the richness of Yahweh's blessing.

The days of Ingathering were nearly at hand. Not only Israelites but also all others who dwelled in Shechem had been busy for weeks. A holiday atmosphere pervaded the entire city.

Attracted by the opportunities to be had, great numbers of foreign vendors and hawkers, pickpockets and harlots, counterfeiters of gold and precious stones also descended upon the city, to tempt the unwary and greedy buyer.

At Kanah's shop, the bartering rate never changed. Boaz, the grain merchant of Bethlehem, a man whom Kanah had known and respected for years, came into view with the travelers from Judah. Kanah left his shop and walked out into the shade of the tent curtain.

"Boaz! Boaz, my friend!"

"Kanah! How is it with you? A joy to behold you again." Boaz left the procession to greet his friend.

Kanah nodded courteously to Elimelech and his wife, Naomi. Although Kanah would be reluctant to admit there were people he disliked, he had never cared for Naomi, for she wore a perpetual expression of discontent. The two boys, Mahlon and Chilion, though tall like their father, were pale, uncommunicative shadows of their mother. Kanah sighed. How often it was that a man like Elimelech was saddled to a family like that, whereas a perfect scoundrel might have a sainted family. Privately, Kanah thanked Yahweh for his blessings—not for the first time that morning.

Boaz was reaching for his wineskin. Kanah stayed his arm. "Oh, no, my friend; the honor is mine. Come and sit in the cool shade."

As Boaz was a shrewd businessman, Kanah had no doubt he had come ready to settle a few business arrangements in intervals when the religious nature of the pilgrimage would not occupy his attention.

Boaz beamed at him. Kanah's broad face glowed with health. "Truly, Kanah, Yahweh smiles on those he loves. You look as fit as a young bull!" he declared.

"Your eyes are blinded by affection," laughed Kanah. "I hope Yahweh has blessed you."

The habitual good humor of Boaz's face altered. "In truth, Kanah, the drought plagues us for a second year. All of Judah is dry. I intend to seek out those whose harvests were abundant. The elders of Bethlehem have empowered me to purchase additional grain."

Kanah's face grew thoughtful. "In order to increase our own harvest, some of us planted to the west, where the slopes level off into the plains."

"You did what? In Sisera's domain!"

Kanah made a gentle gesture. "Moses declared them for Manasseh, though our tribe has never been able to take them. However, we reasoned that Sisera's troops cannot be everywhere. An occasional band of Canaanites roamed near our fields, but they didn't disturb us. Yahweh sent rain, and we plowed and planted."

"Excellent!" cried Boaz. "And the harvest?"

"Came to naught. We plowed and planted, the Canaanites reaped and burned."

Boaz uttered a cry of dismay. "And they prey upon the caravans.

Travelers must keep to the byways." He drained his wine. "You are in no better straits than we."

"Not much. But while the house of Kanah eats, so shall the house of Boaz." The two friends embraced, and Boaz went forth to give his friends the disturbing news.

14

I KNOW IT'LL WORK, thought Joash. He had tethered the horse in the last decent patch of grass in the camping area and was currying him with sweeping strokes. *All it takes is—*

"Hail, Joash. I heard you were back." Hamid came up with quick steps.

Joash raised an arm in greeting. "Good barter?"

"Very. Not this," he added, slinging his pack down. "My weights. Merchants have new tricks every year. Some would help themselves along with their weights. Therefore, I carry my own."

"And what if the merchant declares his are true?"

"Then I say, 'Let us find another party. We will compare his weights with yours.' So far, no one has." Hamid spread his cloak on the ground and sat upon it, leaning against his pack. "I have just come from Lapidoth. We were discussing you. No offense, now!" he added as Joash stopped currying.

"And?"

"This: Lapidoth has no plans to hire you for the present; therefore, I speak. You are a quick scribe, and you have courage. I think merchants would not find it easy to intimidate you. Work for me, lad."

Joash felt the horse's warm rump quiver under his hand. He stared off, across the milling campground. "I have thought much while journeying to Shiloh," he said slowly. "Lapidoth's people rarely see him."

"But you have no people."

"I have parents, although it is not safe for me there as long as Sisera lives." Then, brusquely, "No, Hamid. The life of the caravan is not for me." He brushed more vigorously. "I can grow richer off the merchants here in Shechem."

"What? You would not rob *them?*"

Joash threw him a sensual grin. "Not at dagger point. In a few years, I shall be as powerful as the richest man in Shechem."

"Oh, me," groaned Hamid. "The man is desolate when Lapidoth refuses to hire him. Now he is bitten by delusions of power. How came you to this?"

"I reason thus." Joash dropped gracefully beside the wiry factor. "If you set great store by a gem, Hamid, do you set it on a hillside for all to see, and then leave it? Do you come back only in season, to admire and use it?"

"Lapidoth and Deborah, you mean?" Hamid nodded. "And you wish to take a wife?"

"Sometime," agreed Joash. "And to bring my parents out of Harosheth. But I will have a home to bring them to."

"Well." Hamid seemed to ponder this. Then abruptly he sprang to his feet. "When I am coming to Shechem, hot and tired, it will be good to think a friend awaits me with a cool drink under a shady olive tree." He leaned over for his cloak and shook out the shreds of weed and dust. "I know you will prosper, Joash. Good scribes are always in demand."

"Scribe?"

"Not a scribe?"

"By the baals, no!" Joash got to his feet. "Lapidoth has a protective army for the caravans. I propose such a force for Shechem."

"An army for the town? But who would pay?"

"He who has the most to lose—and to gain," said Joash confidently. "This is an open city, filled with brigands of every stripe, deserters from Sisera's army, men from Moab, Ammon, Philistia." Joash stopped and chewed on a weed stem. "Now, a man by the name of Kanah is head of the biggest clan in Shechem. He could gather the money from those who want protection. And that will not be any small number, I can tell you."

Hamid gazed at the young man in some wonder. "I know Kanah. He's in woven goods. And you think you will just seek him out and proceed to general an army?"

Joash laughed. "Well, perhaps not thus. But eventually, Hamid. Mark me. I shall organize it, and I shall hire only the best men, as Lapidoth has done."

Hamid thumbed his lip judiciously. "And think you not any will protest hiring an unbeliever to protect the children of Yahweh?"

"What is that to anyone? I do not follow Dagon of the Philistines, or Chemosh of the Moabites, or El Baal of Sisera, either. Each shall have his own—no matter. I, Joash, am my own destiny! I follow where *I* lead!"

"Best not let Deborah hear such talk!"

Joash smiled indulgently. "If it pleases her to go mooning that Yahweh whispers in her ear, what harm is there? As long as Lapidoth doesn't take her too seriously."

Hamid raised a hand and glanced about uneasily. "Some say she is truly Yahweh's prophetess."

Joash considered this, then dismissed it with a laugh. "So be it. Oh—one other thing." Joash flicked at the rivet in his ear. "I want rid of this."

"See Heber. I am not a metalsmith."

"Come, good Hamid. Cheer up. Let me buy you some wine. Later we will find some ladies!"

Joash did not need wine to feel in high spirits. Yet as he approached Heber's tent an hour later, he began to feel misgivings. Heber's fire crackled and spit. Several tools were resting with their ends propped in the blaze. Heber was stroking the gleaming blade of a dagger upon the surface of a fine-grained black rock.

Heber glanced up and nodded at Joash. "Already swamped with orders." He paused to sprinkle the black rock with a few drops of olive oil, then bent again to the rhythmic stroking.

Joash dropped to his haunches beside the metalsmith. He fingered the rivet in his ear. "Heber, can you get this out?"

Heber spared it no more than a glance. "I can beat it out. Of course, that would also beat your ear to a jelly." He grinned.

Joash returned the grin in a sickly fashion.

"Or we could slit your ear."

Joash drew a deep breath. "Then do it. I will wear it no more!"

With a sigh for all the work he had ahead, Heber glanced around, sighting Ira and Lapidoth. Beckoning them, he bade Joash sit upon the ground. Heber waggled a thumb at Joash as the men drew near. "He wants to be circumcised."

Joash threw his arms about his legs. "What?"

Heber laughed. "Give us a hand. He wants rid of the rivet."

Lapidoth glanced at Joash's ear, and clapped his shoulder encouragingly. "Good idea." The tip of a spear was already propped in the fire and beginning to glow. Casually he drew his dagger. "Ready, lad? Hold his head, Ira."

Ira pulled the hair away from the side of Joash's head. Joash stared into the fire, the muscles of his jaw working. Lapidoth placed the tip of his dagger at the hole from which dangled the rivet. Deftly he slit the ear. Joash flinched as the rivet rolled upon the ground. Blood guttered down his neck. Heber picked up the spear. As he brought the reddened tip closer, Joash could feel its heat and averted his eyes. Lapidoth pinioned his arms and Ira's grip tightened in his hair. Joash felt the hot, searing pain, and a scream burst from his lips. The odor of burning hair and sizzling flesh offended their nostrils.

Heber kneaded his rigid shoulders. "Jael has some ointment for the burn, Joash. You'll be good as new."

As evening encroached upon the dusty fields within the walls of Shechem, Lapidoth made his way to the tent of Dimon the Ephraimite. Hair still damp, wearing a soft tunic of fine linen caught in a girdle that was studded with stamped metal discs, he spoke tenderly to the woman absorbed in skinning a fruit.

"Mother."

At the sound of his voice, Dorcas dropped the knife. "Lapidoth!" she cried joyfully.

He swung her off her feet in a crushing embrace. Together they entered the tent. He leaned over and clasped the shoulders of the man who lay within. "My father. How goes it with thee?"

"Still trying to get your mother to stay put." Dimon broke into a grin. "She insisted on coming, too. Not that she gives a fig for Yahweh, but she says after religious feasts people always overbuy. So," Dimon swung a hand back toward the recesses of their tent, "in the cart you sent, she packed every pot we own. If she has her way, we won't have so much as a slop jar left!"

This was too much for Dorcas. "Except the pot I'll crack over your foolish head!"

Lapidoth chuckled. Instantly he felt as close to them as if they had last seen each other at breakfast, instead of half a year ago. "Mother, I brought thee a gift from Babylon."

"Perfume?"

"You know I cannot select perfumes. My nose is too used to goats and camels!"

Dorcas reached up to caress his face. "What, then?" she asked.

"A potter's wheel. I have never seen another like it. It spins around, driven by the feet, and both hands are free to work the clay as it turns upon a pedestal."

"In truth? Where is it? Oh, Lapidoth, what a wonderful thing!"

Lapidoth glowed with pleasure. "I'll unpack it in Shiloh. You'll have the rest of your days to play with it, mother." Lapidoth settled on a rug across from his father. His mother sat beside him and reached for his hand.

"Art still alone like the desert wolf, my son?" she asked.

"No. How did you know? I have found myself an incomparable woman. She has eyes like an eagle's and the courage of a lion."

"And claws, too?" asked his mother slyly.

"Aye, probably," he admitted. "I am taking her to wife."

"But Lapidoth, your father should—"

"I know, I know. There is no time." His voice grew boyish again, as he told them of Deborah. He spoke of the manner in which she had left Hammath, of the attack and her slain brother. When he had finished, his parents were silent.

His mother's eyes were troubled as she stared into the fire, remembering. "It is not easy to be uprooted from one's own land."

"Yahweh is with her. She did not have to leave her God behind, as you did, my flower," said Dimon.

"And what will she do, now that her brother is dead and her father in Sisera's capital?"

"After the celebration of the harvest, I will bring her home to you."

"Thy wife will be as welcome as a good rain, Lapidoth," said Dimon. "But what of her father? How will you secure his blessing?"

Lapidoth frowned. "I had thought to send word through friends. But I now believe any contact with her father will be dangerous for her. She will be safest when she is merely wife to Lapidoth the Ephraimite and dwelling with his parents. Let Sisera try to claim her then!"

His father, thoughtful, shifted on his pallet. "Tell me before

Yahweh, Lapidoth, is it only to protect this woman that you would marry her?"

"Nay, father. If I thought she belonged to another, it would drive me mad! She is for me. As surely as Yahweh is our king, Deborah was meant to be mine!" He sprang up. "With your permission, I will bring her to you."

He left his parents, to seek her out from the tent of the Kenites. From the hammering and banging, Heber and Jael evidently planned to work into the night. Lapidoth beckoned to Deborah. Eagerly, she scrambled to her feet and hurried beside him, not quite able to match his strides.

He took her arm. "I have spoken to my parents about thee. They want to meet you. We have no time for a proper wedding, dearest. With thy consent, we will marry here in Shechem. After the celebration of Ingathering, I will take you to the home of my parents, to dwell until my return."

"Oh, let me go with you, Lapidoth! Jael accompanies Heber; many of the women go on cara—"

He shook his head. "No. Not this time. I will return before planting season."

"Then find another means of livelihood!"

Lapidoth stopped.

"Oh, Lapidoth! A month ago I saw thee for the first time. I could not imagine that any man could make me ache and be glad at the same time. Now—to hear you speak of leaving me—I cannot bear it!"

Lapidoth's voice gentled. "Have you not learned, Deborah, that the import of time lies in how it is spent?"

They were now near the sheepfold. A night hush had fallen, seeming to gentle beast and man. Soft, modulated voices, speaking distinctive dialects, made little pockets in the silence. Lapidoth's arm encircled Deborah's waist and drew her close. His fingers plunged into her hair. What began as a gentle kiss soared into passion. Finally Lapidoth pulled away. "I confess, a long betrothal would be the death of me!"

"And thy parents are waiting," Deborah teased.

When Jael and Heber heard the news of the coming marriage, Jael grinned at her husband in wicked delight.

"I know that look, Jael. What pleases thee?"

"Deborah. 'Kenites are pagans,' " Jael mimicked. " 'How can you serve Yahweh, when you are Kenites?' "

"So?"

"Wait until she finds out about Lapidoth's mother."

During the days that the caravans traded and rested before the Feast of Ingathering, Lapidoth, son of Dimon the Ephraimite, and Deborah, daughter of Shamer of Naphtali, were married. For Deborah there was grieving for Gemalli and sadness in knowing her beloved father could not stand with her.

At Lapidoth's direction, Hamid had scoured the marketplace and haggled for the finest cloth and foods and wines to be found. Setting aside their grief for their son, Jael and Heber had become Deborah's surrogate family. Jael found and applied lotions to restore the natural color to Deborah's hair. She joined others in preparing a tent, thick with borrowed rugs and tassled cushions, for the wedding couple.

The day before the wedding was spent by the bridal couple in ritual purification, while friends of Lapidoth toasted with his wine and traded lewd jokes. For wasn't it a fine joke that Lapidoth, who had whored and drank too much from Babylon to Egypt, should find himself smitten by this mystic girl from Naphtali, who had only to look at him for his knees to turn to jelly and his voice to the squeak of adolescence?

15

ONE WEEK AFTER LAPIDOTH'S caravan entered Shechem, four Levite priests carried the Ark of the Covenant in procession through the streets, out the city gates, and up the rocky slope of Mount Gerizim, to the high place made holy by Yahweh's covenant with Abram and Isaac. Servants ran ahead to spread rugs for their masters. The Feast of Ingathering had begun.

By sheer numbers, clans within Manasseh dominated the field. Nearly surpassing them in richness and strength were the clans of their southern neighbor Ephraim. Tribesmen of Judah climbed the holy mountain, the clans girded together in pride and strength from the towns of Bethlehem and Hebron, with a bare few from the city of Jerusalem, which remained a Canaanite stronghold.

In lesser numbers came clans from the more distant tribes of Dan and Benjamin, of Asher and Gilead, of Issachar and of Deborah's own tribe, Naphtali. Ingathering was, in fact, a reunion, with acquaintance looking up acquaintance, with wives calculating how fared the fortunes of other wives.

The woman Naomi, from Bethlehem, admired the imposing figure of Lapidoth as he strode up the hill. Behind him came the pot mender from the caravan and two women. Naomi craned forward curiously for a glimpse of the woman Lapidoth had taken to wife. She seemed a very young woman, by her step, her head veil flipping tartly from side to side as she climbed. Naomi caught a glimpse of a lock of burnished red hair beneath the robin's-egg blue stuff of the veil.

So this was Deborah.

Lapidoth found a spot to sit. As Deborah reached her husband's side, her eyes caught Naomi's bold stare. Deborah's face lighted with a smile.

A brief, automatic smile touched Naomi's lips. In confusion, she busied herself with her sons. The smile of the young woman, coupled with the intentness of her gaze, disconcerted Naomi.

Elimelech touched her arm. "Well, what do you think, wife?
Lapidoth took her with no dowry, either."

"His poor parents."

"She is not your usual young maiden," said their kinsman Boaz.

"Are you saying she is not a maiden?" Naomi's eyes gleamed.

"Naomi!" Elimelech scolded.

"Not at all," said Boaz mildly. "I have heard her devotion to
Yahweh is singular, for one so young. The wonder is that she
married at all. It is a holy marriage. Mahlon and Chilion would do
well to take such wives."

"Humph. Then I suppose I shall have to meet her, so I shall know
what to look for."

Boaz disregarded her sarcasm. "You would do well, Naomi."

Naomi's gaze traveled again to Deborah. Boaz was right about
one thing: she was no ordinary girl. Well, she certainly wouldn't
want a girl like that for Mahlon or Chilion! Imagine living out your
days with someone who looked right into your soul. Naomi shivered, despite the brightness of the spring morning.

As the Ark of the Covenant was settled on its altar of unhewn
stone, the high priest led the people in songs of praise to Yahweh.
The mountains resounded with their strong voices. Then men of
each tribe brought forth pairs of sacrificial animals, to be slaughtered upon the altar. And even as their prayers rose to heaven upon
the smoke of the fires, the aroma of roasting meat filtered throughout the congregation. When the priests had blessed the sacrifice and
eaten of it, the remains were divided, that all might feast and praise
Yahweh for the harvests and, above all, for his great gift of the land
of Canaan.

For three days the feasting and rejoicing went on. Among the
celebrants were nomads who did not belong to the Twelve Tribes,
but who had chosen Israel's God to be their God. Even thus the
Kenites, Heber and Jael, worshiped in their sorrow with the children
of Israel.

Deborah was enraptured. Never had she seen so many worshipers
in one place. How pleased Yahweh must be, hearing thousands of
voices praise him! Seated upon the hillside with the Kenites and
Lapidoth by her side, her heart filled with joy. In the responses, her

voice rang out in strength and gratitude.

Suddenly she grew aware of Jael's eyes upon her. "You really do praise Yahweh for all that has happened, don't you? And yet he has caused you to leave your home and your father to dwell under Sisera. He has taken your brother from you, even as he took our son. How can you praise him for this?"

Deborah remembered how carefree had been the spirit of the metalsmith less than a month ago. "I can sing praise for Lapidoth."

"I cannot sing. I cannot thank Yahweh for this!"

"Then do not curse him for it, either, Jael. For Yahweh's purpose is hidden. We see only the tiny grain that he casts in our eye. I will pray for thee, Jael!"

Jael was astonished at the fierce love consuming the younger woman's face. Slowly Deborah turned and raised her head toward the altar where the priests stood. Her face, her body seemed completely absorbed in the rapture of Yahweh's felt presence. Jael found a tiny core of warmth beginning to grow in her heart. She turned from Deborah to the priest and listened.

"As Moses charged the people, saying, when you have passed over the Jordan, these shall stand upon Mount Gerizim to bless the people: Simeon, Levi, Judah, Issachar, Joseph, and Benjamin. And these shall stand upon Mount Ebal for the curse: Reuben, Gad, Asher, Zebulun, Dan, and Naphtali."

Jael could see the lips of many people moving, as they renewed the history of their people to themselves.

"Cursed be the man," cried the priest, "who makes a graven or molten image and sets it up in secret."

"Amen," thundered the crowd.

"Cursed be he who dishonors his father or his mother!"

"Amen!"

"Cursed be he who removes his neighbor's landmark."

"Amen. . . ."

When all the curses had been pronounced, the high priest raised his palms in blessing. "And if you obey the voice of the Lord your God, all these blessings shall come upon you. Blessed shall you be in the city, and blessed shall you be in the field."

"Amen!"

"Blessed shall be the fruit of your body, and the fruit of your ground, and the fruit of your beasts."

"Amen!"

"Blessed shall be your basket and your kneading trough. Blessed shall you be when you come in, and blessed shall you be when you go out."

"Amen. Amen. . . ."

Upon the fourth day, celebration and ritual gave way to business. By this time, all knew which tribal matters were to be considered, for at night hundreds of campfires had burned brightly, with much laughter and conviviality and exchange of gossip.

One by one, the problems that plagued the tribes were aired: the drought, the incessant raids, the powerlessness of their scattered tribes against better-armed adversaries.

"What is to be done?" cried Mamre, chief elder of Not, wringing his fat hands. "Nowhere can we plant our seeds where the raiders do not discover them!"

A man sitting cross-legged ahead of Deborah poked his neighbor. "I don't suppose he means the seed he scattered last night, eh?"

Jael sought Deborah's eye and giggled.

Before the leaders could address themselves to Mamre's plea, a dispute broke out among the people seated before the altar. Finally a man stood in the midst of them and claimed the right to speak. The sun haloed his white hair and lent dignity to his enormous girth. By his manner, he was a man of great import. "I am Kanah, elder of Shechem. Our complaint lies not with the invader from without, but from within. I speak of our neighboring tribe, the Ephraimites. Within the bounds of land given the tribe of Manasseh, Shechem is by far the largest and richest city. Caravans stop almost daily. We welcome all who come in peace.

"The Ephraimites have availed themselves of our good offices and now reside in Shechem in great numbers. Many of them are my friends. Nevertheless, the elders wish it said here that though the Ephraimites came with smiles upon their lips, there was larceny in their hearts. They set up their shops in competition with ours. They married their sons and daughters into families with much land. With the years, they have grown nearly as powerful as the Manassehites."

"If you can't retain your holdings, that's your problem," called out an Ephraimite.

"Moses did not tell us we should have to fight off our brothers to secure our inheritance!" Kanah reminded him.

Suddenly Deborah felt Lapidoth stir beside her. He stood and made his way to the high place. "I am Lapidoth the Ephraimite," his deep voice rang out. "No city is my home, for I am master of caravans. My soldiers have fought Midianite and Bedouin, Canaanite and brigands in our own hills. And I tell you one thing: Kanah is right to be concerned. The problems we face within are as dangerous to us as those without. Who is our most powerful enemy? King Sisera. And how does he wield such power? He combines under one headship all the city-states and lesser kings of Canaan. The force of Sisera is the force of all Canaan.

"Everywhere I travel, our cities feed upon their own problems without regard for their neighbors. To be sure, the Canaanites keep our cities apart from one another by their raids. Yet do the tribes act together? No. Ephraimite fights Manassehite, Benjamite fights Judahite. None comes to help the other. We must act as a people to aid all Israelites."

"But how?"

"If I knew that, I would be a prophet." Laughter rippled through the crowd. "I can only tell you what I see, and that is all I have to say."

"He is right," cried someone, as Lapidoth left the high place.

"We are a people. We need a king, like other peoples," cried another.

"Yea! Yea!" responded the crowd. "Yahweh should give us a king!"

16

"I AM . . .," PIPED HEBER THE KENITE. He was unused to being the center of attention. Happier for him to sit at the campfire while others told stories. If only Jael hadn't insisted! He cleared his throat. "I am Heber the Kenite. . . ."

As tradition demanded, he began with a recital of his family history, then related the events of the stolen silver and its recovery, and of the three soldiers who tried to abduct Ehi and Deborah. ". . . Our son fought with the strength of ten lions, but he was only half-grown, and these men slew him. I believe my son was sacrificed by Yahweh to protect this woman. Thus his eternal life is assured, and by his blood is Deborah spared.

"Since that time, she has spoken many times with the voice of an oracle. Captain Lapidoth has said he is no prophet. Yet it is said the Lord will raise up a prophet in time of crisis. Is not Deborah a prophetess? Is not Sisera after her because his own prophets have foretold something of her to him? Let us ask for divine guidance through her."

A delicious sense of excitement swept the listeners. The wife of Lapidoth, a new prophetess? Heads craned. Few had known of Lapidoth until he addressed them, and fewer still could recognize his wife.

Deborah heard Heber's words in stunned silence.

"But we do not know Deborah," Phurah, one of the lesser priests, was saying. "If she is a prophetess, what has she said that has come to pass? Yahweh is always pleased by righteous and virtuous women, but your silver might have been returned without Deborah's help. If Yahweh speaks to her," Phurah added, not unkindly, "we will know it."

The speaker's right passed to other men. Heber felt sweat running down his back as he sat again beside his wife, who followed him with rapt expression. "I am so proud of you, Heber, for what you have said is true! Our blessed son died a hero!"

Deborah stared at him. "What have you done?" she whispered. "I am no oracle!"

Lapidoth heard the fear in her voice, as she repeated to him, "I am no oracle! Yahweh does not speak to Israel through me. It is blasphemy! Oh, Lapidoth, let us go away from here!

"Why would he say that?" cried Deborah, when they were alone.

"Heber and Jael are still grieving for their son," said Lapidoth. "Perhaps 'tis easier to bear that he died in a noble cause."

"Oh, that Yahweh plays such jokes!"

"What do you mean?"

Deborah told him of Ehi's deception at the time of the attack on the caravan. "Oh, Lapidoth! I would this meeting were over and we could be as we were on the caravan."

Lapidoth smiled. "You still want to be a caravan wench?"

"Yes!"

Lapidoth grinned and kissed her. "Come. I promised my father a visit."

A short time later, Dorcas and Deborah were strolling through the marketplace. Dorcas seemed to shed years as she walked.

"Caring for Dimon must be a great burden to you, Dorcas," observed Deborah.

Dorcas straightened. "He is my husband."

"Aye. Dorcas, look!" Deborah picked up a heavy, golden fruit. "Hammath has no such fruit as this! Oh, and look!" Deborah held up a girdle of supple hide, studded with gems. "Isn't it magnificent?"

"It looks big enough to saddle a camel!"

"Oh, not for me. For Lapidoth. How much is it?" she inquired of the tradesman.

"For genuine chamois, five shekels' worth of silver."

"Five! But the leather is only goatskin!"

The tradesman cast rheumy eyes at the girl with the north-country accent. "Look, lady, how these gems sparkle. Now, who would put gems like these on goatskin? It is chamois."

"Indeed not. Two shekels."

The tradesman's eyes bulged in their watery sockets.

Suddenly Dorcas added her voice. "The father of my daughter-in-law is a tanner. Perhaps you should look again at the girdle."

"I am being robbed!" he cried. "Very well. It is a mean bargain. Take it. Take it, and leave my stall!"

As the two women walked away, Deborah stole a glance at Dorcas. Suddenly they pealed into laughter, and Deborah tucked the new girdle into the string bag looped over her arm.

"Lady! Lady!"

They turned. A little maid stood before them. She was veiled and draped very simply, and wore no jewelry. Deborah guessed her to be about thirteen. "Peace be with you."

The maid bowed. "Peace to thee. Are you Deborah the prophetess?"

Deborah shot a startled look at Dorcas. "I am Deborah, wife of Lapidoth," she answered.

"My mistress begs that you will wait upon her."

"Who is your mistress?" asked Dorcas.

"Hannah, wife of Raham the Canaanite."

"Tell your mistress we have no truck with Canaanites!"

"Wait." Deborah laid a gentle hand on her mother-in-law's arm. "May it not displease thee, Dorcas, to hear further what the maid has to say. Why does she wish to speak to me?" she asked the girl.

"I . . . I do not know," the maid stammered. "She has been unhappy for so long. Please, please say you will come."

"We are going to the well near the north gate. I will gladly wait upon her there."

When the maid left, Deborah cast a tentative glance at Dorcas. She was tight-lipped, her arms crossed against her breast. Deborah smiled at her. "Thank you, Dorcas. It is your love of your son that prompts you to be so protective. It is one of the things I love best about Lapidoth, too." As though nothing were wrong, Deborah slid her fingers through the tense arm of Dorcas. In silence, they began to stroll.

"Lapidoth will have his hands full," Dorcas burst out ruefully. Deborah squeezed her arm.

When the women reached the well, Deborah pulled on the wooden arm that brought up the leather water bucket. With her own cup, she dipped a cool draught for her mother-in-law.

"You are a strange young woman." Dorcas accepted the water.
"How is it you agree so readily to speak with an enemy?"

"No one is my enemy, save he be the enemy of Yahweh."

"You speak of Yahweh like a friend," Dorcas mused. Everyone
knew gods cared nothing for people. They were too intent upon
their own pleasures, capricious or malicious, according to their
moods. One feared the gods, placated them with sacrifices—but
who had one as a friend? Trust Lapidoth to get all this nonsense out
of her head before it went too far. Dorcas studied the girl as they
rested.

A nice girl, overly serious, but strong and capable. She wondered
fleetingly if her hips were wide enough to bear healthy children.
Well, by all the gods, to be with child was probably just what
Deborah needed to relieve the strange ideas she carried in her head
—before all that thinking made her infertile.

A chair approached, carried by four huge men with glistening
dark skin. Beside the curtained chair walked the young maid. Upon
seeing Deborah and Dorcas, she spoke a few words. A moment
later, the chair was set to rest beside them.

A soft, pale hand drew the veil aside. The woman who gazed at
them had once been very beautiful. Now she was neither old nor
young. Rather, she seemed to be a person who had borne some
tragedy that had stopped the aging process, and in place of aging,
decay was setting in. Thus, although her skin was soft and wrinkle
free, it had a sallow, sagging quality. And though the whites of her
eyes were pure milt blue, they were the eyes of a soul whose light
traveled vast distances to be seen at all.

Deborah rose. "My lady."

The woman's lips were full and sensuous. "You are Deborah?"

The words were spoken with such sadness that Deborah reached
for her hand. "I am Deborah. Tell me how I may help thee."

The woman looked fixedly at her as though neither Dorcas nor
the serving maid nor any of the bustling shoppers existed. "You are
so young. Pray sit with me."

"Don't you do it!" Dorcas, who had been glancing everywhere to
avoid the impression she was at all curious, suddenly leaned nose
to nose with Deborah.

"Be patient, mother." Deborah entered the canopied chair.

"I am Hannah, wife of Raham of Harosheth in the northern kingdom of Canaan. My maidservant, Aida, whom I love, has heard your name in the marketplace daily. She says you are a wise woman. Perhaps the gods brought me here to find you."

"The gods?"

Hannah didn't seem to hear her. "My husband is a wealthy man. He owns a large tract of the most fertile soil in Harosheth. Ten years ago, we had not even a servant. We raised vegetables and sold them in the marketplace; that was how we lived. I did not want our children to grow up with no future. Now many fathers sell their daughters to the priests of Ashtoreth. 'When there is no money for a dowry, is that not better?' they say. 'They are cared for; they have good food and beautiful clothing,' they say. That is what the priests say, their voices oiled and smooth. But we loved our child. Though only seven, she was already beautiful, with hair like a raven's wing and eyes that sparkled like a lark's song.

"Our son, who was then ten, toiled with his father, but he hated being a farmer. He was a sensitive boy, a dreamer. He begged me to persuade his father to apprentice him to one of the craft guilds in the city. Thus, after seven years, he could become a tradesman himself.

"It was true he had no talent as a farmer. It would not be losing a son as much as having one less mouth to feed. I did as my son asked. I could not deny him anything." Hannah appeared lost in thought. "Perhaps I dreamed he would come back to us rich and powerful after seven years and seven more, and that we could then afford a noble dowry for our daughter." The air grew stuffy as the sun burned upon the top of the canopy. Deborah listened on.

"Our son did well in the city and drew the notice of the king. It was then he invited us to visit. Ah, that we had never set foot in the city! And that the king had never set eyes upon our daughter! She was taken for his use, later to be sent to the temple. We were banished and have never heard since from our son or our daughter."

Seeing the tormented woman's face, Deborah found herself already praying. For were not all women alike in their love for their children?

"Deborah, I would give all we now possess to have my children again! It would not matter what has been done to them, or what they have been made to do!"

"My heart goes out to you, Hannah, wife of Raham, but I do not see how I can help."

"In my heart of hearts, I fear my children are lost to me forever. My gods are no comfort! I have sacrificed faithfully, but peace is denied me. You have brought peace to others; I have heard it. Tell me, Deborah, how can one have peace when one is at the mercy of gods and their wicked kings?"

"We have no king but Yahweh," Deborah said softly. "In Yahweh there is peace."

"And do his temples also claim the best and comeliest of the children?"

"The very thought is an abomination! Yahweh is father to us all!" Deborah saw pools of agony reflecting in the woman's eyes. In her mind's eye, she saw a sea gull beating upon the ground with broken wings. She took her hand again.

"Then . . . then will your Yahweh give me peace?"

"You are not one of Yahweh's children," Deborah said, gently. "Yahweh did not call the Canaanites. But I will pray for you to have peace, though I do not know if Yahweh will listen."

Hannah began to cry silently.

"This I can tell you. From Yahweh nothing is hidden. Though you are not one of his, he knows that you have repented of your covetousness, which you believe did cause the loss of your children. Though they may be gone, it is not right that you should suffer all your days. It was an evil act in an evil world that took them from you, and not evil in your heart that caused it."

A light flickered briefly in Hannah's eyes. "Oh, Deborah! That you can tell that!"

Deborah stepped out of the chair. She smiled encouragingly to the woman in the litter. "Empty your heart of all that feeds on thee, Hannah of Harosheth, and perhaps thou will see thy children again. Yahweh's peace be upon you." Deborah let the curtain drop.

Dorcas did not know whether to be indignant or merely amazed. "Do you realize you have been seen consorting with a Canaanite by everybody in Shechem? Wife of my son, what ails you?"

"In truth, Dorcas, I see no more evil in her than in thee!"

Dorcas gasped.

"Good Dorcas, how can she obtain the peace of Yahweh if she

knows him not? It is well with Yahweh that I do this," she concluded seriously.

"Well, young woman! I wonder just how well it will sit with Lapidoth! Let us return to camp."

"Yes, mother of Lapidoth." Deborah fell into step half a pace behind the formidable figure of Dorcas.

17

THAT NIGHT DEBORAH AWOKE SUDDENLY, within the circle of her husband's arms. Through a gap in the tent curtain she could see a vast stripe of stars glittering at her from their midnight home in heaven. She arose. Lapidoth's arms dropped away. Throwing on a cloak, she slipped out.

A strange aliveness tingled in the air. Perfume filled her lungs as she moved through the sleeping camp. Not an animal stirred. The night called her. She hurried, as Yahweh's love descended on her in dizzying ecstasy. In the midst of a small field of stubble she halted —the tents behind her, the sleeping town before her, the animals far to the side. Slowly she circled, arcing her arms and her face to drink in the mystery and the glory of Yahweh. Her heart pounded and filled with exceeding joy.

"I am here, Yahweh. I am Deborah!"

When again she grew aware of the passing night, faint lightning illumined the sky far to the south. Distant thunder vibrated over the land. She was not cold, but warm, alive to every stub of straw underfoot, aware of the lumps of earth, of the dew on the weeds, aware that the water in Jacob's well would be pure and clear, that everything in the clasp of this magical night had slept the sleep of enchantment. Praise moved her lips. Now she lowered her arms, looking curiously about the field. Gray peaks of tents and smudges of trees were becoming distinguishable. She saw with some surprise that fog hovered over the land. And, between her and the tents, at the edge of the field, stood a shadowy figure. She walked toward him.

Lapidoth held his arms out to her, and she went into them. Beneath his cloak, she moved her arms under his and held his chilled body close, warming it. "I shall speak to the tribes, before the Ark of the Covenant at Shiloh." She could feel him tense.

"But the Ark of the Covenant is here, at Shechem. It has never been at Shiloh. You must have misunderstood him."

Deborah hugged him. She loved him for that. He had not denied her union with Yahweh, only pointed out what seemed to be an inconsistency. "No, my dearest heart. Did Israel hear, when you spoke? They cried for an earthly king, not Yahweh. The ears of Israel are hardened against Yahweh.

"I shall speak to the people, but the priests will hear me not. When the Ark is in Shiloh, all will hear."

Lapidoth held his wife at arm's length. Around them, they could hear a faint baa from the goats and sheep, the clink of a dropped pot. Never had they been so close.

"I know Yahweh has given you to me, Deborah. But sometimes I am afraid for you."

"I am the gift of Yahweh. Greater than the gift is what is given in return."

Lapidoth did not understand his wife's words, but for the moment, clinging to her in a cloak of fog, he was content.

In the morning, Deborah told Jael and Heber that she would speak that day upon Mount Gerizim, to all who would listen. Then she disappeared into her tent.

Eagerly the Kenites sowed her words. Dorcas, tending an array of clay bowls and trinkets before her tent, received the news with tight lips. Those metalsmiths were certainly making hay while the sun shined. Dorcas would not have been surprised if they were secretly making idols of Deborah to peddle—especially after that shameless outburst by Heber yesterday up on the mountain. Dorcas's heart ached for her son. What would Lapidoth make of this new embarrassment?

She had not had an opportunity to tell her son of yesterday's folly with the woman of Canaan, but this new madness swept thought of it away. Had she been back in her girlhood home in Philistia, she would have sought the soothsayer. Unfortunately, the art of the soothsayer was forbidden by the god of her husband. But surely her son had married a madwoman!

Unaware of his mother's ire, Lapidoth had slipped away after Deborah slept and gone to the great stone temple. Phurah the priest met him inside the heavy cedar gates of the men's courtyard.

Phurah marked the change in him. "I thought marriage made a man's heart light, Lapidoth." Phurah gestured, and they sat upon a bench that was worn to a satin smoothness.

"It is about my wife I would consult you." Somberly, Lapidoth told the priest of Deborah's midnight vigil and her intent to address the assemblage on this, the last day of the confederation.

Phurah's calm voice broke in with an occasional question, as he probed tactfully into what Lapidoth knew of Deborah's past.

"She is not mad, I would swear! What say you?"

"Moses said by the truth of their utterances shall we know his prophets among us."

The big man gazed bleakly at the priest. "What do you mean?"

"Let us see what she has to say."

Relieved by the calmness with which Phurah had received his words, Lapidoth thanked the young priest and rose to go. He paused. "Oh, yes. She says the people will not heed her until she speaks before the Ark of the Covenant."

"Women are forbidden to speak before the Ark."

"Nonetheless, that is what she says."

"And when will that be?"

"When the Ark is borne to Shiloh."

A laugh burst from Phurah's lips before he could repress it. "I think you need have no fear, brother Lapidoth. Know you Shiloh?"

"It's my home, a poor village of farmers and herders."

"Then you know there is not even a temple. I would say, just take good care of your wife, Lapidoth."

Lapidoth gazed at the solid, square structure about him and at the beautifully wrought chamber in the center of the court of men which housed the Ark, the Holy of Holies. He felt a sense of relief. "You are right. Yahweh would not give up his home to live in a tent in Shiloh. Thank you, Phurah!" He reached into a bag at his waist and pressed a few shekels of silver upon the priest.

"Yahweh bless thee all thy days, Lapidoth, and give thee many fine sons."

As Lapidoth left the temple, cries of the street vendors visited his ears. "Last day of the feast! Get your sacrifices here! Guaranteed unblemished!" A hawker prodded a mixed flock of sheep and goats past the temple. "Last chance to sacrifice!"

As the hawker passed him, Lapidoth realized he was the subject of many curious glances. Words drifted to his ears. "That is the husband of Deborah! The husband of the new prophetess!" Lapidoth's brow gathered in rage. By all that was holy, he could not wait until Deborah was packed off to Shiloh.

"Double your blessings!" called a voice, in the clipped accent of the Canaanite. "Buy a silver Ashtoreth, direct from the temple of Taanach." A gnarled fist thrust a slender silver statue before Lapidoth's face.

"Be gone!" he roared.

The hawker's hand dropped, and his voice failed in midsentence. "All right, all right. Has Ashtoreth done you evil, friend? I also have Dagon and Chemosh. The Moabites swear by Chemosh. He's the best god of the lot."

Lapidoth seized the man's tunic in one fist. "There is only one God!"

"Why didn't you say so?" gibbered the trader. "Praise Yahweh, too, friend. Praise him, praise him!" Lapidoth left him clutching his gods to his breast.

Deborah was not in her tent when he charged into the campground. Indeed, the entire camp seemed deserted. Even his mother, who had not gone up the mountain all week, and his father and the oxcart, were gone. Lapidoth strode rapidly through the west gates of Shechem, heading for Mount Gerizim.

The robes of the people there and on Mount Ebal formed a bright, moving patchwork of color on the hillsides. He spied an oxcart, and with it, his parents. Before he reached them, he heard loud, angry voices rolling down from the speaker's promontory.

Unbelievable as it seemed, a robed woman was arguing with the priests before the Ark. He saw Phurah not far ahead of him, his coarse gray robe flapping about his heels, laboring toward the top of the hill.

"It is the law of Moses," boomed the stentorian voice of a huge-bellied priest. "Women are forbidden to speak at holy gatherings!"

"Deborah is a prophetess," Jael shouted back. "Do you dare stand against Yahweh's prophetess?" Jael planted her fists on her hips. She stood only a few feet below the priests as they moved together in a body, effectively screening her from the Ark.

"As well to expect sense from a sheep, as to listen to a woman!" shouted a second priest.

"Look! She's coming!" cried a voice.

"This is blasphemy!" shouted the first priest. His voice cracked. "We will not permit it!"

Moving through the crowd toward the high place, Deborah's tall figure parted the throngs like a lance.

The priests' eyes widened. Flinging his arms up, the first priest shouted, "I declare this holy assembly to be over. The Feast of Ingathering in this year of Yahweh *is no more!*" Seizing one of the poles used to transport the Ark, he shot it through its moorings. With alacrity, priests sprang to the other pole.

"Wait!" cried Phurah, reaching the Ark well ahead of Deborah. But the other priests raised the Ark from the altar and shouldered their way downhill at a fast pace. The people stood by uncertainly. Jael glanced at Phurah. He remained beside the barren altar, folding his arms within his robe, as he watched the approaching woman.

Jael clasped her hands. "Yahweh is with us," she murmured. She felt someone behind her, and turned to find Lapidoth, his mouth a rigid line, watching too, as his wife drew near.

The stirrings of the crowd ceased. An expectant hush fell over them as Deborah stepped quietly up to the high place and faced the crowd.

Her eyes lifted over the people of Israel, as though seeing ahead, to a time not yet at hand. "Thus saith the Lord." Her young voice rose as clear and piercing as a clarion. " 'My servant Deborah shall speak for me at the Ingathering of the harvest. She shall tell my children of the storm gathering against them. She shall chastise them, for they lusteth after other gods.

" 'I will make the drought to cover the land. I will plague my people, because they are unruly and refuse to act as one. Unless they repent, I shall deliver them into the hands of carrion, who will pick their bones one by one. I shall surely punish those who do not keep my covenant. These are my people. I am Yahweh. I am the Lord.' "

A strange fear gripped the multitude. Outcries of protest reached the altar. "We are helpless against men who thunder across the plains in chariots and burn our fields. How can we fight the desert raiders on camels, who strike and vanish? Is this how Yahweh shows his love for his people, by sending droughts to add to our perils? What does it mean, Deborah? Tell us what it means!"

Deborah stretched forth her hand. "Ask your leaders; ask the judges and the priests. Examine your own hearts. I can only tell you what Yahweh hath said."

As Deborah faced the sea of angry faces, a great weariness overcame her. Then Lapidoth was by her side, and Jael. Deborah moved down the hill, passing among the throng. Hands reached out to touch her garment. But here she met a stare of anger, there of hatred. And Naomi, she who with her husband and sons had met the family of Lapidoth on the road, put herself in Deborah's path.

"Last spring Yahweh allowed the Midianites to burn half our fields. Already a drought creeps over our land. How have we been unruly, Deborah?" she demanded. "We do not honor foreign kings! There are no false idols in my house!" Naomi's hostile stare swept those pressing in on Deborah. "I say your visions are pipe dreams!" Several eager nods agreed with this.

"Hold, Naomi," said an authoritative voice. A man about Lapidoth's age shouldered up beside them. "I am Boaz, kinsman of Elimelech, the husband of Naomi. Forgive Naomi, Deborah. She speaks from bitterness, not from lack of obedience. It is always tempting to discredit bad news."

"Thank you, Boaz," said Lapidoth.

"Why do you defend her?" demanded Naomi.

"Can't you see?" replied Boaz. "Yahweh has called her."

18

True to his vow, Lapidoth left Shechem the next day. Charged with command of the caravan, Ira had already left for Hebron, a week's journey to the south, in Judah. Lapidoth planned to rejoin them as soon as he settled his family in Shiloh.

From the wall atop the north gates, Joash, in high spirits, watched them go. His ear was nearly healed. Lapidoth had given him a new short tunic with a wide embroidered border; Deborah, sandals which she had fashioned for Gemalli; Hamid, a girdle; and Ira, a dagger, spoil of a long-forgotten skirmish. Joash would miss his new friends.

As the last of Lapidoth's party passed beneath, Joash ran his fingers through his thick, short hair. The curls sprang immediately forward again, as he took the steps down the inside of the wall several at a time and went off to seek Kanah.

He found him sitting placidly on a rug before his shop, shaded by a loosely woven curtain that billowed gently in the morning breeze. Kanah was broad in girth but sparse on top. Wisps of his white beard straggled down his chest, and the barest breeze was enough to lift the fine hairs crowning his pate. Behind him, in the shadows of the shop, heavily veiled women worked at looms and hand spindles near huge baskets of fluffy wool.

Courteously, Joash greeted the elder and waited for an invitation to sit. After wine, he broached the subject of his visit. "Kanah of Manasseh," he said earnestly, "I have heard that you are the wisest Israelite in Shechem."

Kanah's face crinkled in amusement. "Am I being oiled for a purpose, young Joash?"

"No, lord. I say this because it is true. I have a proposition to put before you."

Kanah clasped his hands and settled back. He loved nothing

better than theoretical propositions. "Well, let me hear it."

"When I raided caravans to live, lord—escaped slaves have not much choice of occupation—many nights we boasted of the *real* easy marks: little towns and overbusy marketplaces. Then I met Lapidoth on his caravan. I saw the value of a strong armed force. The numbers of Shechem are a thousandfold greater than the numbers of a caravan. Thus, should not the city have the same protection?"

"We have walls. A caravan does not."

"You spoke at the tribal meeting of not having to fight off brothers to secure your inheritance. Lapidoth said it, too. The problems you face are from *within*, Kanah—the dangers within the walls! What you need is an army!"

Thoughtfully, Kanah stroked his beard.

Joash pressed on. "Even when the elders vote to punish a wrongdoer, wrongs go unredressed, because there is not the army to back up decisions made at the gates! Behold, if someone cheats a maid who works in your shop, who redresses the wrong?"

"Her brothers, naturally."

"And if she has no brothers?"

"Her uncles, her father, her cousins. Joash, if you are saying we need an army to protect the widows and orphans, we have laws designed for that."

"And if families have a dispute over ownership of a particular field with Ephraimites who also live in Shechem, or even Canaanites or Philistines, are there enough men, Kanah, to assure justice for the Manassehites?"

Kanah frowned. "What you propose is meant to divide us, not bring us together. As long as men rely on one another, what need have they of protection by mercenaries? Is it not better to depend on your neighbor for aid, than a stranger?"

"I have seen cities where one man has all the power. His soldiers take and never rue, inflict wrongs that are never righted."

"You speak of the Canaanite kings, no doubt. But, Joash, here Yahweh is our king."

Joash snorted, full of impatience for this simplistic view. "Then form an army obedient to Yahweh, controlled by the elders who sit at the north gates! I have heard that any man may go to you, Kanah, and receive justice. But what if that justice involves judgments against the thousands who do not obey your god? Then how do you enforce your righteousness?"

"We leave it in the hands of Yahweh." Kanah recrossed his hands over his ample belly.

Joash swooped up his cup of wine. Only by accident did he glimpse Kanah's eyes shrewdly upon him.

"I understand from Hamid that you are a scribe by training, Joash. As your friends have departed, how do you propose to make a living? I trust you are not reconsidering your former line of work?"

Joash grinned. "You need a scribe?"

"I have far more need of a scribe than a soldier. But—just as a curiosity—how would you go about organizing this army you propose?"

Swiftly Joash outlined his plan. "I am certain that, with each family paying a small sum, we can train and feed a small, effective fighting force that will patrol the streets of Shechem, so that its citizens can walk in safety, and the thieves and pickpockets will do their biting in another town. In harvest, we can patrol fields against raiders, as well."

"Such a force would discourage such crimes, it is true. You are a Canaanite, Joash. Why concern yourself with our fate?"

Joash leaned forward over his folded legs. "I do not. I seek to earn a living. As you have said, I could be a scribe. But I will be more! I can organize this force for you, Kanah. It will be well run and disciplined. Each man in it will be passed on by the elders. It will be no legalized band of cutthroats." Joash's gaze was unflinching. "You will pay me well, and you will receive full measure."

Kanah leaned back, impressed in spite of himself. "Men who become farmers and shopkeepers lose their taste for fighting."

"And well they should. Let soldiering be done by soldiers!"

"I will speak to the others at the gate tomorrow."

Naomi and Elimelech and their sons, and others from the tribe of Judah, were among a band of pilgrims returning home after the Feast of Ingathering. For two days they traveled south, ever watchful for bandits, not building a fire at night, but hiding themselves within caves and behind rocks.

As they neared Bethlehem, Naomi sighed so bitterly that Elimelech stopped and took her arm. "What ails thee, Naomi?"

"Next year is the year that Yahweh decreed the land must remain fallow."

"Does that sadden thee?"

"This year and last the drought has been so bad we might as well not have planted. And now, when it is nearly harvest, that woman speaks of new troubles." Naomi began to sob. Staring toward the hills of Moab, which lay east of the Jordan, she said softly, "There is no drought in Moab, Elimelech."

"We won't starve, Naomi. We will get by, as always."

"Not if the drought goes on. And that woman said there could be a war. Oh, Elimelech, our sons would have to go, too! Let's go to Moab! Moab isn't under the law to remain fallow. We have our seed grain to plant next season. We can plant in Moab!"

"Yahweh does not dwell in Moab!"

"We can keep faithful to him!" pleaded Naomi. "Oh, please, my husband! Why should you and our sons die for the sake of a few warmongers and a prophetess who is the daughter-in-law of a—"

"Peace! Do not blame her." But Elimelech grew thoughtful. He, too, had entertained such rebellious thoughts, though Naomi had always been more outspoken. "It would mean depriving our sons of their inheritance. They would have no lands for their children and their children's children."

"Then do not sell our fields! Can you not hire some trustworthy men to watch over them and our house? If the land must remain fallow anyway, dear husband, that would not be against Yahweh's wishes."

Elimelech smiled in self-contempt. "Yahweh's wishes are that we stay in the land he gave us."

"Those are only the words of the woman Deborah."

"She is a prophetess."

"So she says." Naomi glared at her husband. "It is easy for her; she has no sons!"

Elimelech looked around uneasily. "Take care, Naomi." He looked at his sons, lounging against a gigantic rock. Both were now taller than he. Soon he would be arranging their marriages. *To pagans in Moab? Surely not!* "If we abided in Moab but a year, then we could come back home and plant. Perhaps talk of war would be over, and life could go on as before," he said slowly. "Surely the drought will end before then."

"Yes, my husband!" she cried.

"Very well, Naomi, it shall be as you say. We will make arrangements and move to Moab."

Two others who had observed the feast left Shechem in more jubilant states of mind. Gaius and Sacar, staffs in hand, urged the ass that carried their belongings down the western foothills and across the desert to Taanach. A fierce ball of sun was in their eyes, and a lust for gold in their hearts, as they dreamed of the price Sisera would pay for news of the prophetess.

19

KING SISERA leaned upon the parapet of Taanach. Across the Pass of Megiddo, a bare four miles distant, he could see the ridges and crests of another fortress, which now lay in ruins. A century ago, Megiddo had been considered impregnable, as Taanach was now. A chasm separated the two. Through this narrow pass traveled the richest caravans in the world. It was the vertex of the main route from Damascus to the Great Sea and from Phoenicia to Egypt. He who controlled the pass controlled the wealth of nations—and collected the tribute for the passage.

A good breeze swept in from the cooling waters of the Great Sea, fifteen miles west. Absently, Sisera lifted his face to it, then began to pace. His eye caught the lowering sun's illumination on the cone of Mount Tabor, which rose, fifteen miles to the northeast, out of the flatlands. Between Mount Tabor and the fortress of Taanach, the fertile Valley of Jezreel lay in a wide, uneven crescent. Here slaves cultivated wheat and barley, vegetables and fruit. His expert vinedressers worked in his vineyards, and on sloping hillsides too steep for farming, his shepherds herded flocks of goats and sheep and maintained his horse herds.

The previous year, Israelites from Manasseh had sacked and burned the fortified city of Jezreel, a pretty little city on the eastern rim of the valley. The Israelites were madmen in battle. With clubs and staves, they beat off metal spears. None of the things that mattered to ordinary soldiers—women and other spoils of war—could be counted on to sidetrack them.

Those stubborn tribes! Why could they not have stayed across the Jordan? Why had they entered Canaan at all? Holed up in their little hamlets, they were nigh impossible to dislodge. His chariots were useless in those mountains, and Sisera had no wish to risk losing horses to those mindless peasants. They would probably run them in flocks, like sheep, and expect to harvest horsehair!

A generation ago, Sisera knew, the Israelite tribe of Ephraim had launched a campaign against foothill cities in Philistia, south of Canaan. Eventually the Philistines had drawn together in a confederation and driven them back into the hill country. Any way Sisera looked at it, he, too, would eventually have to fight the Israelites. And he did not want to be bothered—yet.

It was not invasion that Sisera feared, but internal strife. He had been a soldier in the days of King Jabin. Jabin's power had been dissipated by bickering among the lesser kings of Canaan. Sisera had learned the effects of consolidating by observing Philistia. Fortunately for Sisera, Philistia's concern with building internal stability after repelling her invaders had allowed him time to strengthen Canaan's borders unchallenged, while ridding himself of minor city kings who opposed him.

By shrewd statesmanship, Sisera had achieved a wary peace with Philistia and with Phoenicia to the north. He had made generous trade agreements with each of them, including minimum tribute for use of the Pass of Megiddo and protection while their caravans were in his domain. Thus he had managed to make Canaan the fulcrum in the balance of power against Egypt.

The Israelites, still occupying Jezreel, threatened that balance. They were like sand fleas: visible and stinging everywhere, but gone when one tried to swat them. *Not only they. . . . Not only they.* His eyes again rested on the peasants laboring in his fields. How many of his own people belonged to the revolutionary Habiru, Canaanites by name, but traitors and mercenaries by profession? More than once he had suspected that they, and not the Israelites, were attacking the trade caravans that were under his averred protection.

Thus far the kings of Phoenicia and Philistia were impressed by his chariot army. At least for that, he could thank his Egyptian patron. But what if he were to stop sending tribute to Rameses IV? At present he could ill afford to antagonize Pharaoh. But once he extended his reign through Phoenicia and Philistia, controlling the entire eastern shore of the Great Sea, it would be another matter! Phoenicia would be first. Sisera ran his hand over the fine stuff of the cloak over his arm. He would have the secret of their purple blue dye. Yes, better Phoenicia than Philistia. Philistia was his buffer against Egypt. No need to alarm Pharaoh by having Canaan at its very border!

"King Sisera."

Sisera turned. A young soldier—clean-shaven, like himself, and bareheaded—climbed the steps. "Yes, Omar?"

"That new tanner you brought, sir. He wants to know if you will be coming to the tannery today. It's something about the new harnesses."

"Tell him. . . . Never mind. I'll see him now." Sisera followed the young soldier down the circular stone steps and crossed the courtyard.

Twin walls encircled the city of Taanach. Between the outer and inner walls lived her citizens. Here were their shops, their food stalls, their homes, wells, and meeting places. Here was space aplenty to pasture animals, if the city were threatened, and room for caravans.

Within the second wall was Sisera's palace, fronted by a spacious courtyard paved with stone. On the left of the landscaped courtyard was the temple of El Baal, nearly as magnificent as the palace. Skirting the right wall of the palace was a broad avenue, down which Sisera now went. Here was the heart of inner-city life. Behind the palace grounds, the avenue widened to an area that contained all the crafts needed to sustain an army.

In Taanach, no craftsmen were banished beyond the walls! Sisera considered their skills most precious. Here were the weavers, the tanners, and the metalworkers, whose great ovens smelted tin and copper to forge the bronze for chariots.

Sisera paused at the tannery. What in the name of El Baal was he going to tell Shamer when his men appeared with Deborah? He wondered that they had not yet returned. But he had cautioned patience. Her complete safety was of first importance.

Sisera stepped inside. Shamer the Naphtalite was directing the activity of half a dozen men while engaged in scraping a huge horsehide. His heavy face was red, and his muscles bulged. When the king appeared, he stopped work and wiped the sweat from his face with his arm.

"Good morrow, Shamer. I've seen your expert hand in that new harness for Shassbar."

Shamer nodded. "Aye. The trouble you had before was using a leather that couldn't take the strain. About the new harnesses for the chariots, lord. . . ."

Sisera listened attentively. In the month since his arrival, Shamer had proved that a man who loves his work can give no less than the best, no matter for whom he toils. Shamer's best was very good. Sisera had provided him with everything he asked for. The tannery was three times the size of his poor shop in Hammath, with fine engraving tools and stamps wrought of bronze, infinitely harder than the copper stamps Shamer was used to.

"How like you Taanach, Shamer?" he asked when they had finished their discussion. "Are your quarters satisfactory?"

Shamer's blunt fingers seized a scrap of leather and worked it, as though finding comfort in the familiar act. "If it wasn't for missing my children—begging your lordships's pardon—I would be happy as a man could be."

"I will invite them to visit, if you wish," said Sisera.

Shamer's face lighted up. Sisera laughed inwardly. He looked up as Omar reappeared at his side.

"Sire, there are two peasants at the inner gate. They beg to see you."

"What about?"

"They said to tell you they come from Shech—"

Hastily Sisera pulled the soldier away from Shamer.

"—from Shechem."

"Is there a woman with them?"

A ribald gleam flickered in Omar's eyes. "No, my lord," he answered gravely.

"Oh." Obviously they were not the soldiers on his private mission. "Let them refresh themselves. Then bring them to my chambers."

The men who presented themselves before Sisera an hour later appeared more nervous than travel weary. One kept opening and shutting his mouth in a vacuous grin, exposing a mouthful of black and broken teeth.

"He is Sacar, and I am called Gaius," the other said. "We are herdsmen, lord."

Sisera detected a shard of fear beneath the obsequiousness. "You are safe here, and welcome."

What Gaius and Sacar had to relate to Sisera at first enraged and then troubled him. "And there were Habiru on this caravan, who saw my soldiers killed?"

"Oh, yes, sir. It was all about the red-haired woman they called Deborah. Then, in Shechem, the Habiru leader, Joash—"

"Joash, you say. I had a slave—"

"Oh, the very same, sire. His ear was bored," said Sacar. "Why, in Shechem he and two of his men were riding your horses."

"And you say the woman then *married* the captain of the caravan?"

"Yes, sire. A Captain Lapidoth."

Sisera scowled. He knew the big Philistine. What lies Shamer had told! Deborah betrothed to an Ephraimite, indeed!

Gaius picked up the story. "Then we went up on Mount Gerizim —just to see what went on at one of those meetings—and this Deborah got up and said she was talking for their god."

"What did she tell them? No. Wait," Sisera snapped his fingers and sent for Darkon, high priest of El Baal. Darkon was experienced in the ancient religions. While he waited, Sisera plied the men about Deborah and the manner in which the people responded to her. Finally, Darkon made his appearance. Sisera understood the message of the delay. Darkon was not a minion, to be summoned imperiously. He came because he chose to.

"I am glad your sacred duties did not forestall my invitation," said Sisera wryly.

Darkon nodded slightly and rearranged the fall of his robe.

"Darkon, think you that you could tell a prophet of another god?"

"Which god?"

"The unknown god of the Israelites, called Yahweh."

"Little is known of him, King Sisera. But I will try."

Sisera nodded.

Gaius sucked in his breath. "This is what she told the people: 'Thus said the Lord: My servant Deborah shall speak for me at the Ingathering of the harvest. She shall tell my children of the storm gathering against them. She shall chastise them, for they lust after other gods.' "

A smile flickered across Sisera's face. Darkon betrayed nothing.

"Go on."

" 'I will send droughts to plague my people, because they are unruly and refuse to act as one. I shall deliver them into the hands of carrion, who will pick their bones one by one, unless they repent. I shall surely punish those who do not keep my covenant. These are my people. I am Yahweh. I am the Lord.' "

Sisera slapped a hand on his thigh. "By the baals! Their god is on our side! Well, Darkon? Tell me, what see you? Did the people believe her?" he asked, turning to the informers.

"Don't know, sir. There were plenty of angry people when she got through."

"People are like that when they hear what they do not wish to hear." Darkon turned to the king. "I do not know, Sisera. If she had spoken of good fortunes, it would be easy to dismiss her. No one in his right mind conjures a storm against himself."

"You could say she acted crazy, sir," said Sacar eagerly.

"Deborah's father is in my service," mused Sisera. He enjoyed Darkon's astonishment. One had always to keep a step ahead of these priests. "I believe I shall speak to him. Only today, he mentioned that he would like to see his children. Think you not we should invite her?"

Gaius and Sacar exchanged glances. Gaius shook his head slightly, but not before Darkon caught the movement.

"Shall I reward these worthies, King Sisera?" Darkon's smile was unusually gracious.

"Please."

While Darkon led the two men to the portal, Sisera picked up an ivory figurine of Anath. The goddess Anath was sister and consort of Baal, son of El, god of vegetation and god of storms. Anath represented the twin female functions of fertility and sexual pleasure. She was also a goddess of violence. Sometimes she was depicted as wading to her hips in the blood of the slain. But this was his favorite pose. Anath astride a plunging horse, brandishing a weapon. His fingers caressed the figure while his mind imagined a certain red-haired prophetess.

Sisera was beginning to enjoy himself immensely. As Darkon returned, he said, "I have never conversed with a prophet of the unknown god."

"You have never been interested in religion."

"How can you say that?" The hand that held the Anath swept

around the room, indicating a variety of gods on pedestals. El the Bull, father of the gods, stood slightly higher than the others. Next to him was a wooden image of Asherah, the lady of the sea. Dagon, ancient god of Philistia, with the body of a fish and the head and hands of a man, was next to her, then a variety of lesser deities.

"Mark me, Sisera. This woman is trouble. Banish her from your thoughts."

Sisera stared imperiously at Darkon. "I will invite her, and she will come." He motioned a servant. "Send for my scribe."

"I do not think so."

"No? Who tells King Sisera no?"

"Take care, Sisera, that you are not drawn beyond your depth. I mislike your fascination with this self-proclaimed prophetess."

"Pah! Tell me, Darkon, do you believe our own prophets?"

"Then it is not that she may be a prophetess." Darkon's tone was faintly mocking. "She is but another woman."

"Of course! Of course!" *She is not just another woman. She is she who dominates my thoughts!* Sisera's pace quickened. He went on, "I will send ten trusted men and two maidservants to attend her. I will have her father make her a special gift."

Darkon drew his robes about him. His lips widened in a superior, humorless smile. "Before you invite the Israelite, O *noble* Sisera. . . ." With a stony expression, Sisera faced the high priest. "The herdsmen have related to me a most unfortunate circumstance. One of those killed in the raid on Captain Lapidoth's caravan was a certain Gemalli, brother to the Israelite."

Sisera was stunned. Then an oath flew from his lips. Darkon's eyes gleamed. "Leave me!" snapped Sisera. *Oh, the fools! The utter fools!*

By the gods, now he was in a dilemma. If he told Shamer of the death of his son, no power would persuade him to urge Deborah here. Yet, if he did not tell him, Shamer would hear it from his own daughter. He could kill Shamer. Kill his best leatherworker for such an inconsequentiality? Not likely! Oh, why did incompetents continually bring him to such impasses? He had sent three of his most trusted and discreet soldiers on the simple task of abducting a peasant woman. Instead, they had killed her brother and gotten themselves killed, to boot. And more, they had given three of his prize stallions into the hands of peasant rebels.

No woman was that important. He would forget Deborah. What

was a woman? What was a night's pleasure next to the incomparable glory of thundering across one's own domain, of feeling the power of plunging beasts pulling your chariot? He would tell Shamer himself of the death of his son. A commander did no less for his men.

20

DEBORAH RAN THE TIP of her tongue over her cracked lips. She longed for a cool drink as they passed the well in the deserted square inside the gates of Shiloh. Yet no one else seemed to feel the burning heat, so she kept silent. Shiloh, like Hammath, was a small tribal village, but there the similarity ended. No cooling breezes off a sparkling sea nourished the hot, dusty land.

At last Lapidoth reined before a whitewashed hut. On the roof, flush with one wall, was built a small room. Extending out from the wall on that side, a long, low roof of palm thatch shaded some sort of workshop.

"We're home!" cried Dorcas, sliding off the ass and disappearing into her house. Lapidoth lifted his father from the bed of the oxcart as his mother emerged with an armload of cushions and rugs that she arranged over a bench with back and arm supports resting against the wall of the house.

"Ah." Dimon sank gratefully into the cushions. "Nothing like your own home and your own family." His smile included Deborah.

Deborah smiled tentatively at him, then glanced around for Lapidoth. Her husband was busy supervising the unloading of a bulky, wheellike object.

"Here it is, mother. Your new potter's wheel." His voice was as eager as a child's. "You'll be able to make pots faster than father can decorate them. In Babylonia, they use them thus." Clumsily, Lapidoth tried to demonstrate the workings of the wheel.

Dimon's voice filled with awe, as he contemplated the wheel. "What a marvel! Why didn't we think of it?"

"Let's take it into the pottery, mother. Where do you want it?"

Two of his men followed mother and son under the thatched roof beside the house. Deborah trailed along. She saw racks of dyes, bronze tools, scores of wood implements, various dry pots, and a stone cistern, which smelled of wet clay, built in one corner.

Lapidoth suddenly looked around for Deborah. He frowned and ushered her outside. "What troubles thee, Deborah?"

"Stay here with me," she whispered urgently. "Moses said that when a man is newly married, he shall be free at home one year, to be happy with the wife he has taken."

An expression of great tenderness came over his face. Cupping Deborah's face in one big hand, he said, "Moses must have meant that a man should treat his servants thus. For how can I lead a caravan and yet remain at home with thee?"

Before Deborah could reply, Dorcas' voice intervened. "Lapidoth! Why makest thy bride stand in the hot sun?" To Deborah she added, "My poor home did not expect to receive a bride. All that is here is yours," she added gracefully.

"Thank you," Deborah whispered.

They followed Dorcas into the darkened interior. Black soot climbed the white limestone wall above the hearth. Wooden shelves on the wall next to it held a variety of spices and oils and linen sacks, which Deborah supposed contained dried foodstuffs.

In a niche above the sleeping quarters, Deborah found something that made her blood freeze. She shot a swift look at Lapidoth. Seven little household idols of Dagon lined the niche.

They heard Dimon's voice. As Dorcas excused herself, Deborah turned on Lapidoth. "I cannot stay here! What were you thinking, to bring me here? Yahweh has warned that when we worship the gods of the pagans in the land, he will deliver us into their hands!"

Lapidoth's hands came up in a gesture of futility. "My mother is Philistine, Deborah! She has a right to her own gods."

"Only Yahweh is God!"

"Half the houses in Shiloh have gods like these! Also in your precious Hammath."

"Your father is an Ephraimite. How came he to allow this?"

"What right have you to ask?"

Deborah wrung her hands. "He should have forced your mother to leave her gods in Philistia. Oh, that such abominations are here —in the home where you brought me to dwell!"

Suddenly they realized Dorcas was in the doorway. "My gods are my own, Deborah of Naphtali. Before you came, they were here. Just because you are here, I shall not abandon them."

"And I shall not live in a household that worships false gods!" Deborah flung herself past the woman. "Lapidoth, I am coming with thee!"

Lapidoth caught up with her in the village street. He took her arm roughly. "No, you are not. And now you will apologize to my mother."

"I won't! I won't live here! Your father had no business marrying a Philistine!"

Suddenly Lapidoth struck her, in full view of his parents and of his men. Her headcloth flew off, spilling her red hair about her shoulders. Deborah lowered her head in shame. Standing in the dust before the house of Dimon, she slowly covered herself with her veil. She felt Dimon's eyes upon her. Beside him, Dorcas stood victoriously in her doorway.

Her glance flickered to the men. They grew suddenly engrossed with their horses. Lapidoth strode away from her to speak to them. One began to unload the asses. *O Yahweh!* she mourned. *Deliver me from this hour and this place!*

Lapidoth turned, stepping away to avoid her. With cold eyes, he disappeared into the house with his mother.

"Deborah." Dimon patted the cushions on the bench. "Come and sit beside me. I know everyone in Shiloh like my own calluses. Come and speak to me of your city in Naphtali. Could you see Galilee from your home?"

Head down, she walked slowly to the crippled man and sank by his side. Lapidoth came out and leaned over to embrace his father. "Yahweh keep thee, father. I will return in three months." He turned away.

"Three months!" gasped Deborah. He was going to leave! He wasn't even bidding her good-bye! "Lapidoth!" she sobbed. "O Lapidoth!" She reached him as he prepared to mount. "Forgive me, dearest. I beg thee!" She lay her head on his shoulder, so she could not see his eyes. His body felt unrelenting against hers.

"You have much to learn, daughter of Shamer." He put her away from him and swung up on his horse. "Look at me," he commanded.

She lifted her face, read the pain in his eyes.

"Your ways are sometimes strange to me. But Yahweh speaks to you. Therefore, you may raise a separate tent on the far side of the pottery. Yahweh keep thee, Deborah."

"My husband. . . ."

His expression softened. He leaned over. But then he saluted his parents and wheeled away, down the dusty village street with his men, to rejoin the caravan.

Deborah watched until they turned the corner that led to the square. Slowly she turned back to the house. "Mother of my husband," she began softly, "I beg thy forgiveness. I . . . I may not abide in thy house, but I will try to be an obedient daughter."

Dorcas had retreated to the center of the small room, her arms folded. Deborah fancied the line of Philistine gods rocking triumphantly behind her.

"We cannot always have what we wish, Deborah. You are Lapidoth's choice. Therefore, I too shall honor the wife of Lapidoth." But saying this, she turned away.

Deborah turned back to the yard. Her few possessions had been piled in the baking sun beside the pottery, together with her tent. Slowly she headed toward them.

The next morning, after breakfast, Dorcas picked up her water jar. In a detached voice, she invited Deborah to accompany her to the well.

"Please, mother, may I remain here and grind the barley?" Deborah responded.

"But the grinding stone is in my house," said Dorcas caustically.

"Pray give her leave to bring it out here," said Dimon, from his cushions. "She has not heard my stories," he laughed.

Dorcas was torn. Grinding the barley was tedious, backbreaking work. She would much rather spend her time shaping pots, or being in the happy company of her friends. On the other hand, she did not see why she should go out of her way to make life easier for this young high-and-mighty. In the end, she did as her husband asked, for she knew that fresh ears to hear his tales were as welcome as spring rains to a dying plant.

So they drifted into a pattern. The mortar and pestle were left outside, beside the cushions where Dimon spent his day. Every morning before she left to fetch water, Dorcas would pour out upon the stone a pyramid of barley to be made into bread for the following morning—double portions before Sabbath, for Dimon insisted on strict observance of that day.

The tales that Dimon told Deborah during these morning hours were of Lapidoth's boyhood and before, to the time when he himself was a young soldier and the Ephraimites had warred upon the Philistines.

At that time, the Philistines were beset by internal struggles, and the Ephraimites saw that as direction from Yahweh to extend their grasp upon Canaan. The Philistine strongholds faced the Great Sea. Inland stretched vast, fertile plains, where Philistia was sparsely settled and poorly defended. In the center of this agricultural paradise was the little town of Lachish, targeted by the Ephraimites for their first campaign. They conquered it easily and claimed its fields, its vines, and its orchards in the name of Yahweh.

As a member of the occupation force, Dimon became greatly attracted to the Philistine people, and soon took a woman as concubine. The occupation of Lachish did not last, and when, three years later, its recapture was imminent, Dimon prepared to flee with his infant son and the mother, Dorcas.

Dimon had considered leaving her behind. But the knowledge that she could be stoned made him uncomfortable, for she had given herself to him willingly. True, she was overtall for a woman—taller than most of the stocky Ephraimites, including himself—but she was comely and had a certain bearing. Other Ephraimite soldiers might suddenly and piously remember Yahweh's admonition against consorting with foreign women, noisily and tearfully abandoning them, but Dimon could not forget another of Moses' teachings: that there be but one law for the stranger and the believer. In their three years together, he had grown genuinely fond of her, never doubting her steadfastness and her love for their child.

Dimon had cause to rejoice in his decision. Philistine soldiers, cutting through the recaptured town on their magnificent horses, were sniping at the rear of the retreating Ephraimites. Dimon took an arrow in the joint of his hip. Dorcas managed to hide him and the baby; then she crept back into Lachish by night, where she boldly made off with two horses of her celebrating countrymen. She deliberately chose a mare and a stallion, and thus rescued her master.

They traveled to Shiloh, a hamlet deep in the mountains of Ephraim, and there Lapidoth grew to manhood. Dimon was permanently crippled, but for many years was the equal of any on horseback. From him Lapidoth attained mastery of horses, which were a rarity in Shiloh.

Lightened by Dimon's tales, grinding the barley became a pleasurable task to Deborah. It reminded her of life in Hammath, and it helped to fill the endless hours. Afternoons, when Dorcas could find no further chores for her until it was time for the goats to be milked, she would beg her permission to walk. At first Dorcas was surprised. "Walk where?"

"Upon the hills, mother of Lapidoth."

"But why?"

"Yahweh speaks to me when I am alone."

And Deborah heard from her lips the same question that Lapidoth had put to her so earnestly: "How does he speak to you?"— a question for which now, as then, she had no answer.

Each day, as she walked through the hills around Shiloh, she discovered new favorite places. From a certain crest, she could see the caravan road from the south, on which Lapidoth would one day return. In another place, the wind seemed never to be still. Here she went when she felt deeply troubled, to spend hours in prayer. In yet another place, an ancient oak overlooked the gates of Shiloh. Sitting here, she could see over the gates into the tiny square. Occasionally she spotted the sedately moving robes of the women as they made their way to the well, and scampering youngsters involved in endless play.

These were the days in which only the gentle spirit of Dimon kept Deborah from despair. Word of her rebellion against the gods of Dorcas had spread throughout the village. For years the people had chosen to forget Yahweh's commandment. As in other towns, they had grown comfortable with many religions and with unbelievers of many tribes. Dorcas was a good woman. Did she not care for her husband, who was crippled? Was she not an obedient wife? The consensus among the elders was clear: An obedient pagan was preferable to a willful fanatic.

21

TALES OF DEBORAH were relished in Shiloh. Shiloh was too small to support a priest of its own, so until the traveling Levite next called, the people pondered her among themselves. Some were in awe of this tall young woman with the fiery hair, who, in denouncing the home of her husband's parents, chose howling winds and searing heat above the cool, thick walls of a well-made house.

Since Deborah was Lapidoth's wife, Dorcas suffered her to work in the pottery. In spite of the coolness between them, Deborah admired Dorcas. Dorcas the Philistine—for so she mentally labeled her—was a gifted craftsman. The pots she threw with increasing skill on the new wheel became, with Dimon's designs, works of art. Dimon's stories of her courage and the manner in which she coped with a crippled husband without it seeming a burden gained Deborah's respect.

In her daily roaming of the hills, Deborah often brought back roots and flowers unfamiliar to Dorcas, from which in Hammath they had extracted dyes.

As the weeks passed into months, Deborah became a familiar figure in Shiloh. Though she did not cast down her eyes, as was becoming in women, yet she addressed only those who spoke first, and then with quiet respect.

To Dorcas's initial relief but now growing disappointment, Deborah seldom joined her and the other women at the well.

"How is your new daughter this morning, Dorcas?" inquired a friend at the well, as they were dispersing one morning. The other women paused. Dorcas had steadfastly refused to be drawn to gossip about Deborah. Yet, neither did she defend her.

"She is well," replied Dorcas. "By the way, Nedra has not been to the well for days. Is she ill?"

"No. She draws water when no one's about."

"Since her husband died, she seems to have lost interest in living."

"Do not her husband's kin care for her?"

"Oh, they look in on her. But you know how it is, after the mourning period is over. She'll be all right in time."

"I don't know; it's been almost a year now," Dorcas answered slowly. Suddenly, through the city gates, Dorcas caught a glimpse of Deborah arranging her skirts upon a rock under an oak overlooking the town. She had an idea. Perhaps Deborah, if her god was really powerful, could discern the reason for Nedra's unrelenting grief. And what if a tiny part of her would revel if Deborah failed?

"Well," Dorcas announced with finality, "I have things to do."

Curious glances followed her. "How is she getting along with that strange daughter-in-law of hers?" The words drifted after her.

Dorcas stopped at a doorway beyond sight of the well. "Nedra?" she called. No answer. "Nedra?"

A bleak, puffy-faced woman opened the door. "May I come in?" Dorcas walked boldly past her.

Ten minutes later, both women emerged, Dorcas heading for her own home, and Nedra, pausing for a moment to shade her eyes, skirting the musical voices at the well, whisking through the gate, and plodding stolidly up the hillside.

Perched upon the hill, Deborah recognized the approaching woman. Her husband had died—so Dorcas had told her—after the poor woman had nursed him for years. Indeed, she had spent her youth giving life to the dying man. Her suffering spirit touched Deborah's heart, and she called on Yahweh's name to share it.

The older woman nodded at her and sat down heavily. "I am Nedra, widow of Nathan," she puffed. "And you are the new wife of Lapidoth."

"I am she."

"Forgive me that I am not gracious. I have lost the art of gentle talk. I am like barley broken before harvest and left to wither on the stalk. Dorcas has told me that Yahweh speaks to you. Will he speak to you of me?"

She turned her careworn face to Deborah. In her eyes was the despair of a caged animal who knows that only death will bring release. "I have no sons, no line of inheritance to care for me in my old age. Nathan's family sees that I do not starve, but oh, I am

starved in spirit! I have no one to care for, and no one truly cares
for me!"

Deborah reached for Nedra's hand with both of hers. It was dry
as parchment.

Nedra's chin quivered. "You are the first to touch me in a year."

Deborah's arms opened. Nedra came into them and wept quietly.
Deborah praised Yahweh for Nedra's devotion to her husband. She
drew back with a smile and stroked the sad face. "Nedra, thou did
serve Yahweh well, when you cared for Nathan. He hath not forgotten thee. Do you know Eladah, widow of Suppur?"

"Of course. But she has cousins—nay, children of cousins.
Though she lives alone, her house is like a beehive."

"Hast thou baked bread this morning?"

"Why should I? I am the only one to eat it."

"This is what you shall do, Nedra. Bake two loaves of bread.
Grind the flour exceedingly fine, sweeten it with honey made from
the nectar of fruit, and spice it with herbs, so that it is irresistibly
fragrant."

Nedra arched away from her. "What? Make an offering? Is Yahweh punishing me? Haven't I been punished enough?"

"Patience. Wrap the hot bread in linen and take it to Eladah."

"What need has she of bread? She does not want for kin."

"Did you come for Yahweh's wisdom or to whimper?" asked
Deborah sharply.

Nedra's heavy lids dropped. "I will do as you say, Deborah," she
muttered.

The following morning, Nedra arose early. She picked through
the barley grains before she ground them. Impulsively, she poured
in a handful of her little store of red wheat and added a generous
pinch from her preciously hoarded spices. While the bread was set
to rise in the warmth of the sun climbing over the windowsill, she
arranged bundles of grasses and chips of dried dung in the oven and
lit it.

By late morning, the bread was ready. Wrapping the hot loaves
carefully in linen, she hurried to the dwelling place of Eladah. All
was quiet within. It must be lonely, too, at times. Ah, she knew how
that was! She could imagine the unbearable loneliness of the other
woman, after the sun had gone down. She knew what it was like
to labor for hours, baking succulent goat-meat stew and crusty

bread, and have no one across the table to wipe his mouth with relish and say, "Such a one, to make a feast out of plain food!"

Nedra's heart warmed with compassion. "Eladah?" she called softly.

Eladah appeared at the door. She saw the linen bundle in Nedra's hand and looked questioningly at Nedra's face.

"I have brought you a gift."

"For me? For what? Oh! How good it smells!" Taking the bread, she uncovered it and drew a long, appreciative breath.

"I . . . I have no one to share it with. I thought . . . I thought you would like to share my bread with me."

Eladah's face radiated a smile. "Oh, yes. . . ."

The next day, Nedra climbed Deborah's hill. Puffing rapidly when she reached the top, she lifted her head. She did not seem quite so unhappy.

"How did you know Eladah was in such poor spirits? Did Yahweh tell you? The poor woman! We talked so late into the night she begged me to remain, rather than go home to unlit fires."

Deborah laughed and embraced her.

"She . . . she needed me, Deborah. We are alike in so many ways. How could I have thought the bread was only an offering?"

Deborah rejoiced. "Behold, serving Yahweh is serving one another."

Every morning for a week, Nedra climbed the hill to spend an hour with Deborah, questioning, listening. The seventh morning, Eladah came, too. After they had greeted one another, Eladah spoke.

"Nedra has made such a difference in my life, and she swears it came from you."

"Not from me," protested Deborah with a joyful laugh. "I can only tell her what Yahweh gives to my heart."

"May I come back every day with Nedra, and will you speak to us of what Yahweh gives to your heart?"

"Gladly, Eladah."

As Eladah and Nedra returned through the gates of Shiloh, Nedra called to her friends at the well. The women crowded around the pair, eager to know what had caused this miraculous change in the grieving widow.

"It was Deborah!" cried Nedra. "O Dorcas, blessed thou must be, with such a daughter-in-law! For she did perceive my grief as a loneliness of the spirit, and she showed me that conquering loneliness means seeking to help another's loneliness. What we give away, so Deborah teaches, Yahweh shall return a hundredfold." She slipped her arm around Eladah. The two women exchanged a smile. "I took Eladah's loneliness, and Yahweh took mine, and now my heart is so full I cannot remain silent!"

Dorcas was struck dumb. Was Deborah then truly a prophetess? Had she angered Deborah's god by testing her? It seemed the women would never stop talking so Dorcas might depart gracefully. She went seeking her daughter-in-law.

Deborah was in the pottery, crumbling dry, purplish leaves into a mortar. She rose respectfully when Dorcas entered.

"Deborah, I have just seen Nedra. What did you say to her?"

Obediently, Deborah related all that had transpired.

Dorcas appeared disappointed. "But any of us could have told her the same thing. Someone probably did say to go forth and make some new friends." She shot a keen glance at Deborah. Ruefully she added, "But not I. Truly, you seem to have remarkable wisdom, for such a young woman."

Deborah warmed at the grudging praise. "Thank you, mother."

Dorcas glanced inside, where Dimon lay dozing upon his pallet, then caught her lip between her teeth before asking in a low, urgent tone, "Deborah, *how* does your god speak to you? Here. Let me crush that. Is it color for a new dye? Did he speak to you of Nedra? Oh, what foolishness! The gods aren't interested in such things as loneliness."

"Yahweh is," put in Deborah meekly.

Dorcas went on, as if to herself, "They are interested in causing mischief. They urge forgetfulness in wine and pleasures of the bed; they consort with mortals and laugh at the consequences." Punctuating each statement with a downward thrust of the pestle, she continued. "They flooded the earth for their own pleasure. Did you know that?" Dorcas fixed her with an accusatory stare. *"Why* is Yahweh different? And why cannot his people see him? When I pray to Dagon, I can see his spirit in his idols."

"Does Dagon speak to you?" Deborah challenged her. "Does he ever answer you?"

Dorcas threw her a look of superiority. "When does a god ever stoop to that?"

"O Dorcas, if you knew Yahweh! He speaks to what is good in us. He chastises us when we forget him. He brought us to this land —this holy land. He took us to be his people, he made a covenant with us, that we would be his people and he would be our God forever. He is God of all, Dorcas! The fish and fowl, the land, the heavens! Sit, and let us speak of Yahweh!"

Thus began a new way of life for Deborah.

Lapidoth returned in three months and stayed in Shiloh nearly a week, while the caravan traded in Shechem. So eager were Lapidoth and Deborah to see each other again that the bitter words at parting were forgotten. Deborah had filled her tent with fragrant wild flowers, that their first night together might be as in a field. In the morning, she knew that no other love could have been possible. She prayed that their coming together might bring a child.

That morning, though she protested, Lapidoth engaged several young men to begin construction of a stone house. Lapidoth sent word to her father of their marriage and of Gemalli's death, though not of the fact that Gemalli had died at the hands of Canaanites. He feared Shamer's wrath would serve him ill as long as he lived in Taanach.

Lapidoth had brought news of Dorcas' friend Naomi, whom she had taken a liking to at the Feast of Ingathering. The family from Bethlehem had migrated to the land of the Moabites, east of the Jordan. And the drought in Judah and in Benjamin had not broken.

There was news of Joash from Hamid, who came riding in one afternoon to pay his respects. The elders of Shechem had responded favorably to the young Habiru's plans for a city army, and work to organize such a force had begun.

Weeks passed into months. One year, and then two, went by. Amidst a maelstrom of increasing boldness by Canaanite raiders against outlying communities and unwary travelers, Shechem became an eye of peace. The Israelite elders and their families rejoiced that Yahweh had sent Joash to be their protector.

Deborah still did not become with child. Nor did the land bloom, for Deborah's grim foretelling bore true. No rain had fallen in the hills of Judah, in Benjamin or Ephraim, in Manasseh or Issachar, or in Naphtali, for over two years. In the cities, wells sank to frightening levels, while those in oases that the caravans depended upon were jealously guarded.

The crops of barley, planted early and nourished by cooling fogs while young and tender, did not come to head. Roots withered and could not draw nourishment from the soil. Sheep and goat herds began to dwindle. The older animals, the sick and weak, died off. After the first swing of the seasons without rain, lambs and kids failed to prosper. Their bleats were as thin as their mothers' milk, and their coats afflicted. The goat cheese and sweet curds that were a staple of the Israelites' diet were tough and dry and fell apart to the touch.

The price of grain shot higher than any man remembered, as caravans brought wheat and barley, guarded more preciously than gold, from beyond the stricken land.

Those who recalled Deborah's ominous words recalled them in tones of fearful wonder. Later they spoke in anger of the woman they perceived to be cause of their misery. On the trade lanes, Lapidoth heard these mutterings against his wife from those who knew Deborah only by hearsay.

Meanwhile, in Shechem, standing upon the sacred hills of Gerizim and Ebal, the priests gazed westward, beyond Jacob's well, toward the Great Sea. They could see storm clouds rolling up, hear the distant roar of thunder. But the rains fell agonizingly short, watering the fields of Sisera. And they knew Sisera's flocks increased, and his granaries filled to overflowing.

And the Israelites said to their priests, "Behold. Yahweh is a wilderness god. See how the gods of the Canaanites and the Philistines increase that fertile land!"

As prices rose in the vendors' stalls in Shechem, civic lawlessness mushroomed. Joash's army was all that lay between the people and anarchy.

As the drought entered its third year, a new cry was heard upon the land: "When will Yahweh deliver us?" Even as in their wretchedness they cried to Yahweh, some also sacrificed to the Canaanite god El, praying for him to send storms, and to Dagon, the Philistine god of agriculture, that he not let his land die.

The length and breadth of the land of the Twelve Tribes shimmered and curdled in the heat, and the rivers became tombs of cracked clay.

22

In the village of Shiloh, these three years wrought more subtle change. The house in which Deborah dwelt was built where her tent had been, on the other side of the pottery, where she labored diligently under Dorcas' critical eye.

Deborah spent hours each day in prayer and communion, often while walking the hills or sitting under her favorite oak. In a tradition begun by Nedra, it was here people sought her. In the beginning there was only a trickle. Then two or three pilgrims a day, from distant cities, would come to hear her words.

Increasingly, Lapidoth met travelers who asked, "Art husband of the prophetess?" They would then seek the protection of his caravan to reach her. From Shechem and Beth-shan, from as far south as Bethlehem, from her native village of Hammath, people of the Twelve Tribes sought her counsel.

Some she could answer directly. More often the supplicants remained in Shiloh while Deborah carried their problems to Yahweh, summoning them when she had received an answer.

In the third year, the trickle swelled to a stream, and with it came an increased demand upon the tradespeople of Shiloh for goods and services. Prospering, Shiloh found a civic pride replacing its initial embarrassment over having the prophetess in its midst.

Time passed quickly for Deborah. Often she wondered about her father, yet Yahweh had not lifted his command against visiting Taanach. Of late, Deborah's nights had been troubled. She longed for Lapidoth, who had been away two months. Within the reality of his arms, the horror of strange dreams would flee.

Following one such night, she fled to the hills to beg Yahweh's guidance, but heard only the voices of children playing tag in the fields below. Silently she returned home. Dorcas arched a questioning glance. She returned it with a smile that quickly faded.

That night she dreamed again. In the morning the skin over her high cheekbones seemed nearly translucent, and her eyes were shadowed. Silently she took her place in the pottery. She picked up a heavy pestle and, with a rhythmic motion, began to pulverize chunks of dried clay on a large, flat stone.

Dorcas watched her for an hour and finally laid down her tools. "Daughter, whatever is on your heart, pray speak. Art ill? Hast thou conceived?"

Deborah looked at her brick-stained hands and rubbed them together absently. "Lady mother, I wish it were so." She sighed deeply. "How I wish Lapidoth were back!"

"Tell us, Deborah. What is it?" asked Dimon.

"For three nights I have had strange dreams," she began. "In them, a great gold chariot, driven by ink black horses, did thunder over newly planted fields. The horses' hooves and the wheels did crush the new shoots, leaving the ground bare and red. For two nights there was nothing more. Then last night I saw a threshing floor containing forty tents. The chariot tried repeatedly to gain the threshing yard, but wherever it smashed through the tents, more tents rose behind. Each time it gained the yard, the sacks of barley spilled and mired the wheels." Her face was anguished. "And now I fear I know the meaning of the dream."

"But what is it, Deborah?" cried Dorcas. "Tell us!"

"It . . . it is a message for King Sisera."

Dimon and Dorcas exchanged frightened glances. "King Sisera!"

"We must send a messenger to Taanach. We must say that Deborah, prophetess of Yahweh, bears a message to Sisera, king of Canaan. We must ask for safe passage."

"You can't mean you are *going* to Taanach! I forbid it! If Lapidoth were here—"

"I know, lady mother," said Deborah passionately, "I know. But even were he here, it would still have to be."

"But Deborah, would you risk the lives of Ephraimites?" asked Dimon. "They would be killed before they reached Taanach. Who will carry the message, and how will you be sure of safe passage?"

"I don't know, father," said Deborah miserably. "I only know what must be."

"Let us send for Joash," said Dorcas.

"He will not dissuade me, gentle mother."

"Perhaps," she said grimly.

Dimon chewed his lip thoughtfully. "Prepare your message, Deborah. We will send a man to Shechem for Joash. He can secure a messenger. Will you grant us one promise?"

"If I can."

"You must not go if Sisera cannot guarantee your safety."

Deborah squeezed his hand. "I will do my best."

"I'm going with you," announced Dorcas. Dimon shot his wife a look of surprise.

"Who will manage the pottery?" Deborah asked. *And care for Dimon,* she thought.

"You need an attendant," Dorcas said flatly.

"Then I shall ask Nedra."

Less than a week later, Joash rode into Shiloh with two aides. Success agreed with Joash. Gone was the pugnaciousness that Lapidoth had first marked, replaced by the confidence of the professional soldier. He had filled out; his neck and shoulders were now corded with muscle.

He lost no time in coming to the point, as they all sat under the olive tree before the pottery. "My messenger reports that Sisera promises you safe passage. But before I tell you the rest, I want to know if your god also says that you will be safe."

"Israel will be safe. Perhaps I can avert a war."

"War?"

"Even so."

"All that from dreams, Deborah?" Joash's face was troubled. "I will go with you! I know Sisera's ways."

Dimon nodded. "Do as he says, Deborah."

"Dear Joash. Many times you told Lapidoth that you would be murdered if you returned to Taanach!"

"Surely your god—"

"Thou must not fling down thy gauntlet! We do not throw ourselves into the teeth of serpents and then dare Yahweh to rescue us!"

Joash laughed. "And what are you doing, my lady?"

"Obeying Yahweh."

"You think because your father is in Taanach you will be safe." Joash uttered an oath. "Sisera cares nothing for a life, only for what is expedient. Deborah, this is too dangerous. Your god cannot mean you to walk into the jaws of that jackal." He flung aside the messenger's parchment. "It may even be. . . ."

"What, Joash?"

He ran a hand through his unruly hair. "Have you thought what Sisera gains by having the wife of Lapidoth in his power? The caravans! What might Lapidoth not bargain away to regain your safety? If Lapidoth can be broken, where can Israelite merchants trust their goods? Then where will be the trade links that bind our cities?"

Deborah put her hands to her temple. "No, no, no! This has nothing to do with Lapidoth!"

A sneer curled on Joash's lip. "Your brother was killed because you refused to go to Taanach three years ago! Now you believe Yahweh sends you. Then why did Gemalli die?"

"Joash! You would not speak thus to Lapidoth! Do you prey upon me because you expect womanly tears? I obey Yahweh, in this as in everything!" The others forgotten, Deborah and Joash had risen to their feet.

"I have prepared a message. You will take it to Lapidoth!"

Joash planted himself before her and thrust his head forward. For a moment they stared at each other.

Suddenly Deborah relaxed. With a coaxing smile, she said, "What I want or you want means nothing, dear Joash. Yahweh is all. Your words of anger are born of fright, because Lapidoth is not here to counsel me. I am frightened, too. I fear—"

"Then let me go with thee." Joash's voice was husky.

"No." Her voice grew firm again. "I will have the messenger's words."

Joash turned away. "Sisera will send soldiers and handmaidens to attend you in Shechem in two days. This ring is a symbol that you are under his protection." Joash took the ring from his finger. As Deborah accepted it, a sigh escaped her.

Joash beckoned his men and strode apart from the family under the olive tree. "Return to Shechem at once. Tell Kanah what has happened. Take two other men and extra horses and ride for Lapidoth. You will find him on the road to Damascus."

"But what about you, commander?"

"I will take her to Shechem. Then I go to Taanach," he said in a low voice.

"But the prophetess said—"

"*Deborah* said." Joash's face was grim. "Living among the Canaanites makes it easy for one to promise one thing while contemplating another."

"By thunder, commander, prophetess or no, this woman has scrambled your brains! If Sisera catches you, your life won't be worth that crop in your ear!"

"Dost want to die old and rickety, good friend?" Joash clasped each of them by the shoulder. "Tell Lapidoth I will never be far from his wife. If Deborah's god is going to protect her, perchance he'll keep an eye on me, too." Joash grinned carelessly. "Anyway, what would my life be worth to Lapidoth, if I let Deborah face the jackals alone? Come. We each have a journey before us."

The following day, Joash accompanied Deborah, Nedra, and several of the elders of Shiloh to meet King Sisera's emissaries in Shechem. Word of Deborah's mission whipped like fire through the city.

When the Canaanites' procession appeared at the north gates, half of Kanah's force and many of the private citizens were on hand for their first real look at the enemy.

The suspicious and the curious followed the rich train through the city streets to the field where the Ephraimites from Shiloh waited. There were ten Canaanite warriors, richly mounted upon spirited stallions and garbed in fine woolen cloaks. In their midst rode two women arrayed in thin, shimmery fabric that gleamed softly in the sunlight, fluttering out from beneath billowy capes. Below hems trimmed with golden flowers, they wore tiny slippers embroidered with pearls and flashing gems. Gold coins were strung across their flawless brows. The women rode milk white asses and led a third. At the end of the procession were the pack animals.

Deborah rose to meet their leader. Dismounting, he brushed back his burnoose. He was a man well into middle age. His gray hair was richly curled, his face oiled with aromatic herbs. He brought his hands before his face in semiobeisance, and Deborah caught the glitter of heavy rings.

"May the gods keep you," he said in a soft, cultured voice. "I am Beno, adviser and emissary of the great king of kings, Sisera. We are honored by your desire to visit. And here," Beno produced a bundle wrapped in fine linen, "is a gift from your father, Shamer."

Eagerly, Deborah accepted it. It was a chamois-skin bag, to carry her personal things. The leather was butter soft, stamped with an intricate and lovely design. She could imagine the hours Shamer had labored over this for her. Sudden longing for him welled so strongly that tears fused in her eyes. "Thank you, lord Beno," she said. She caressed the bag. Her father must be well treated, else he could not have the peace of mind to create such a beautiful gift. Perhaps Yahweh had set his hand upon King Sisera and was about to deliver the rest of Canaan unto the Israelites! But her dreams were not dreams of peace.

Beno misinterpreted her silence. "Fear not for your safety, lady. Sisera recognizes the natural fears of one who travels in an unknown country. These maidens will serve you on the journey to Taanach and upon your return home. While you are his guest, they shall attend your every need and desire."

"And spew it out to Sisera," Joash muttered in her ear.

"This is Joash, a commander of the Manassehites," said Deborah, as though she had not heard him. Then she presented the elders from Shiloh. Beno acknowledged each with a formal bow. As they gathered ceremoniously on a thick rug and Deborah ordered refreshments, Beno's gaze flickered back to Joash. Joash's hand went casually to his dagger.

"May I caution you, lady, that this man is an escaped slave? He attempted murder upon the person of the king."

"This man is friend to my husband and to all of us," Deborah replied firmly. "What happened before does not concern us. In Shechem he is a free man. But I should like to bring a companion, if I may," she added in final dismissal of Beno's charge.

"Of course. We will begin at dawn, if this is convenient to you. It grows very warm in the valley this time of year." Beno arose.

The two Canaanite women, Deborah realized, had been casting sidelong glances at her since they arrived. Under their scrutiny, she grew aware of her modest clothing and the dye ingrained in her hands. Their complexions were as smooth as wet clay. Their raven hair gleamed beneath their costly veils. Their nails were tinted with a red dye, the like of which she had never seen. The same unnatural dye colored their lips. *Why,* she wondered, *do they paint their lips?* Beautiful shadows of twilight colors appeared to be brushed around their eyes, lending a mysterious allure.

"I have no need of handmaidens, noble Beno," said Deborah, "but I shall welcome their companionship."

"As you say." Beno bowed courteously. His eyes narrowed as he studied Joash, who remained cross-legged upon the rug, watching him as a fox watches a snake. "Had I been king, Joash, you would have been put to death, rather than made a slave."

A few short years ago, Joash would have been at him like a maddened bull. Now he merely leaned back with a mocking smile. "But you are not king."

"Are you one of them?"

"A follower of Yahweh? Paugh! I am my own god and my own destiny!"

23

A DAY AND A HALF LATER, a peddler in a coarse brown cloak, with a tower of bird cages on his back, passed bent and unnoticed through the city gates of Taanach. Ignoring the soldiers everywhere, he made directly for the main section of the bazaar. Here, with colorful and obscene chatter, he offered his birds. Suddenly he uttered a curse and shrugged out of his harness straps. He turned to a peddler of spices and oils beside him. "This ill-made and worthless harness! Where is a tanner who can mend it?"

"There's a nest of them in there." The peddler pointed a knobby finger in the direction of the gates to the inner city.

"All the tanners?" That was both good and bad.

The peddler nodded. "Sisera's got nothing on his mind these days but his demon horses and chariots. The tanners about got to live with the beasts."

"Huh. Thanks." The peddler shouldered the bird cages, clutching both ends of the broken harness strap, and headed for the gates.

It was nearing sundown. How closely were the gates guarded? People appeared to move freely in and out. If he did not find the right tanner, where would he hide until morning? What if he were recognized? Boldly, he scuttled through the gates, his cages swaying precariously.

"Peddler!"

He stopped, screwing his face into a vacant grin. "Me, your worship?"

Leah, queen mother of Sisera, dallied over her morning meal. Her robes were a handsome blue, bordered with silver embroidery and costly gems. Even at this early hour, her hair was elaborately dressed and her skin carefully made up. Between long, tapered fingers, she twirled a silver goblet filled with juice of the pomegranate. On the beaten gold plate were a few wafers of cracker and slices of fruit. Her appetite was not good this morning. Perhaps she should send for the physician. Behind her, her personal maid leaned sleepily against a pillar. Her mistress had awakened her at dawn to help her get ready.

But what silliness, Leah scolded herself fondly. *My son has other women. He has other wives. No matter what he does with this one, nothing will change. He is a connoisseur of women.* To be a connoisseur, one must sample freely and often. Had not she taught him that? Did she not herself practice it? Fondly she caressed the cold silver image of Ashtoreth, her favorite goddess. In truth, she and Sisera were responsible for the continued fertility of their fields, their success at tax gathering, and their plundering.

Other women of her years were past middle age, but not she. She had borne but one son. Her breasts were as firm at forty-five as they had been at fifteen, when she had been delivered of Sisera. She knew what it took to keep a body young. And she kept her women on the watch for likely young men.

A sigh escaped her lips.

There was one young man she had not forgotten, though several seasons had passed. If only her foolish son had not made sport with the youth's little sister! But, by his own indulgence, Sisera had created an enemy and set up the chain of events that led to the young man's escape from Taanach. A remembrance of him stirred a quiver in her. For she had seen him, sweating as he labored in the stone quarry. Before he had unfortunately learned of his sister's death. Well, that was too bad. What she needed, Leah reasoned, was a new man to take her mind off this strange woman coming to the palace.

Since Deborah the Ephraimite had sent word that she would visit, her foolish son had turned the palace inside out. He had even presented that awful-smelling peasant from the tannery with new robes in honor of his daughter's visit. Leah sniffed. She wondered if the daughter had the rank odor of a tanner, too. She was probably a big, flat-footed woman with gaping teeth and pockmarked skin and hair like lank ropes. But even as she conjured up this pleasant vision, Leah had to smile, for Sisera was a connoisseur, after all.

In his quarters behind the tannery, Shamer scratched under his arm. This new woolen garment itched like nettles! How did the soldiers abide such tunics? Ever since Sisera had ordered the pouch for Deborah, Shamer had wondered uneasily about the means the king had used to persuade her to come. He could only trust that Yahweh still guided and protected his daughter.

This decided, Shamer forgot the ramifications of her visit and gratefully took off the new tunic, deciding he might as well work until word came of her arrival.

The guard who had called to the bird peddler from the inner gate kept his distance, lounging in the shade of the stone archway. "No peddling in here," he repeated.

"No, your worship. I need a new harness. See? It broke." Joash waggled the broken strap. Suddenly, the end flew out of his hand, and the bird cages tumbled down about him, with much squawking and flapping.

"Oh, unlucky wretch that I am! The baals are frowning on me. Do you want a bird? Let me give you a bird. Here. Here's a pretty one." He scrabbled sideways toward the guards, a cage clutched in one grimy hand.

"Get those licey birds out of here! You're cluttering up the gateway. Be quick! And if I catch you selling them, peddler, I'll put *you* in a cage!"

"Yes, your worship." Quickly, Joash gathered the cages and scurried down the street, hearing the guards' laughter behind him.

Directly before him rose the palace. Palm trees set along the walls of the palace lent graceful contrast to the brownish gray stone, while between them, oleander bushes spread the fragrant perfume of their poisonous coral blooms in the air.

Joash followed the broad, familiar avenue beside the palace walls. He passed a crew of slaves repairing a section of wall. Fear mushroomed unexpectedly in his throat. He recalled the weight of the stones, the torn and bleeding fingers, the whine of an overseer's lash, the stinging, searing pain. He bent his head into the neck of his cloak and hurried past.

He heard the clang of metal in a blacksmith's shop: a chariot wheel being mended. Two peasants were standing patiently by, with plowshares to be fixed. Next, a tannery. He paused. Under a canopy worked several men in leather aprons.

By the gods, he hadn't the slightest idea which would be Deborah's father! At least there were no soldiers. Amid the talking and occasional laughter, he heard an accent that was not Canaanite. The speaker was a huge, red-faced man diligently scraping a hide, pausing methodically to pour an oily liquid over the area he worked.

Joash set his bird cages down and began muttering about his strap. Harness in hand, he went in. No one paid any attention to him. There were three others in the tannery besides the man with the north-country accent. He wandered around, seemingly curious and in no hurry. Finally, he stopped next to the huge foreigner. The man fixed him with a smile.

"Son, we can't fix that until we finish the king's business. Why don't you leave it?"

"Are you Shamer of Naphtali?" Joash asked in a swift, low voice. The man's expression changed. He glanced quickly at the others. He picked up the bowl of oil and motioned Joash into the recesses of the tannery.

"Who are you?"

"Someone with news of Deborah. Where can we talk?"

"Is she well?"

"Yes."

"Wait here. The others will go soon." Shamer refilled his bowl from a cask of oil and returned to his labors. When the others left, he lifted a curtain and motioned the peddler within, lighting an oil lamp. The floor was of smooth, hard clay. The room contained a bed off the floor and a well-made table.

Shamer pulled a wineskin off a hook and brought a loaf of bread and a bowl of fruit and cheese to the table. "Come and sit, please."

"Shamer. . . ."

"Peace. You are?"

"Joash."

"Peace. Let us eat first, Joash." Shamer blessed the bread. While they ate, he spoke of affairs of Taanach—simple gossip, as any peasant might know. Joash ate with increasing anxiety, casting glances at the curtain. Finally, Shamer washed down the last of his bread with a swallow of wine. He leaned back. "Now, Joash, what can you tell me about my daughter?"

"You know she is on her way to Taanach?"

"Yes. Though I cannot fathom why she comes to see me now."

"She comes to see Sisera."

Astonishment lighted Shamer's broad face. "But why?"

Joash emitted a whistle of exasperation. "She says her god gave her a message for him in a dream. She speaks of stopping a war."

"I thought. . . . I had almost forgotten. Then Yahweh speaks to her still."

"Some believe it. People come from all your tribes, seeking her judgment."

"They do? My daughter?"

"They call her a prophetess."

Shamer digested this with effort. Shaking his head, he said, "There is no talk of war here. No, I cannot believe it. Sisera is an honorable man."

"An honorable man! After killing your son?"

Shamer stared at Joash. "Gemalli was killed in a Midianite raid."

"By the baals, they were not Midianite. I was there. They were Canaanite."

"Canaanite! But you are Canaanite!"

Joash had no choice but to trust the bewildered tanner with part of his own story. At its conclusion, Joash pushed back his cloak and revealed his scarred ear. "This is from a slave ring like those the stone fitters wear. Though he may not have intended Gemalli's death, Sisera is all treachery, Shamer. He ordered the raid to steal your daughter, and now she walks into his hands."

Shamer's giant head swung back and forth.

"How can you abide here, so far from your people and your god?"

"Yahweh is with his people, no matter where they are. Sisera treats me so well!" Shamer argued with himself. "I have more business than I ever had. He pays me so well! Oh, treacherous king! He has ruined my family! And Deborah, married to a Philistine!"

"His father's Ephraimite. He is a good man. You know Lapidoth."

"Yahweh is punishing the house of Shamer." Shamer buried his head in his hands.

Joash rose and paced miserably in the flickering light. Finally, Shamer lifted his head and ran his sleeve across his eyes. "I am a virtual prisoner here. At the end of the first year, Sisera, true to his word, offered me passage home. He knows I worship Yahweh still. This he allows. But," Shamer lifted his meaty palms, "I had nothing to go back to, with my only son dead. And my business was good. So I decided to stay." Shamer clenched his fists and brought them down softly on the table. Finally he said, "You have taken a great risk coming here, young man. Are you a believer?"

Joash smiled. "I believe in all the gods."

"There is only one God; blessed be Yahweh. If not for Yahweh, then why did you come?"

"Lapidoth befriended me when I was a hunted man. He is on caravan and does not know Deborah comes here. He would not have allowed it."

"What can we do?"

Joash uttered a short laugh. "In truth, I don't know. I know the palace well; but I also am known. I thought merely to see that Sisera kept his word. If he should try to detain her against her will, I have some friends left. Maybe we could get her out."

"Shamer," called a young voice from beyond the curtain.

"Sh-h," Shamer lifted his hand. "I am here."

"Come tell us a tale, Shamer." Without warning, the curtain was flipped aside, and a boy of twelve or thirteen sauntered in. He scarcely looked at Joash. "My father begs to tell you he has several skins of old wine that are best washed down with your tales. Will you come? All of us are waiting."

"Yes. Tell your father I'll come, lad."

The boy cast a curious glance at Joash and left, whistling a merry tune.

Joash looked at Shamer questioningly.

"I tell the tales of our people. The history of the Naphtalites must not be lost. Whatever happens to me, the truth remains—even in Taanach. Stay with me, Joash. You will be the son of my cousin. Surely Yahweh has sent you for a purpose." Shamer paused at the curtain. "Are those your bird cages?"

"Yes."

"I will have the boy keep them until you leave. It would not do to have them noticed too much."

24

CARRYING SISERA'S RING in the chamois bag and seated upon the white ass, Deborah rode in relative comfort to the city of the Canaanite king. Hours before they reached the gates, she could see the fortress against the western horizon. They rode by field after harvested field, patchworked among neat orchards. They began the switchback climb up the mountain to the gates of Taanach through endless rows of grapevines sprawling down the slopes, their luscious fruit a dusky, succulent purple.

As Deborah passed through the gates, the scope of the city filled her with wonder. There was not one marketplace, but many. Every street was overflowing with merchants. People were everywhere. A profusion of colorful robes and turbans and a cacophony of tongues signaled Egyptians or Phoenicians, Philistines or Assyrians. In cages were animals of every description and exotic birds of fantastic plumage. Rugs of intricate design hung on poles for display, side by side with metalware and clay pots in such shapes that she could only wonder at their use.

She peered with fascination up and down the narrow, hilly streets. Houses were built in long connecting rows that fronted directly on the street. Most had no windows. "Where is my father's tannery, Beno?" she asked eagerly.

Beno's horse continued at the same leisurely pace. "Within the palace walls, lady."

"In the *palace?*"

Beno threw her an indulgent smile. "No, lady. These shops and stalls are for peasants and caravans. The craftsmen work directly for Sisera."

"Do not the tanners and the metalsmiths also market wares?"

"All they produce is Sisera's."

Deborah pondered this. She shifted slightly upon the plodding animal. After two days, her backside was becoming tender. They approached the second gates, formed by a jog in the wall. To enter, they had to ride parallel to the fitted-stone wall and turn sharply. Inside, the courtyard was paved with stone. It was immediately cooler and quieter, less dusty.

The people were dressed better, and their feet were shod. Men in the familiar bronze helmet and leather vest of Sisera's army seemed to be everywhere. Several were around one building she took to be a barracks.

The procession drew up before the steps of the palace. Beno dispatched a messenger. Deborah held her breath. Her hands grew clammy upon the reins. She remembered the arrogant soldier in her father's house three years ago, saying, "Young maidens who are too particular may find themselves serving the temple." Her thoughts rushed ahead. *Oh, Gemalli, dearest brother!*

Suddenly King Sisera was there, on the steps, now in the graceful robes of the statesman, welcoming her. She searched the tanned face, the patrician nose, the thin, well-defined lips. He had not changed at all. "I am honored to welcome you to Taanach, Deborah, daughter of Shamer, wife of Lapidoth."

Before she could reply she heard a beloved voice.

"Deborah!" A powerfully built figure hurried forward, arms flung wide.

Sliding off the animal, she rushed into her father's arms. "Oh, father, father! Praise be to Yahweh! Father!" Shamer's hug took the breath out of her. Finally he held her at arm's length and searched her face, tears coursing down his cheeks.

"How often have I thought of thee!" They embraced again. She turned to Beno. "I wish to go with my father."

Beno said smoothly, "There will be time later." He glanced up at the king. "King Sisera has readied an apartment which he begs you to consider your own during your stay."

"Please allow my servants to show you there," added Sisera graciously. "Then we shall sup, and later we shall talk."

"I would stay—"

"My quarters are too small," Shamer said hastily.

Deborah caught his hand. His look seemed to convey a warning. "Then I shall see you soon, father." Shamer nodded, relieved.

Troubled, Deborah followed the handmaidens with Nedra to a spacious chamber on the second floor, partitioned by filmy curtains. The largest area contained a raised sleeping couch. Curious, she went to it, pushed it and plumped it. A murmur of delight escaped her lips. The attendants giggled at her childlike pleasure. How strange to sleep above the floor! What if she should roll off during the night? The covering was a thick-sheared lustrous fabric totally unfamiliar to her.

She glanced around for Nedra. The old woman sat uneasily upon a cushion in the corner. She appeared so miserable that Deborah had to laugh. "Nedra, come and try this!"

"No. I'll be glad to sleep in my own house again!"

"Shall we prepare a bath for you, mistress?"

"A bath?" Was there a pool for women in the palace? She smiled eagerly. "Oh, yes."

While the maids prepared her bath, she walked to the latticed window. Out to the left, a handler led a horse toward an exercise ring. Horses stabled within the palace grounds? Everything was strategic, Beno had said. Then probably the tannery was that direction, also. She would ask for a tour. Beyond the palace walls, the lower city sprawled over the hilltop. She marveled at the task, enclosing such a huge city within walls, and on a hilltop, at that! How many years had gone into erecting the wall? How many thousands of peasants laboring a lifetime?

Deborah felt a stillness settle on her. A breeze lifted her hair. She raised her eyes heavenward and lifted her arms. "I, Deborah, thank thee, Yahweh, for thy leading. Thou shalt uncover my inner ear that I hear not what Sisera says but what he means. In all, I am thy servant."

Turning, she saw the girls staring at her, their faces no longer full of hauteur but of mingled wonder and trepidation. "Do you really speak to your god?" the younger one blurted.

Deborah smiled. "He is my companion."

The girl looked around uneasily. "And he talks to you?"

"Yes."

"Your bath is ready, mistress. And a cool drink and some fresh robes," said the other.

"Who chose the garments?" Deborah asked.

"King Sisera, lady." She draped over her arms a sea green robe and gossamer veil and a golden girdle sparkling with sapphires and rubies.

"It is lovely," Deborah said regretfully. "But I shall wear my own robes."

An hour later Deborah had forgotten the heat and weariness of her journey. She had allowed the attendants to perfume her with oils and to dress her rich hair, though not in the elaborate style they wished. Then she donned an unbleached linen robe, draping a dark blue veil softly about her head and shoulders.

When Beno appeared to escort her to the king, Deborah glanced at Nedra. The attendants followed her gaze. "Don't worry, we will care for the old one."

Beno led her downstairs through an enormous audience chamber, then up again to Sisera's apartments and another chamber, smaller, richly hung with costly tapestries. There were low tables carved of ebony and inlaid with mother-of-pearl, tall marble pedestals with exquisite statues of the gods, huge urns filled with exotic flowering plants. It was the most beautiful room she had ever seen. And on the balcony, silhouetted against the city, was the spare figure of Sisera. Even in repose he carried himself like a soldier.

Beno paused a few paces into the chamber. "Deborah of Ephraim," he announced.

Sisera turned. A smile lit his face. He strode across the carpeted floor and took both her hands in his outstretched ones. "Deborah! You look . . . magnificent!"

"Thank you, my lord." Deborah lowered her eyes, aware of his bold gaze.

"How has it fared with you?"

"Am I to believe you don't know?"

Sisera broke into laughter. "Oh, it is delightful to see you again. Come. Let me show you something." He placed her hand upon his arm and drew her to the parapet. In the distance, sharp shadows of the last rays of sun accented the deep cleavage between two ranges of hills. "That is the Pass of Megiddo, Deborah. You could follow these mountains all the way to the Great Sea."

He smiled down at her. "I am glad you came, Deborah. You have filled out a little. Somehow . . . you do not seem a tanner's daughter. You feared to come to Taanach before. Or perhaps you fear me still, else you would have worn my gift."

"It is a lovely garment." She matched his bantering tone, studying the deep-set eyes used to sunlight, the crisp, curled hair and smooth-shaven cheeks. He was as clean and sharp as new flax. His presence was commanding. She could believe women were easily attracted to him. Turning away, she walked idly around the chamber, pausing before an ivory image of a nude female astride a horse. Sisera reached around her and picked up the carving. "Meet Anath, Deborah. You remind me of her. She is my favorite. She is goddess of war and love." His fingers closed around the figure.

"It is an odd combination."

"Not so odd. Love is always close to war. She is consort to El Baal. Together they are totally powerful."

The pause grew heavy. Deborah tore her eyes away from the figure between his fingers and moved on. "And this, who is this?" Her fingers brushed an ivory figure about two feet high, a female with heavy breasts and hips.

"She is Ashtoreth, goddess of fertility. That is her temple out beyond the temple of El. And here, Deborah . . . for your god."

It was a pillar of white limestone about four feet high, polished to a mirror finish. There was nothing on it. She glanced at him questioningly. "For the unknown god." Before she could protest he went on, urgency and persuasiveness creeping into his voice. "Your people and mine, we are like herds of goats and herds of sheep. We all occupy the same land. We of the city-states of Canaan have learned to live together. I am at peace with all the kings of Canaan and Philistia. We are willing for you to live peacefully among us with your god, even as Shamer does."

"Even as your soldiers let my brother live peacefully among you?"

Sisera looked away. "I am truly sorry for that. It was never intended."

Deborah stifled her bitterness. Yahweh had not sent her here to cry her own loss. "You say the gods desire us to live in peace. Well they might, for they have no power against the one true God."

Sisera seemed amused. "Just like a woman. I speak of living at peace together and you change the subject!"

"I am not just a woman, King Sisera! As Moses and Joshua were not as other men, I am not as other women. I am Deborah, prophetess of Yahweh and judge of Israel!"

Sisera snorted. "Is this what you preach under the oaks of Shiloh?"

"What good eyes you have! Pity your ears are not likewise."

"My ears have heard reports of you for years, Deborah of Ephraim. Who elected you prophetess?"

"Yahweh called me."

"How do you know his wants? Did you go through an apprenticeship, perhaps?"

"You are laughing. What I know, I know."

"You mean he doesn't tell you everything?"

"No."

This seemed to please him. "But still you speak in his name."

"Yes."

Suddenly a new thought seemed to strike Sisera and he frowned. "Then, tell me now, why *have* you come?"

Deborah's hands flew together at her breast, then she dropped them to her sides. "You have the power to strike throughout the land. Nowhere are we Israelites safe outside our own villages. You speak of living in harmony. It is tempting, as when the lion invites the lamb to share his bed. Even now it tempts some who should know better. But know this, O Sisera. Our God is a jealous God. Not only is he first God, he will be the only God!"

"Yes, yes, we've heard this before."

"King Sisera, Yahweh *gave* us this land! He did not say to take it if it is unoccupied. He said, Take it. I your God give you this land in trust for me! And you shall worship no other gods in my land. Clearly, then, if the land is ours, and the people therein are to be Yahweh's people, then pagans who worship false gods must be driven out!"

"That's preposterous! Is this why you came, to tell me this?"

"I bring you a warning. I dreamed of a great gold chariot driven by black horses, thundering, thundering over planted fields. The wheels did crush the shoots and leave the ground bare. I beheld a threshing floor, with forty sacks of barley. Round about were forty tents. The chariot tried to gain the threshing yard. Wherever it broke through the ring of tents, more tents rose behind. Each time it gained the yard, sacks of barley spilled and the wheels of the chariot became mired in grain."

Sisera gave a snort of impatience. "And did Yahweh tell you what the dreams foretold?"

"The tents were the nomads, our people, wanderers, seeking a home. The sacks of barley were the peasants settling in the cities. The wheels of the chariot represent the might of Sisera. No matter how many times you crush the tents of our people, more will follow. The barley grains are like unto our people, who will suffocate you even as they did mire the wheels of your chariot."

"But I have no plans to war upon you."

"Whether the lion consumes the lamb a bite at a time or devours him whole, it is still the same for the lamb."

"That is because the lion will always be stronger."

"Something. . . ." Deborah struggled to voice what she felt but could not. "Something tells me that this will not always be so." The fire of her eyes pinioned him. She felt herself drawing power from the man himself, as though Yahweh were sapping the mighty warrior and infusing her with his strength.

"I see." Sisera sagged away from her.

A tense silence fell upon the chamber.

Deborah said quietly, "May I see my father?"

"Of . . . of course. A litter will be waiting when you are ready." Sisera preceded her from the chamber.

Darkon, high priest of El, stepped from behind a latticed alcove and watched them leave. Prophetess or not, this was a dangerous enemy. Gathering his sable robes about him, he hurried to the temple.

25

THE LITTER, borne by four strong slaves, scarcely swayed as Deborah and Nedra were carried through the streets. The veiled women peered through the curtains. The streets of the inner city were amazingly clean. Here there were no beggars with gaping faces pawing for alms, no slop emptying on the streets to splash the skirts of unwary passersby.

Presently a familiar odor struck her nostrils. "We're coming to the tannery!" she told Nedra.

"Aye!" Nedra wrinkled her nose.

Shamer was waiting for them when they alighted. "Father!" Deborah threw herself into his arms. "Look at you! Where did you get such fine clothes?"

Shamer stroked his tunic. "King Sisera. For your visit."

Deborah introduced Nedra. "It's good to meet another Israelite," Nedra declared. "It is frightening to be so far from home."

Shamer nodded sympathetically.

Deborah drew his arm through hers. "Let us go inside, father."

"But the odor. . . ."

"Father, am I not a tanner's daughter? How I have missed the good, honest scent of new leather!" She could feel him relax slightly.

The tannery was far larger than their humble home in Naphtali. Sisera had been good to him, Shamer insisted, as he showed Deborah and Nedra around the workshop, the fine-crafted tools and expensive dyes. "And he sent to Egypt for these stamping tools." Proudly he displayed the dark metal stamps.

A worker offered Nedra a place to sit and a cup of wine while Shamer drew Deborah through the curtain to his living quarters. He motioned her to a comfortable couch and pulled up a bench.

"And now my daughter," he said with hunger and longing in his voice, "how has it fared with thee?"

Sisera's sandals crunched through the gravel, his mood scarcely matching the gentle splashing of fountains or the serene statues placed in cool grottoes along the walks. He spied Beno at one end of the garden and motioned to him.

"She is with her father," Beno said in a low voice. "A runner just returned."

"Then come, we have an appointment with Darkon."

Beno did not like Darkon, but he was too cautious to express his disapproval. Though Sisera had been his friend for twenty years, the king was not a man to let friendship sway his political judgment. And Darkon had the ear of Sisera.

Shortly, the three men were seated in a secluded chamber within the heart of the temple of El. Beno pulled his cloak about him. No matter the season, a coldness and dampness pervaded these thick stone walls. He repressed a shudder. By the flickering torchlight, Darkon's face was etched in saturnine shadows. Beno longed to be back in the sunlight.

"Well, Darkon," Sisera plunged ahead, "what think you of our guest?"

"You would be well to kill her and be done with it."

This took both Sisera and Beno by surprise. "Do you think there is truth in her prophecy?"

"I think there is danger in any fanatic, especially those girded in holy zeal. People like that have no fear for themselves. Therefore, they are unpredictable."

Sisera moved uncomfortably. "Beno?"

Beno dipped his head graciously toward the priest. "I have not heard the words she attributes to her god."

"Yes, yes, but you've been with her for several days. Does she seem fanatic to you?"

"She seems like a very normal young woman, a trifle overserious at times. If she says she represents her god when she speaks, then. . . ."

"Then what, Beno?"

"Then I believe she . . . believes it. She was fearful of coming to

Taanach, afraid of you, my king, but she came in full belief it was the will of her god."

"There!" crowed Darkon. "Religious fanaticism at its sniveling worst. And thus this foolish young woman will cause her own death."

"She is the incarnation of Anath," mused Sisera.

"Believe that, and she has bewitched your mind!"

"My lord!" said Beno. "If you could be assured she is no more than an unusually adventuresome woman, would this not pull the teeth from her claim as a prophetess? Prophets are holy men. They are uninterested in the venal pleasures that beguile the rest of us."

Sisera thought of the green gown she had refused to wear.

"I see her as a woman with little self-consciousness. Indeed, she has an innocence about her that protects her in diverse situations."

"Paugh!" muttered Darkon.

But Sisera nodded, remembering her as a maiden wading in the waters of Galilee.

Beno hastened on. "Suppose you found her innocence but a sham? Suppose she were like all women, weak and frightened, tempting men with false innocence only to draw back when their mischief carries them too far?"

Sisera exploded in a laugh. "Are you suggesting I *woo* the lady, Beno?"

Beno grinned. "Unless Darkon would rather."

Darkon shrank at the prospect. "It is my suspicion that you would destroy her claim to save the woman's skin."

Beno smiled with an ease he did not feel. "I appreciate anything beautiful and warm, Darkon. It would be a shame to cut off a bloom by mistake."

Abruptly Sisera got to his feet. "I will spend more time with the lady. Whatever she is, she interests me."

Darkon's hand shot up to arrest their departure. "I give you the words of the Moabites, when first they did meet the Israelites. 'This horde will now lick up all that is round about us, as the ox licks up the grass of the field.' Take care, Sisera, that in seeking to prove—"

"Enough. We will discourse later. Come, Beno."

"My lord!"

"Well?"

Darkon uncoiled and rose swiftly. "Speak to your lady mother, Sisera. Truly, women can see into each other more easily than men."

"We will see." Sisera already had a fair idea of Leah's reaction to Deborah. He and Beno stepped outside in the cleansing air.

"If you will excuse me, sire, I must meet the lady Deborah."

"Now she's a lady, is she?"

Beno said nothing.

"I will fetch her myself, Beno."

In the tannery, a troubled silence. At length Shamer shook his bull-like head. "I suppose you know what you are doing, but . . . Deborah, are you sure?"

"Father. . . ."

"Now, now, I know your dreams, but you have grown away from me. This belief of yours . . . that to fulfill Yahweh's covenant all but his people must be driven out."

"How else can the false gods be destroyed?"

"Well, by. . . ." Shamer thought of the chariot makers and the vinedressers and the weavers of Taanach who had become his friends. Already some of them had renounced the gods of Canaan. Some of them knew Shamer's tales as well as he and delighted in pouncing upon details he omitted. Many lonely hours were vanquished in the company of his Canaanite friends. Still, he supposed, his daughter must be right. Spinning tales of the Israelites was only the work of his own weakness. He had thought to bring his daughter to one of their gatherings. Now, he saw, it would not do at all.

Deborah was waiting for an answer.

Slowly Shamer shook his head. "I am only a tanner. You are called prophetess." He placed a fist upon his chest. "I have discovered that these people are not evil, Deborah. Surely, if they cast away their false gods, Yahweh would rejoice."

Deborah frowned. "Yes, but . . . they cannot become Yahweh's *children,* father! The Kenite metalsmiths on my husband's caravans tell everyone they are Yahweh's children. I am happy that they no longer worship false gods, but to call themselves Yahwists. . . ." Her voice trailed off.

"How can you be sure they are wrong?"

"I . . . it is not one of the things Yahweh speaks to me about. And. . . ."

"And what, my daughter?"

Deborah sighed with a sadness he had not heard before. "Perhaps it is because my dear husband was born of a Philistine woman that Yahweh has not blessed us with children."

Awkwardly Shamer put his hammy arms around Deborah and embraced her as he said, "Where is your own faith, daughter? Perhaps you are one of the desolate. Perhaps you will bear no children. But show your faith, and your descendants will be many." A sudden movement behind Deborah distracted Shamer.

She turned to see the curtain drop in place. "Who was that, father?"

"No one. No one. Deborah, I have work I must finish. It must be nearly time for Beno to fetch you and your woman." He lifted the curtain into the outer shop, and plunged back to work with relief.

Deborah left the tannery and wandered outside, her mind in turmoil. Her father had changed so! He had grown deeper, and yet more simple. And how could he compare her with the desolate woman! It frightened her.

A chariot approached, pulled by a pair of trotting white horses, perfectly matched. The driver wore gold gauntlets which flashed in the sun. His bare head was thrown proudly back.

Sisera drew up before the tannery and sprang down lightly, the reins resting loosely in his hands. His eyes crinkled with good humor. "May I offer you a ride, Deborah? My mother is waiting supper for us."

She stepped back. "Thank you, sir, but I do not think there is room for three of us."

"Shamer!"

Shamer came to stand just behind his daughter. "Yes, sire?"

"See that Deborah's woman gets back to the palace."

"Yes, sire." Shamer turned away without a glance at Deborah. Sisera's eyebrows lifted in an unspoken challenge to her.

She hesitated. Surely there was nothing to fear! She found herself allowing Sisera to hand her into the chariot. In spite of herself, and the troubled father behind her, she felt her spirits lifting. She admired the fan-shaped plate of bronze which covered the forepart of the chariot, molded and etched to depict a scene of triumphant warriors on rearing stallions.

Sisera smiled down at her proudly, possessively. Determinedly she avoided his gaze. "You are not afraid of horses?"

"My husband taught me to ride. He is the best horseman in Ephraim."

"Tell me about him. Surely few husbands allow their wives to travel to distant cities alone."

"Surely you know, my lord, that Lapidoth is away. He would not have wished me to come."

Sisera threw back his head and laughed. "Oh, such honesty!"

"He would be astonished at this chariot, my lord, for truly it surpasses even the Philistine chariots. He says they are heavy and not easy to turn."

"Even so. If you could see them sweeping over the Plain of Jezreel, Deborah! Rocks, pits, nothing stops them! And my horses—did you ever see such beasts?"

"Truly, no."

The teeming peasantry in the streets parted like a wave before the chariot and closed again behind it. The rich trappings of the chariot threw off sparks of sunlight. It was a heady feeling. Deborah felt it like wine and laughed for the sheer pleasure of feeling so alive. Suddenly her eyes lighted upon a poor bird seller. He had stood upright and stared at her in astonishment as the chariot clattered by. Sisera felt her start.

"What is it?"

"Nothing. Where are we going?"

"Are you equal to a real ride?" he asked slyly.

Deborah remembered her dream. "How fast can you go in open country?"

His answer was an arrogant smile. Several horsemen fell in casually behind them as through the gates of the fortressed city they rode, to the bottom of the hill. Suddenly, with a shout of exuberance, Sisera cracked the whip over the backs of the startled horses. With a tremendous surge, the chariot leaped over the fields, leaving the horsemen behind. Faster and faster, until it seemed the wheels barely touched the ground. Deborah's cloak flew back and her red hair whipped in the wind. They passed peasants tilling the fields and glimpsed orchards through shadowed arches of trees. Finally Sisera brought the foam-flecked stallions to a halt. Snapping the reins through a holding ring, he stepped down.

Deborah was out of breath and laughing from sheer exhilaration

as he handed her down. He led her into the shade beneath a vener-
able fig tree whose lower limbs had been pruned to provide a shelter
for men and animals.

Sisera's eyes roamed thirstily over her features. "Now," he
breathed.

Before she was aware of it his arm had gripped her waist, pulling
her to him. His other arm pinioned her arms at her sides. She felt
his mouth close on hers, felt the scratch of his beardless face. She
struggled. It only increased his iron grip. His hand moved up to her
hair. He buried his face in its abundance.

With horror Deborah realized she could not fight his strength. He
would do his will. Only Yahweh could save her. She stopped struggling. Yahweh would not let this happen! She felt the trunk of the
fig tree at her back. When Sisera reached for her lips again she did
not resist. It was a long, deep, lingering kiss. To her it was as cold
as a serpent. He pulled back. A slight smile curved the fine, thin lips.

"My Anath," he whispered.

She struggled to control her fear. The words dropped as cold as
well stones. "I am Deborah, wife of Lapidoth, prophetess of Yahweh. Do this thing if you must. My body is nothing and Yahweh
is all."

Sisera lifted a hand to twine a finger in her hair. "And I am Sisera,
king of Canaan. Thou art only a woman, Deborah."

Deborah refused to lower her eyes. They stood thus, he breathing
heavily, she fighting to maintain control. Finally he looked away.
He turned from her. "A king does not take what is not offered
willingly. In time, Deborah, you will come to me."

Days away from Taanach, an Israelite on horseback entered the
gates of Damascus and learned that the caravan of Lapidoth the
Philistine had come in from Babylon just two days ago. The rider
sent up a prayer to Yahweh that he would find Lapidoth in a
benevolent mood.

26

IN THE GREAT DINING HALL of the palace, light flickered from a hundred bronze sconces filled with fragrant oil. The pale glow softened the harsh stonework and softened the features of the small woman who waited with the king. She sat erect upon a ruby couch before a low table laden with delicacies. There were fillets of fish poached in sheep's milk, crisp vegetables marinated in garnet wine, honeyed grapes and berries, pastries filled with dates and almonds, tender, steaming strips of roast lamb on golden plates.

The woman herself seemed a delicacy of art. She wore on her soft, plump arms a score of gold filigree circles. Her silver hair was resplendent with icy jewels which flashed blue lights, as did her painted eyes. Her gown was cerulean blue and frosted with silver.

Deborah appeared on the arm of Beno. Leah extended a gracious hand while her eyes swept the prophetess.

King Sisera rose, signing Beno away. "This is she, mother. Deborah, prophetess of Ephraim. My mother, Leah." Deborah bowed to her as she had to Lapidoth's mother.

"Leah, queen mother of the Canaanites."

"My son's head is filled with your lore, Deborah. I think you have bewitched him." Her voice was light and musical. Leah beckoned Deborah to a plush couch beside her. She smiled significantly to her son and gestured to a place at her other side. Instead, Sisera drew a couch beside Deborah.

Deborah did not glance at him. "A good king must learn all he can of those who dwell about him. Only then can he make wise judgments."

Deborah's answer took Leah aback. She had been prepared for coyness or stupid giggles, but not this.

"I am glad you believe him a good king." Deborah did not rise to the bait. Leah went on. "In truth, I have not met a prophet before.

Oh, of course, we have our priests, you know. And the king must support them all to keep his subjects happy. I suppose your priests do likewise?"

"No, my lady. Our priests are priests of Yahweh."

"The unknown god, mother."

"Oh, yes. The empty pillar." A quick, bright smile at Deborah. "And do all of this god's prophets have red hair?"

For the first time Deborah smiled. "In truth, I do not know. Neither have I met another prophet."

"What do you see? Do you see visions? Do you live in a cave like the holy men?"

"Nay, lady. I abide in the village of my husband. I milk goats, grind barley, weave for my husband, and make pottery."

"Ugh! Have you no servants for these chores?"

"Yahweh blesses all work, lady. The man who tills his own field earns his own reward. He who forces another to till for him and does not share its bounty does evil in the sight of the Lord."

Leah glanced at Sisera. "What is she saying?"

"I think that was a slap at Canaanite ways, mother," he grinned. "Alas, how could I possibly till all my lands? Some men are meant to be servants and some masters, even as birds fly and beasts do not."

"Yahweh has said to us that each man shall own his own land and care for it, and hand it down to his children to be held in trust, even unto the last generation."

"Oh, my," Leah fanned herself. "This talk grows too much for my ears. Deborah, surely you have heard that too much thought renders women infertile? Have you no fears for your unborn sons?"

Deborah drew a sharp breath. The cruel barb had landed truly, though not for the reason Leah believed. "No, lady. I listen to Yahweh. Surely his care for me is better than my care for myself!"

"Hear well, mother! Israelite women are not cradled and coddled like rich men's concubines."

"So!" His mother leaned back with a delighted laugh. "Now we learn the pit of your fascination. Very well, Sisera, but mark you, Israelite women submit to this only because their men are too poor to have it otherwise. If you let them, such women will only too gladly take over all that you have and enjoy it themselves!"

Cutting off her son before he could challenge this, Leah turned to Deborah and said sweetly, "I am most curious, Deborah. You are so tanned. Do you enjoy the sun? Do not you peasant women find it harsh upon your skin? I suppose it is nothing to you. Like birthing babies. When my son was born—"

"Mother, I grow thirsty. Will you serve wine, please?" Deborah stole a glance at Sisera. His mouth was hard with anger.

Leah smiled sweetly at her son. "A thousand pardons for forgetting my duties. I often hostess his dinners," she told Deborah as she poured wine into silver goblets. "His wives are such rabbity little creatures. They would rather play in the warren all day than discourse with strangers—especially women. We have never hosted an unescorted woman, Deborah. Usually women come here as spoils of war. Such a turnover. Women do not hold my son's interest for long. But he does his duty to the gods, don't you, my love?" She glanced fondly at her son, then turned once more to Deborah. "Have you no family?"

Deborah returned the bright smile. Leah knew perfectly well who her father was.

"My husband's home is in Ephraim."

"Oh, yes. I had forgotten. And he permits you to travel about alone in these dangerous times?"

"King Sisera assured me I had naught to fear." She avoided looking at him.

"Oh, yes. Well, Sisera, she is . . . different. Probably we can soften her skin with pumice powder, but those nails—"

"Mother! You have gone far enough. Deborah, please pardon my mother's rudeness. As you can see, she is not used to conversing with women who have more on their minds than themselves."

Leah rose. Two bright spots of red appeared high on her cheeks. "And who is it who keeps you from making a constant fool of yourself! Use this one for the gods and get rid of her. She is evil!"

Sisera rose in swift, deadly motion. "You beg so prettily for the baubles of war, for males upon which to practice your witchery. Think you I do not know you fear losing your place of honor? This does you no honor, mother. Leave us!"

Leah's chin jerked spasmodically. Darting a venomous glance at Deborah, she swept from the room.

Sisera began pacing, his sandals making no sound on the carpeted stone. He felt strangely at odds with himself. "It was not from fear of your god, Deborah, that I did not take you this afternoon. Only once did I allow myself to. . . ."

He stopped before her and willed her to look upon him. A smile played on his lips. "Had you been willing, as I am still . . . then I would forget that you are the wife of Lapidoth and, perhaps, a holy woman." He ran the back of his forefinger down her cheek.

"Why did Yahweh call you?" he asked softly.

"To make his presence real to his people."

"That is not easy when he has no image," he said in the same soft voice.

"There is no image of Yahweh because he is beyond human imagination. He is spirit, he is wind, he is fire. He is *all*, Sisera! He does not play as do your pitiful gods, or engage in human jealousies, or demand human sacrifice. Through prophets he sent the holy laws, which are the same for all, which say a family must care for its poor elderly, that humankind must be honest in all dealings; must love God and forsake images; must love nothing on this earth as much as doing the will of him who made us. For true happiness lies in doing the will of the Father. True wealth is not stored in treasure houses, but in good deeds done for one another in his name."

In the pale robe, with the blue veil falling softly over her burnished hair, Deborah seemed to radiate light. Sisera faltered backward. "Why does your god wish me to know these things?"

"I do not know, King Sisera. Perhaps he desires to work through you."

Fright such as he had never known invaded Sisera's heart. Among the silent images of Anath and El, of Ashtoreth and Dagon, he could live comfortably. But a god such as Deborah proclaimed! A god of such awesome power that he could protect even a woman alone in an alien country. No! Never would he be subject to such a one! His face became a mask. "I pray that you will excuse me now, Deborah. My servant will escort you to your quarters."

As she left, he felt the flickering shadows of the dining hall rise and merge and deepen into a monstrous, palpable void. It would suffocate him. He fled to the balcony and filled his lungs with air. Of one thing he was now certain: If anything happened to the woman Deborah while she was in Taanach, his empire would crash about him.

"S-s-st!"

Shamer awakened groggily. He had consumed a great quantity of wine last night. "What? Who is it?"

"Joash. Sisera is up to something. He has ordered Beno to take Deborah away from Taanach at daybreak, and he's called out a regiment of chariots."

Shamer was sitting now, groping for his sandals. "B-but, why?"

"By the baals, who knows what's in the devil's mind!"

"Does this mean I won't see my daughter again?" Shamer couched his meaty hands between his knees, dangling a sandal.

"Shamer, Shamer! Come, man."

"What? What can I do, Joash?"

"Go to the stables. Help harness the teams. Try to find out where they are going. I'm going back to the palace."

"Are you going to see my daughter?"

Joash stopped abruptly. How to tell Shamer that he had seen her on the arm of Sisera, disporting herself in his chariot. His heart filled with pity for Shamer and with outrage for his friend Lapidoth. By the gods, if Deborah were his wife he would beat her until she could only crawl at his feet! He smiled reassuringly at the old tanner. His voice gentled. "No. One of her maids."

But as far as Joash could learn, Deborah was merely returning home. The maids were to accompany her and Nedra as before, this time directly to Shiloh. Of the reason for the chariots, they could offer not a hint.

Skirting the palace guards, Joash returned to the tannery and cursed the coming daylight. Shamer returned near dawn with the disquieting news that the chariots were forming a war party. There was no talk of targets. But neither Sisera's horses nor his chariot were being readied. "It's probably a minor raid," Shamer concluded.

Or something Sisera doesn't want to be associated with, thought Joash. Shamer was watching him.

"What will you do?"

"I don't know. I can't follow both of them." Joash struck his fist on the table. "Why didn't Deborah stay in Shiloh!"

Deborah and Nedra left Taanach by caravan within the hour. Their way lay along the base of the foothills along the southern edge of the Valley of Jezreel. Almost upon their heels, a regiment of chariots commanded by Lieutenant Sem trotted through the two sets of gates and struck across the valley in a southeasterly course. Shortly thereafter a poor bird seller, now divested of his birds, plodded unconcernedly through the gates upon the back of an ass, acquired undoubtedly by the sale of his birds, and followed in the direction of the chariots.

Deborah's mind was in turmoil. Why had Sisera dismissed her so imperiously? Where was Joash? Why had she not been permitted to bid her father good-bye? Brooding skies overhead matched her mood. Had she done what Yahweh desired? Who could be sure? Sisera had met her words with iron control. Would Yahweh's message persuade him to allow the Israelites to expand peaceably?

"My lady." Deborah looked up. Beno pointed to the flat-bottomed lead gray clouds unrolling across the sky. "A storm is coming. We must make all haste through the valley." He need say no more.

A benevolent rain would cast its seed lovingly and gently over the plain, readying the stony soil for the plow. But sometimes the rain came like a raging beast, thrashing down the sides of the hills, causing the shallow wadis of the river Kishon, which crossed and recrossed Jezreel like a web of stones, to spew forth the very rocks of its beds. Unfortunate the man or animal caught in its wrath.

The little procession pushed on through the valley, hugging the foothills. The first drops of rain began to hit as they gained the far side of Jezreel and began the ascent into the mountains. They had made not nearly enough progress for one day, yet the ferocity of the storm sent the soldiers seeking shelter.

The party settled in under a ledge that jutted forth like a stele to ancient gods. By dawn the storm had passed, and they set their faces once again toward Shiloh.

The unexpected rains had disrupted the mission of the chariots, too. Thus midday of the second day found Sem and his men lying in tall grasses on a knoll overlooking fields of barley planted in the foothills of the Manassehite village of Not.

Sem watched the graceful figures of the young women and men in the distance moving methodically, peacefully, tilling their scrawny rows of barley. The rain had fallen short of the Israelite lands. It was peculiar, all right, this drought that stopped and started at the Israelite borders. Not a bad trick for a mere wilderness god. Sem's mind dwelt for a moment in speculation. What was so urgent about this mission that he had had to call his men from a night's sleep, or a night's pleasure, in the case of some? What was to be gained by sacking a poverty-ridden village of ignorant peasants?

The crop was almost an embarrassment, unworthy of destruction. Sem heard a horse moving in its traces behind him. He settled more comfortably on the hillside. Only a short while now until the gleaners completed the swing around the near end of the field, closest to his men and headed the other way, farthest from their own defenses.

27

When Deborah and nedra reached shiloh, the entire village poured out to receive them.

"You're back! You're back!" cried Eladah the widow. "Someone call Dorcas. Deborah has been delivered from the Canaanites!" Spying her friend Nedra among the soldiers, Eladah shrieked with joy. "Nedra!"

"Praise be Yahweh, we're home!" cried Nedra, suddenly finding her tongue. "Oh, Eladah, wait till you hear!"

Beno dismounted and offered Deborah his hand.

"Stay and be refreshed, noble Beno," said Deborah.

"No, lady. With your permission we shall water the animals, then repair to the wells at Shechem. My men will feel more at home there." Nor would he let his men tarry long at the wells. By Sem's timetable, Beno would have to be out of Shechem by nightfall to escape the wrath that was sure to come.

Deborah smiled. "Thank you for your good care."

Beno lingered a moment, observing the joyful faces of the villagers. The citizens of Shiloh pressed in, eager to miss not a word of their conversation, which he knew would be told and retold at the cooking fires tonight.

"I could wish we followed the same star, Deborah, prophetess of Israel," he said. "Farewell."

Prophetess of Israel! The people looked at one another. This Canaanite general had called Lapidoth's wife prophetess of Israel!

As Beno and his men left, the crowd folded in upon them. "Tell us what happened! Did you actually see Sisera? What did he look like? Tell us about the palace! What did you *see*, Deborah!"

Deborah drank in the familiar faces, the shining eyes and flashing smiles of welcome. So dear to her were Yahweh's people! Her heart swelled in thankfulness. She spied Dorcas hurrying toward them, her veil flying behind.

The two women embraced, then Dorcas held her at arm's length. "As thou hast said, Deborah, Yahweh sent thee to Taanach, for he has miraculously delivered thee hence."

Deborah slipped her arm around Dorcas' waist. "Good friends, I shall tell you all about Taanach only after I have told my husband. He is bound to return soon."

And pry though Dorcas might, and even crippled Dimon, leaning precariously on his pallet, Deborah revealed not a word.

But as for Nedra, she reveled in her new status. All day she sat beside the well in a circle of rapt listeners, reciting her tale.

The next day and the day following, Deborah ground the meal for the morning cakes and thought of war to come. She labored in the pottery and yearned for Lapidoth. She strode the hills at dawn gathering herbs and wondered that Yahweh was silent. Had he already given direction, and had she failed to recognize it? She examined her heart. Yes, war was to be. But no other thing, no time of urgency stirred her heart. Therefore, she must be content. In Yahweh's time would she be led further.

At dawn the fourth day of their return, a minute movement on the road from the north caught her eye. She was standing under her favorite oak. It could mean . . . Lapidoth! Deborah flew down the hill. Quickly she looped a halter around one of the horses and struggled up on his back.

Beyond the gates Deborah urged the horse into a gallop. Soon she could make out a large form, and beside it, a flash of blue cloak. Lapidoth and Hamid. Never had she been so glad to see them! Minutes later she stood in the middle of the road in the arms of her husband, with Hamid beside them smiling broadly.

Words tumbled from her as the watery torrent had tumbled about them on their return from Taanach.

Lapidoth's face was struck with relief, then anger. "You in Taanach! You and Sisera!"

"Why say you like that! For three years Yahweh forbade me to go and now he sent me. Oh, my husband, Sisera's might is terrible to behold!" Out of her poured tales of the wealth, the wonders of Taanach. She told him of the chariots, of the thousands of well-fed and trained soldiers, of her father laboring among many in the tanneries there.

"And now?" They began walking leisurely toward town.

"Verily, I do not know. I wait for Yahweh's word."

Later that morning, Deborah and Lapidoth were sitting with the elders before the gates of Shiloh. Suddenly a clatter of hooves interrupted them as horsemen in the vanguard of a procession rode through the gates. Deborah rose with an exclamation of gladness. "Joash! Thou art safe! Blessed be Yahweh!"

Behind him was a full company of soldiers and, still coming in, a score of civilians on foot.

Lapidoth left the circle of elders and greeted his friend. "Hail, Joash! What brings you and Kanah's men to Shiloh?"

"Hardly the best of news," Joash said tersely. He swung a leg over and leaped lightly off the horse. As he pulled off his helmet to wipe the damply curling hair on his brow he glanced at the assemblage. When he saw Deborah, contempt flickered briefly on his face. "Sisera's legions sacked the village of Not. It happened three days ago."

The elders rose with cries of dismay.

"Neither man nor child is alive. Not a house stands. The fields are gutted." Joash turned to Deborah. There was no trace of the appealing, boyish earnestness of three years ago in the harsh voice that now said to her, "There are no bodies of young women."

Deborah gasped. She remembered Mamre, the fat chief elder of Not, his wives and his children. . . . Why? Why had Sisera's wrath fallen upon Not? Behind her, the women of Shiloh began to wail.

"Where is your caravan?" Joash demanded of Lapidoth.

"Damascus. When your runner came, Hamid and I rode ahead. Thank you, Joash. I know the risk you took to protect my wife. I am in your debt."

A priest elbowed his way through. Deborah recognized Phurah, the young Levite whom she had met at the Feast of Ingathering.

"Commander Joash," whispered Phurah urgently, "the Ark. . . ."

"Yes," nodded Joash. "Behold, everyone! Since the raid the Shechemites are at each other's throats. A man who lived there for years was murdered yesterday because he happened to be Canaanite. We're on the verge of civil war."

The silence in the normally bustling square was like a shroud suffocating the new day. "The priests and elders of Shechem ordered the Ark brought to Shiloh for safekeeping. Lapidoth, I must speak to you."

Grasping the big man by the shoulder, he pushed his way out of the crowd. While the villagers watched, four priests carried the Ark of the Covenant to the center of the marketplace. Deborah felt Dorcas at her shoulder.

"What is the matter?" whispered Dorcas. "Thou art white as curd."

Deborah reached for her hand and grasped it tightly. The enormity of what was happening began to dawn upon her. The Ark rested in Shiloh. That night in the field in Shechem so long ago, Yahweh had told her that when the Ark was in Shiloh she must speak to the tribal confederation. Yet there was no confederation planned. But surely the Israelites would avenge the destruction of Not! Together they could fight!

Why had Sisera done this! Had her challenge to his power incited this vicious act? He had cast down the gauntlet. He had flaunted the words of Yahweh delivered by his servant Deborah.

She swayed against Dorcas. "O mother of my husband! I am frightened!"

"What frightens thee, Deborah? We are safe here."

"No one is safe, mother. Now no one is safe!"

Around them, the elders babbled excitedly of constructing a stone temple to replace the Tent of Yahweh. Suddenly Lapidoth burst upon the two women, his face terrible with rage. "In the name of Yahweh, woman, what hast thou brought upon us?"

Dorcas intervened. "Not in the streets, Lapidoth. Come. We shall sit together at home with your father. Joash and his men need refreshment."

"You entertain Joash. I would speak with my wife! Deborah. Come!" Rapidly Lapidoth strode down the dusty street toward their house. Deborah hastened after him. Who was this menacing stranger? It was a side of Lapidoth she'd never seen.

He was waiting in the cool dimness of the house, poised as if he would strike her. Her heart pounded. She halted just inside the door.

"I knew, before I took you to wife, that you were not like other women, Deborah. But I hoped that marriage would change you. I hoped that when we had children—but no, it's not the sons of Lapidoth they speak of but Deborah's husband. Husband of the prophetess! It is as if when I married you I ceased to be Lapidoth the Philistine and became Lapidoth the husband. And now I find no honor even in that—if honor it ever were! I find you have been disporting yourself like a harlot, riding in Sisera's very chariot! Tell me this is the work of Yahweh!"

She tried to answer. Her voice could not break through the boulder in her throat.

"Deborah. . . ." His voice betrayed his agony.

"Nay," she whispered. Then her courage returned. "Sisera parading me in his chariot was the folly of an enemy who shows off his armaments as though to a child! Think, my husband, would Sisera have boasted of his chariots, his horses, the skills of his men, or exposed the might of his armies to such as thee or Joash?" She placed her fingertips to her temples and closed her eyes for a moment. "The stories are true," she went on, "the rumors whispered of the speed of their chariots, the terrible manner in which they may affright a man who has only himself on foot, armed with a cudgel. Oh, Lapidoth! Yahweh has shown us what we face!" With her face tipped inches from his, Deborah searched his eyes.

Slowly he relaxed. His hands came up to rest on her shoulders. "Forgive me, Deborah. The words of Joash were hot because he does not understand thee. It was not Sisera the king, but Sisera the man I beheld."

"Thou art the only man for me, husband." She almost cried with relief.

"And thou the woman for me," he said heavily. "What's done is done. When Ira brings the caravan to Shechem, I will draw my men. Joash is already under orders."

Deborah shook her head. "No, dearest. The Ark is in Shiloh, don't you see?"

"I see that we must avenge Not!" he said grimly.

"The Ark is in Shiloh, Lapidoth, *as Yahweh hath foretold!*"

"Deborah, this is no time. . . ."

She drew herself up. "Shall we waste our men by dribbling them in small doses to be crushed under Sisera's iron wheels? Well have I listened to thee, Lapidoth, when thou didst tell of the forces on horseback which strike a caravan and vanish before the dust settles. To follow Sisera's men now, when they are long gone, is to sacrifice the blood of Israel to El Baal. This shall be a matter for all the tribes!"

Lapidoth searched her impassioned face. Well he remembered the night in the field when Yahweh had called her, when he had awakened and she was gone, when upon discovering her in the field overwhelming relief had given way to grudging jealousy that Yahweh demanded first claim on his wife. In the mystical union between his wife and the unseen power of Yahweh, she had been for a time lost to him.

"Very well, Deborah. I do not understand, but I must obey Yahweh in thee. Let us join the others." Something in his face closed to her. He dipped his massive shoulders and went out through the curtain. Deborah felt suddenly bereft. *Desolate.* She remembered Shamer's description with a shock of recognition.

In the courtyard before the pottery, under the lacy shade of the olive, they found Joash on his haunches on a rug next to Dimon's pallet. Lapidoth's father looked up at him. For a man of his years, crippled with pain, it was not fear of war which had the power to move him, but contemplation of the sadness of loss sure to follow. Dorcas placed a cup of wine in her husband's hand and a tray of sweetmeats within reach.

Deborah gestured an offer of help. Dorcas shook her head and Deborah sank to the rug beside her husband. She sighed deeply, her gaze resting on Joash. He met it with a mixture of hostility and embarrassment.

"Why didst follow me to Taanach, Joash?" she inquired gently.

"What choice did I have? No Israelite in his right mind walks into the mouth of the lion. Lapidoth was gone. Who was going to protect you?"

"Yahweh."

Joash snuffed a retort and turned to Lapidoth. "I do not understand you. There was Deborah, joyriding with the king of the Canaanites. Yet here she sits in honor beside you."

Lapidoth fixed Joash with an impassive stare. "Do not question what you do not understand."

Joash got deliberately to his feet, his lips pulled back. "Don't pretend with me! I will tell no one else what I saw, but as for myself, I may wonder which side—"

Lapidoth's coiled fist carried the impact of his entire body as he sent Joash sprawling in the dust. Dorcas screamed. For a long moment Joash didn't move. Then his limbs responded jerkily and he hauled himself to his feet. He looked at all of them, his full lips working. When he spoke, his voice was low and hoarse. "We're going after them."

"You won't find them."

"It doesn't matter. A village of theirs for a village of ours." He stumbled away.

"Lapidoth, don't let him go! Joash," cried Deborah, "wait. We must wait for Yahweh's call. Now that the Ark is in Shiloh. . . ."

Joash stopped and faced them, blood trickling from his dust-caked mouth and nose. His chest heaved. "My men thirst for enemy blood." There was dignity in his bearing as he said, "Think no more of your debt to me, Lapidoth. I will never claim it. Not was a Manassehite village. Ephraim can sit home and tend its fires. Manasseh has already heard the call. I know a Canaanite village near Jezreel, with few soldiers. Tell me how your Yahweh can better those odds! Fare thee well, *prophetess!*"

"Lapidoth!" cried Deborah.

"Let him go." Lapidoth spat in the dust.

Dimon's quiet voice broke in. "If Kanah has ordered him to retaliate, that is what he will do. Be thankful it is not our responsibility to avenge Not."

"It *is* our responsibility, but only with Yahweh." Deborah's voice rang with conviction. She scrambled to her feet and shook out her skirts. "I am going to the hills."

All day the tall, graceful figure of Deborah was seen among the wild flowers upon the hills above Shiloh. Dorcas fretted that she would be hungry, but Lapidoth forbade his mother to disturb her. As evening neared, when the lowing of the animals pressing together filled the twilight with song, Lapidoth prepared to go to his wife. Dorcas made ready a packet of food and a skin of cool goat's milk.

He found her upon a rocky abutment which presented a smooth shelf half the size of a small room, cradled on two sides by the hills. Her face was set toward the flame of sunset which had already deserted the valley. She had pushed back her veil and the red beams glinted in her hair. Her eyes were smoked in shadow. She neither spoke nor moved. Lapidoth removed his cloak and settled it around her shoulders. Watchful, he sat a little way off. Deep in the night she suddenly arose. She raised her arms in a wide circle beneath the starry sky. Her voice rose clear and strong, chanting a paean of praise to Yahweh.

Hours went by. Still she stood in an attitude of obedience. Lapidoth must have dozed. When he awoke at dawn, Deborah was curled in his cloak, asleep. The food was untouched. As though she felt his gaze, her eyes opened.

"Good morrow, my husband."

"Good morrow. Hast slept well?"

"Oh, so deeply." Deborah rose and stretched.

Lapidoth opened the food packet and blessed it. Together they broke the fast. At length Lapidoth said, "Hath Yahweh spoken to thee, Deborah?"

"Yes, lord. There must be a meeting of all the tribes in Shiloh before the Ark. There I will deliver his words." Her face was filled with a calm and terrible beauty.

A tremor rippled through Lapidoth's body. How much he loved her, and how inadequate he felt to protect her from whatever must befall! He would give all to Yahweh to spare her, for he knew that in the mere matter of speaking before a confederation there could be trouble. Many of the tribes would not accept being ordered about by a woman, even as they had fought her right to speak in Shechem at the Feast of Ingathering.

"It shall be as you say, prophetess of Yahweh."

28

LAPIDOTH KNEW DEBORAH THAT NIGHT, with tenderness and passion beyond anything they had experienced together. The next morning, in half-awake contentment, he felt renewed stirrings and reached for his wife. She was gone. He listened, but did not hear the familiar sounds of breakfast being prepared, or voices in the pottery. He smiled ruefully. What now had taken her?

Deborah had gone first to the hills and then to Yahweh's Tent, on a quiet street under a grove of tamarind trees. Having sent word to the priest, she waited within the first courtyard. For though Yahweh's prophetess, she was still subject to the laws forbidding a woman to enter the inner courtyard or the innermost Holy of Holies containing the Ark itself.

Phurah hastened to her, robes flapping about his ankles, hands extended with pleasure. "Deborah, I'm pleased to see you looking so well. Living in Shiloh agrees with you." He led her to a bench and sat beside her. "Your fame has grown. In Shechem people speak your name with reverence."

"Thank you, Phurah. But now I need your help."

"My help?" Her plea took Phurah by surprise. "Thou art closer to Yahweh than even I, though guardian of his Covenant."

"I have taken the Nazirite vow."

"You have *what?*"

"War is coming, Phurah. I must separate myself to Yahweh until we have won."

"That is not a vow taken lightly, Deborah."

"No." Deborah bowed her head. Her fingers plucked at a strand of hair which fell forward across her cheek.

"And it has made thee unhappy."

"Yes," she whispered. "O Yahweh condemn me for such weakness! Lapidoth, my poor Lapidoth, my dear one. . . ."

"Does he know about a Nazirite vow?"

Deborah shrugged. "I . . . I suppose."

"Does he know you've taken it?"

"Not yet. It wasn't a thing . . . open to discussion. I . . . I was afraid I would be dissuaded." She raised her head swiftly and Phurah could see the torment in her eyes. "In the arms of Lapidoth. . . . I have forsaken his bed. Nothing must separate me from Yahweh. I must be ready when he speaks!"

"It is not just thy bed Lapidoth loves, Deborah." Phurah's voice was gently reproachful. "This will pass. I will go with you into battle. I will be there when the time has come to complete your vow."

She thought of that time, after the battle should be won. Certain things were required, one of which she dreaded, and cursed her weakness. They sat in silence. Finally she burst out, "Oh, Phurah, some things are so hard to bear!"

"But you are also a woman!" thundered Lapidoth that night as they faced off in their house. "How could you do it! How could Yahweh demand that you separate yourself from my bed! That you drink no wine, or eat grapes? Deborah. . . ." His face was purple with anger. "By thunder, it is h__ to be married to a prophetess!" Lapidoth seized his cloak and disappeared into the dark streets of Shiloh.

Deborah sighed wearily. *O Yahweh, is nothing easy?* If only she had a babe to cradle, to comfort her when she felt so terribly, completely alone. She picked up her cloak and climbed the outside stairs to the roof. There she sat with her chin propped on her knees. Thus she had sat as a young girl many times at Galilee's shore, dreaming as each ebb and flow of the current carried tides of tiny phosphorescent fish. And she had stared, fascinated, at the silvery, vulnerable creatures, marveling that any had lived to become grown.

Her head would look like a melon, he'd said, for he loved to thrust his fingers through the vibrant mass of her hair. Suddenly she lowered her head upon her arms and wept.

Lapidoth did not return until morning. He stared at her through bloodshot eyes, his stale breath reeking of wine. "I meant to lie with a harlot," he croaked. "I could not do it." He stumbled past her and fell on their mat. Soon she heard him snoring.

"We took him prisoner, King Sisera, because he had a hole in his ear you could spit through."

"Let's get a look at him." Sisera moved to the dais at the end of the audience chamber and sat on a chair carved to resemble a huge predatory bird, two high, arching wings forming the arms. He leaned back, stretching his legs before him. Strange, how lacking in energy he had felt lately. How boring was Taanach!

Two palace guards dragged the unfortunate into the chamber. Blood streaked his face. A deep gouge appeared in his vest where it had deflected a spear. A guard ripped off his helmet and kicked his legs out from under him. As he fell before Sisera, the guard placed a foot on the back of his neck.

Sisera leaned forward on his elbows. Of course he knew him. Beno had said he was now an Israelite commander. "If it isn't my Habiru scribe. How is it your military talents escaped our notice when you worked for us, Joash? Now you seem to be everywhere, mostly in my hair."

The man struggled against his bindings.

"By Anath, get him to his feet! I despise men who cannot look me in the eye."

The men hauled him upright. Joash planted his feet apart and stared defiantly at the king.

Sisera sighed. The whole affair of Joash had been badly managed. "It would have been simpler if you had been killed on the battlefield. And nobler, Joash. A soldier's death is better than an escaped slave's. Well? Surely after all these adventures you have many tales?"

Joash coughed and spat a gout of blood on the marble floor. "All that I am I have learned from you, Sisera."

Sisera left his chair and stalked around Joash. "Tell me, did your prophetess send you to make war upon me?"

Joash's expression remained carefully unchanged.

Almost to himself Sisera continued, "I brought you to my palace, had you educated, allowed you to participate in the temple rites. I treated you nobly, Joash," he reasoned quietly.

"I served you well and would have to this day if you had not—"

"Enough." Sisera waved his hand tiredly. "Kill him and be done with it. Stone him."

"Oh, no!" Leah parted a curtain and hurried into the chamber.

Sisera glanced up in surprise. How long had she been listening? "No, my son. There is a better way." Her blue eyes widened innocently.

"What now, mother? The man is a traitor."

"He has used his eyes against you. Shall you grant him escape through death? Why should you lose a trained servant?"

Sisera sighed. He had no doubt at all that his mother had something special in mind for Joash. And within, he knew what it was. He preferred not to dwell on it.

"He cannot serve thee dead, my son."

"Then how shall he serve me, my wise mother? Shall I hamstring him, that he cannot run away? Lop off his hands, that he cannot climb the walls? Cut off his manhood, that he—"

"Put out his eyes," said the mother of Sisera. "And then give him to me."

"No! Kill me, Sisera, as you killed my sister! Does not even a peasant have feelings? Should not even a peasant avenge his family? Who are you, that you can rip the flower of maidenhood from little children! What gods tell you this is good?"

Sisera's cuff sent Joash reeling to the floor. The soldiers wrenched him to his feet. "Enough! Stone him and be done with it."

Leah laid a soft hand upon his arm. "Please . . .," she wheedled, "call it my spoils of war."

"But why this one? You can have any man."

"I want this one. He can listen to my thoughts. He can compose poems for me when I am lonely."

"Then why put out his eyes?" But even as he asked, Sisera saw the wrinkled face, the shapely but liver-spotted hands. A wave of discomfiture settled in his breast. Sisera looked into the eyes of the tormented man.

"I know what I want," Leah whispered coyly.

Joash strained forward to catch Sisera's answer.

"And you know you will get it," he said slowly, facing Joash.

"No!" Joash screamed. "Kill me! Kill me! If you don't I will do it myself! I will not live blind! Mercy, Sisera! Your sword!" Joash fell to his knees, exposing his throat. "One thrust, Sisera. Do it!"

Sisera felt the gorge rise in his throat. What weakness! Joash knew a peasant was like a beast, no more. Why shouldn't his mother have the wretch if it would keep her off his back in her old age? He turned away in scorn. Suddenly an image of Deborah appeared before him. Sisera started and a shudder passed through his body.

His mother asked, "What is it?"

"Nothing. Take him to the metalsmith's forge and put his eyes out," he told the soldiers. "And have Shamer the tanner hold him."

Joash's shrieks rent the air. His screams echoed in the halls of Sisera's palace even after the heavy doors had closed.

"Leave me," said Sisera.

When they had all left, he clutched his head. Anger at Joash had released a flood of memories. Joash had come to his attention as a young man of perhaps seventeen. He came from Sisera's own native province of Harosheth to be an apprentice to the palace scribes. Daily he worked in the library, copying old texts, perfecting his script.

In a flight of fancy the young man wrote a battle poem detailing one of the king's successful campaigns. The chief scribe showed it to Sisera, and soon Joash became his personal scribe. More, recalled Sisera, a companion. Then Darkon suggested inviting the boy's family to the palace to visit their son, having learned of the close ties between Joash, his parents, and his younger sister. Darkon arranged for the king to observe the child being bathed and refreshed (even as he had done when the prophetess came).

Sisera's measured strides carried him up and down the audience chamber. He paused before the dais.

"She is very young, Darkon," he remembered saying. Indeed the girl was but thirteen or fourteen. "I could bestow upon her father lands in his own name, as a mark of honor for the family of a temple maiden."

"Even so," agreed Darkon.

"Send for Joash."

"My lord . . ." Darkon said, "Joash is a brash young man. He sets great store by his sister. Perhaps even more than the gods would deem proper."

"Hmm. Perhaps I should send him away until the child . . . ah, the young maiden. . . has been initiated."

Darkon managed a wintry smile. "I will arrange it, lord, and then an audience with the parents."

The parents, Sisera recalled, did not grasp the honor. They refused permission to make their daughter a temple maiden. At last they were banished from court without her, under threat of death should they return.

Afterward, Sisera had kept his part of the bargain, generously deeding them fertile lands north of Harosheth.

But for days Sisera could not shake the feeling that he had erred badly. He longed to forget the episode.

When Joash returned to court he was like a demented soul. It was necessary to enslave him in the rock quarry, where his madness could be contained. Beno lamented the years wasted in training him as a scribe, to which Darkon responded that it only proved the uselessness of educating the peasant breed.

Privately Sisera wished the whole affair had never happened. Later that year, in the temple, the maid had died in childbirth. Not only that, Sisera had been deprived of his scribe; his ideas, his joy and appreciation of living. Joash. And now this final degradation—to be a pet for his mother's fancies. Sisera sighed. Power had its unpleasant side.

Joash awoke. It was dark. At first he felt nothing. Then pain seared through him. He moaned. He felt hands about his head. Something was lifted. A coolness descended, and he passed again into unconsciousness. . . . A familiar voice, gentle and sorrowful, aroused him.

"Here, eat . . . no, put your hands here. That's it. It's not too hot, go ahead."

Joash tasted the soup. "Who is it?"

"Shamer. I'll take care of you until you are well." Joash put a hand to his eyes. His fingers felt the empty sockets. He flung the bowl aside and screamed and screamed.

Enveloping him in a grip of iron, the big man rocked him like a babe. "Yahweh will deliver us . . . Yahweh will deliver us," he crooned.

Phurah hurried through the morning ablutions. Lapidoth had summoned him to the elders' gate with word that Deborah would speak to them. Since she had visited him two days ago, everything was moving at a faster pace.

Deborah had not been far from his thoughts since he had learned in Shechem that the Ark was to be moved. Never in his wildest imaginings had he dreamed it would come to the sleepy village of Shiloh. Why, Shiloh was not even a caravan stop. And as for a temple, it had little more than an altar of unhewn stone. Its sanctuary was separated from the outer rooms only by goat-hair curtains —surely no better than Moses knew in the wilderness! He thought with longing of the gleaming, whitewashed walls of the temple in Shechem, its library of sacred tablets, and scribes on padded sandals moving with quiet reverence. Who would have conceived the Ark endangered in Yahweh's own temple in Shechem?

He thought of the change in Deborah since moving to Shiloh. Her cheeks, though never rounded as other young maidens, had become more hollow. About her eyes was a remoteness, as though in Yahweh's service she had gone to another plane, from whence she returned only sometimes.

The night had been chilly. As an afterthought, Phurah threw on his wool robe before leaving for the gates.

Phurah arrived just as the elders were seating themselves along the stone benches on the sunny side of the marketplace. From their appearance, the hasty summons had also caught them unaware.

"Greetings, Phurah," said Shoshoma, gray-haired chief elder of Shiloh.

"The Lord be with thee," responded Phurah.

"Deborah is coming," announced one of the elders.

Side by side, Deborah and Lapidoth came down the peaceful street. Deborah's face was radiant, her eyes reflecting a deep inner joy. The dark blue wool cloak over the mass of red hair shaped her being like the hands of Yahweh. The elders rose. Shoshoma offered her his seat. As he was not an elder, Lapidoth stopped at the fringes. With strength and pride he gazed upon his wife.

"Men of Shiloh," she began without preamble, "Yahweh has given thee an important task. He has caused his sacred Ark to be delivered to Shiloh. In the days to come he shall lead us against the Canaanites, and he shall deliver the mighty Sisera into our hands."

Shoshoma left his seat. *"War?* Are you saying there is to be war, Deborah?"

Deborah's glance pierced the elder. "Thus saith Yahweh."

A murmur arose among the elders.

"Throughout Israel thou art to go, men of Shiloh, and speak to the chiefs of the clans which are the most powerful of each tribe.

Thus shall you speak: 'Deborah, prophetess of Israel, does summon thee to the Lord's bidding at Shiloh, in the land of the tribe of Ephraim.' After you have spoken to each chief, he shall send runners to each village, that throughout the land all shall know Yahweh has declared a holy war. We will fight the Canaanites!"

The elders sat in stunned silence. Finally their voices struggled through their thoughts. "Not since Joshua has Yahweh sent a deliverer . . . a holy war? Will the men of Gilead, beyond the Jordan, agree to fight Canaan, too . . . who knows?"

"By this act shall they show their faithfulness and obedience to Yahweh. In ten days we shall meet under the grove of oaks. There will I speak to the gathered multitudes. Great is Yahweh, defender of Israel against her enemies!" Deborah allowed her gaze to rest upon each of them in turn. At last she turned to Lapidoth. "Let us go home, my husband."

"Lapidoth . . ." began Shoshoma, a plea of bewilderment in his voice.

"I shall return directly, Shoshoma." Lapidoth held out his hand to Deborah.

Later, with Lapidoth's counsel, the men of Shiloh planned how to accomplish Deborah's bidding.

"What of Joash, Kanah's commander?" Shoshoma wanted to know. "He has a score of horses and a hundred fighting men."

"Joash is Habiru. He is not bound to do battle for Yahweh." Remembering Joash's fiery haste to avenge the sacking of Not, Lapidoth added, "But, in truth, I know of no man with more hatred for Sisera."

"Then we can count on him," said Shoshoma positively.

"By now, Ira should have the caravan in Shechem." Lapidoth glanced at the gray-haired elder and smiled. "I will speak to Joash there."

Shoshoma nodded. "With your permission I shall accompany you. I would speak to Kanah myself."

One by one, the other elders agreed to travel to Benjamin and Asher, to Naphtali and Dan, to Issachar, Zebulun, and Judah, to the sparse tribes of Gilead and Reuben beyond the Jordan.

Later, as he prepared to leave for Shechem, Deborah clung to him. After the night she had revealed her vow, they had grown closer in every way but the marriage bed.

He kissed her tenderly. "I will be back as soon as possible, dearest."

Emerging from the house, Lapidoth sought his parents in the pottery. "Watch over Deborah, mother. Yahweh's burden is mightily upon her, and I fear she will forget to eat."

"Yahweh certainly knew what he was doing when he gave that woman to you. I don't know who else would put up with it all."

Lapidoth scowled. "Do you really think a mere woman could accomplish all that she has? You have lived beside her for more than three years. Know you another like her? What woman in the village would not change places with thee to be so favored of Yahweh?"

"Why, Lapidoth. . . ."

"Perhaps those gods of yours put it into your head to speak thus!" he stared at Dorcas until she looked away. Then he leaned over to embrace his father and was gone.

Dorcas stared moodily after him. She sighed. Well, maybe Deborah was Yahweh's messenger, but how much more would Dorcas have enjoyed just an ordinary daughter! Absently she brushed the dried chips of red clay on her hands against her apron and walked across to Lapidoth's house. She listened at the curtain. "Deborah?" Lifting it aside, she peered within. Deborah lay curled upon her mat, asleep. She looked exhausted. In repose, her face appeared vulnerable. Crescents of shadow appeared under the brush of lashes. Dorcas felt an unaccustomed stirring of sympathy.

How must it be for Deborah to be at the beck and call of a master like Yahweh, who demanded attention for long nights when others slept, who bade her deliver messages which brought upon her head the wrath of Israel? Dorcas felt a great tenderness swell inside her. *You are a good servant, Deborah. I hope Yahweh is a good master.*

Then Dorcas did a strange thing. She turned and left that house and went straight to her own. One by one, she lifted her Philistine gods from their places about the walls. "I am sorry," she murmured firmly. "The life of my son's wife is too precious to me. I cannot have you at odds with her god." She tied them securely in a bundle. Taking a stout stick, Dorcas carried the bundle to a lonely spot beyond the walls of Shiloh. There she dug a shallow grave and buried Dagon and the other gods of Philistia.

29

SHECHEM WAS IN AN UPROAR. No one seemed to know precisely what had happened. When Lapidoth and Shoshoma rode through the streets they were bombarded by a babel of rumors. The Ark had been stolen by the Ephraimites, who were jealous that for so long it had been entrusted to Manasseh. No, it had been hidden because an attack by King Sisera was imminent. No, the Israelite prophetess had thrown in her lot with Sisera, and together they planned to conquer Canaan. And in the background, from behind walls of houses and courtyards, the men heard the chilling, high wails of mourners, not once but many times.

Ira hailed them as they passed through a central marketplace. "Well glad I am to see you. It's like a siege." Ira spat in the dust and squinted up at Lapidoth. "Just pulled in yesterday, but by thunder, if we don't pull out quickly, the elders will commandeer us to defend the city. As it is, captain, men are pulling out of the caravan left and right."

"Have you seen Joash? There was a raid on—"

Ira nodded. "Soldiers have been straggling in all day."

"And Joash?"

"Haven't seen him, captain."

"All right, I'll see you in camp later. I'll be at Kanah's shop with Shoshoma."

Several of Kanah's clan had already assembled in his shop. Kanah's old face was wracked with grief, his wispy white hair disheveled. "Lapidoth. Shoshoma. Yahweh has cursed this day."

"We have heard your soldiers rode to avenge Not," said Shoshoma.

"The strike was not quick enough to catch them off guard," said a younger man, resting a supportive hand on Kanah's shoulder. "Someone got a warning to the Canaanites. By the gods, I swear—"

"And Joash?" asked Lapidoth with sinking heart.

Kanah shook his head. "He sent a runner back. They rode into a trap."

"The fool! It was an ill-conceived raid! Did you send reinforcements?"

"The runner was thrown from his horse among the rocks of the foothills. For several hours he lay unconscious. By the time he reached us, remnants of our troops were already returning. No, Lapidoth, there is no word of my commander," said Kanah. "No one saw him killed. We have lost perhaps fifty men and a score of horses . . . all that we had."

"We would offer help, but there is no time."

Kanah lifted his palms. "An Ephraimite offering help?"

"Kanah," Lapidoth's glance included the others in the crowded shop, "Yahweh, through his prophetess Deborah, has pronounced a holy war."

Kanah's ample bulk struggled upright. "War!"

"Upon King Sisera himself," declared Shoshoma solemnly. "All the tribes are summoned to a meeting in Shiloh before the Ark, ten days from today."

"War," Kanah repeated to his clansmen, when Shoshoma had finished. "By all that's holy, we are ready for it!"

Lapidoth left the elder and made his way to the caravan ground to find Heber and Jael.

"Good morrow, Lapidoth," called Jael as she laid out tools for the day's labor. Heber sat contentedly beside a fire. "How is Deborah? How are your parents?"

Lapidoth swung off the horse. "They are well, Jael. Heber, I have a mission that concerns you both."

Jael tossed a mallet toward a neat bundle of nails and joined the men at the fire.

"What is wrong, captain?" asked Heber.

"Heard you the news about Joash?"

"Only that there is no news."

Lapidoth nodded. "Deborah says there is to be a war against Sisera. Yahweh's war. There is a call out to all the tribes."

"Then we will fight, too," said Heber promptly.

Lapidoth smiled. "I know, old friend. But I have something that must be done first. I cannot say there is no danger."

Jael leaned forward and laid a hand on her husband's arm. "If it will help destroy that monster, we will do it."

Lapidoth knew that their slain son, Ehi, was never out of their thoughts. "Then hear. Deborah's father, Shamer, abides in Taanach. He is a tanner in the inner city."

"I remember," said Jael.

Heber nodded. "We know Taanach. We've worked there."

Lapidoth lowered his voice and leaned toward them. "Think you that you could reach him without Sisera's knowledge?"

"Sisera would think nothing of two metalworkers doing business in their travels," replied Heber.

"What shall we do when we see him?" whispered Jael.

"Get him away. When Sisera hears of Deborah's call he may try to get at her through him. She will not waver from Yahweh's path, that I know," he gave a rueful laugh, "but if we can help. . . ."

Heber nodded. "It shall be as you say."

"Getting him out will be no problem," boasted Jael.

"But now it is wartime. It may not be so easy," pondered Heber. With a sudden movement he stood up. "We shall start today."

Lapidoth rose also and embraced them roughly. "Yahweh bless thee!" He turned away and then stopped. "Your story must be that you have come lately from the city of Pharaoh by way of Gaza. Be ignorant of war talk."

"We'll probably be conscripted," remarked Heber. "That might not be too bad. I can make a wheel look solid that will fall apart when it goes."

Lapidoth grinned. "Just get in and out in one piece, please."

"Lapidoth!" called Hamid, from a few lengths away.

He found his friend in the midst of a squabble among factors and merchants. In one rapid-fire breath Hamid said, "Explain to these men that anyone who would remove his goods from the caravan has the brains of a sheep. Everybody knows if the Canaanites are busy fighting a war, they won't have time to harass us. Tell them it's business as usual."

Lapidoth judged the knot of worried, angry faces. He saw few Israelites among them.

"We want no part of any Israelite war," said a Phoenician who factored for his father's business. "There are rumors that you are pulling your men out to fight. Without your soldiers, Captain Lapidoth, who is left to guard our goods? We've all got a lot tied up in these shipments. You gave your word they would be safe."

"And while you're off fighting the Canaanites, don't you know the Midianites will be beating the harvest!" added a factor from Damascus.

Hamid shot his countryman a look of disgust.

Ira, with some of his own men, joined the group. Lapidoth acknowledged him with a grim smile. "A call from Yahweh is greater than a contract for my services," he told the factor.

Rebellious mutterings filled the air.

Lapidoth raised his voice. "Those among my men who are not Israelite are under no obligation to fight."

"You Israelites!" said the Phoenician. "You always come up with some law that forbids you to do what you don't want to do anyway." He turned to the others. "I say we wait in Shechem."

"It's as good a place as any," said the Damascene.

"When will it come, Lapidoth?"

"Soon. You will not have long to tarry. Put your stores together and set guards," he advised them, "as though you were soldiers. Set others to guard the flocks and the asses and camels. Remember, Shechem is an open city."

"There's not enough grazing. You know what the drought's done."

"Then you must move them as you see fit. I will return as soon as the war is over."

Finally, a factor spoke who had not said a word. "Are you Israelites actually going out against Sisera?"

"At Yahweh's command."

The factor shook his head. "I think you're mad."

Lapidoth smiled grimly. "That is because you do not know Yahweh."

"What now, Lapidoth?" asked Ira.

"You'll take the rest of the caravan to Egypt."

"Yes, captain. But I want to fight, too."

"There will be no fighting until after a council of the tribes. Appoint an overseer to remain with those who stay in Shechem. When can you be ready to leave?"

"It depends on the factors who go with us."

"If you threaten to leave without them, they can wind up their business here in a day."

"Aye." The men clasped hands as Ira grimly promised, "I'll deliver everyone safely and be back in time to slit Sisera's gullet."

30

LESS THAN ONE HUNDRED YEARS had passed since Yahweh had given Moses the sacred tablets of the Law, and less since Joshua had gathered them together to divide the land of Canaan among the Twelve Tribes, their portions to subdue and settle.

Since that time the tribes had grown apart in speech and habit. Where enclaves of Canaanites remained, the tribesmen had adapted to their words and ways. Some had remained nomadic shepherds; others clustered together and formed villages, practicing useful trades.

As the day of meeting arrived, the hills of Shiloh were a babel of dialects. Arrayed in a new coat, upon which his wife had worked for days, Shoshoma labored up the hillside through the multitudes. Ahead of him, under a massive oak, Phurah and several priests busied themselves around Yahweh's Tent. Within the tent, too sacred for unjustified eyes, rested the Ark of the Covenant. Shoshoma reached the knoll. Below him waited a sea of faces.

"Where is Deborah?" he whispered to Phurah.

"No one has seen her for three days. When Lapidoth got back she wouldn't even let him stay with her."

Since issuing the call to war, Deborah had not returned to her little house beside the pottery. Instead, attended by Nedra, she had erected a tent upon a knoll in the midst of the pilgrims.

As Shoshoma's eyes roamed over the hundreds, nay, thousands waiting restlessly upon the hills, he smoothed his new robes nervously. "You don't suppose she's run away, do you?"

The young priest smiled and shook his head.

Shoshoma heard a murmuring wave before he could distinguish the words. "Deborah . . . Deborah . . . Deborah is coming! The prophetess is coming. Hail Deborah, prophetess of Yahweh!"

And there was Lapidoth, rising from his parents' side. His tower-

ing figure plunged through the crowd. Following his direction, Shoshoma spotted a single figure upon an adjacent hill, robes sailing
behind in the wind, a staff in hand. The solitary figure marched
across the windswept hill with powerful strides. Surely not Deborah! By now many had seen the figure. The familiarity of calling her
name diminished as she approached. A wave of awe stilled the
crowd. Few among the thousands were old enough to remember
Joshua. For the rest, to actually be in the presence of a prophetess
seemed a stunning experience.

Now Lapidoth was with her. She did not pause. Rapidly they
approached the hill and the oak where Yahweh's Tent was situated.
Shoshoma scanned her face. He was shocked. It was the same Deborah, yet he knew her not. She looked neither right nor left.

When she reached the tent, Deborah turned and faced the people.
Lapidoth dropped a pace behind. The priests attending the Ark
drew back. Her arms stretched out. "Yahweh has heard your cries,
O people of Israel!" Deborah cried. Then her gaze seemed to alter,
as though gradually seeing the people standing and sitting below
her.

"Thus says the Lord, the God of Israel: 'Your fathers lived of old
beyond the Euphrates, among them Terah, the father of Abraham,
Nahor, and Haran, and they served other gods. Then I took your
father Abraham from beyond the river and led him through all the
land of Canaan, and made his offspring many. I gave him Isaac, and
to Isaac I gave Jacob and Esau. And I gave Esau the hill country of
Seir to possess, but Jacob and his children went down to Egypt. And
I sent Moses and Aaron, and I plagued Egypt with what I did in the
midst of it; and afterward I brought your fathers out of Egypt, and
you came to the sea; and the Egyptians pursued your fathers with
chariots and horsemen to the Red Sea. And when they cried to the
Lord, he put darkness before the Egyptians and made the sea come
upon them and cover them; and your eyes saw what I did to Egypt;
and you lived in the wilderness a long time. Then I brought you to
the land of the Amorites, who lived on the other side of the Jordan. . . .' "

As she spoke, Lapidoth's eyes became watchful, as if testing the
attitude of the throngs. Her voice rose and fell. The listeners seemed
enchanted by her words, the oft-told and well-loved recitation of
Yahweh's deeds in behalf of his people.

" 'I gave you a land on which you had not labored, and cities which you had not built, and you dwell therein; you eat the fruit of vineyards and olive yards which you did not plant.' "

Deborah's eyes flashed like twin shafts of light. Suddenly she smiled. "Now, my beloved people, you see the most powerful enemy ever to rise up against the Israelites. You see his caravans ride the broad routes from Egypt to Damascus while we travel by night in the rocky places. You see peasants till his broad fields in valleys that are fertile and sweet and well watered, while we scratch in fields no bigger than tent curtains. You attribute these blessings of King Sisera to the power of his gods. And you seek the idolatrous blessings of Sisera's gods for yourselves!"

Many eyes avoided hers.

"You have yoked yourselves to his Baal. The success of whatever is false and commonplace has made it worthy in your sight. False gods occupy your homes. Your sons and daughters have gone a-whoring after iniquity. Yahweh has warned you and you have not heeded. Therefore, Yahweh has sent droughts that burned your fields. Your herds and flocks have died of hunger, and your tongues thirst for the sweet gush of waters that do not come."

Heads nodded and mutterings of agreement rose.

"You see King Sisera gouge tribute from those who lack power to resist. You see him wantonly destroy villages such as Not. The time is upon us to test the power of Sisera's gods. For the voice of Yahweh sent me to Taanach. I have seen, O my people, the iron chariots of Sisera. In one I have flown over the Plain of Jezreel. They are enough to strike terror in the heart of a soldier.

"But I have plumbed Sisera's weakness. Even so did Joshua prophesy of this time, 'In the Valley of Jezreel you shall drive out the Canaanites, though they have chariots of iron, and though they are strong.' Yahweh has tried us sorely that his people might turn to him in their distress."

"But Deborah," said one of those nearest, "my family lives in Jericho. We've never had trouble with Sisera."

Deborah replied, "There is no peace until every man and woman can live unmolested in the shade of the fig."

"Yes, yes," moaned the people. "Yahweh has turned his face from us."

"But you are still his people, the very children of Yahweh. This

land of milk and honey he has given us. We are his people," Deborah's voice coaxed them and then lashed them anew: "But now that
you dwell in Canaan, you have forgotten your promise. You have
seen the Canaanites worship gods which seem to bring forth the
fertility of the land, and you have forgotten that Yahweh alone is
responsible for the earth's abundance. In your puny fear you have
groveled in the dirt before other gods, and sacrificed your precious
seed in temples that are a desecration of the human spirit!

"Did not Joshua warn us, 'Take not the ways of the land you are
entering for they are the ways of evil. Keep to your own ways, for
you are the people, the chosen of God, to bring his witness to the
world.' "

Deborah's words hovered over them in the silence. Her gaze
locked with Lapidoth's, and she felt his strength infuse her. Knots
of conversation sprang up on the hill below her.

Commanders of the clans of Asher, who dwelled to the north
between Naphtali and the Great Sea, approached. Their chief elder
stepped forward and carefully settled about himself a beautiful
cloak of linen, embroidered with fish and seashell patterns.

He bowed slightly. "Deborah of Ephraim," he began in a courte-
ous and cultured voice, "we of Asher have never been as numerous
or as strong as the tribes of Ephraim and Manasseh. What you have
seized by force we have won by guile. We have no quarrel with
King Sisera."

"He is our best customer!" put in another.

"We have trade agreements with Sisera, and with merchants from
Phoenicia to Philistia," continued their leader. "We have negotiated
with the Phoenicians for passage on their ships to other ports, which
are eager for goods from across the Great Sea. It would not be
expedient for us to fight. Surely you understand."

Deborah studied the Asherites. "My sons," she said gently,
"Yahweh blesses your good fortune. Nevertheless, before our personal desires must come obedience to Yahweh. It is not of myself
that I bring you this command. He hath not said, 'Thou who art not
busy,' or 'Thou who dost lust to do battle,' or even 'Thou who dost
hate the enemy,' but he hath called all of Israel. For Yahweh's ways
are not the ways of men, and his commands are not for the glory
of men but for the glory of the Father of this world."

The merchant's eyes fell. He beckoned his countrymen about

him. "We must make a decision," he murmured, and led his contingent away.

Another chieftain approached. "It will be harvest in a few weeks. Who will harvest my fields if I go off to fight this war?" asked the man, who was from the tribe of Reuben. "It's not Sisera and the Canaanites, but the Midianites who bedevil us, Deborah."

Scattered cries of assent greeted his words. "We have to harvest by night, and winnow in the secrecy of the wine press. We dare not leave our fields unguarded. The Midianites come like hordes of locusts with their tents and all their people, and steal our grain after we have labored on it, and drive us away. Then they burn our fields and steal our flocks in scorn for our weakness. Help us fight the Midianites first, O Deborah, then we will fight Sisera!"

Deborah's heart filled with compassion. "The loss of your fields and flocks is great, but it is nothing compared with loss of faith in Yahweh. Trust in Yahweh, man of Reuben. For in the fullness of his time you will be delivered. But not for this has Yahweh called me. The Lord our God marches before us against Sisera! If you disobey the call, then you are betraying him!"

The Reubenite's face blanched before her passion.

"I have seen the legions of Sisera." A chieftain of Naphtali pressed forward. Deborah recognized Buzi, the wine merchant from her hometown of Hammath. She held out her hand with gladness, and Buzi pressed it warmly before releasing it. "He has kept troops in Naphtali for years. The men of Hammath will fight, Deborah, but who will lead us?"

"Yahweh has commanded that Barak lead us," answered Deborah.

General Barak was a soldier of great renown. Not since Joshua had a military commander been so successful against his enemies. A rash of angry talk broke out among Buzi's compatriots. "It seems General Barak did not even come, Deborah," said Buzi, not looking at her.

"Then I shall send for him." Deborah's eyes swept the multitude. Her voice rose again. "I charge you now. As Joshua hath said, 'Put away the gods which your fathers served beyond the river and in Egypt, and serve the Lord. And if you be unwilling to serve the Lord, choose this day whom you will serve, whether the gods your father served in the region beyond the river, or the gods of the

Canaanites, in whose land you dwell.'

"My beloved people, now is the time! Yahweh summons us to battle against the hordes of Sisera!"

One by one the mutterings against her ceased. Those who were faithful cried the ancient response, "We will serve the Lord. We shall not forsake the Lord to serve others. We will follow where Yahweh leads!"

"By this mighty oak, which has heard all that was said, are you witnesses that you have chosen to serve him?"

"We are witnesses!"

Deborah's arms rose and she blessed the multitude. "Take good care to observe the commandment and the law which Moses gave you: Love the Lord your God, walk in all his ways, keep his commandments, cleave to him, and serve him with all your heart and with all your soul. Return now to your tents. Prepare yourselves with sacrifice, prayer, and fasting for the mighty battle which is to come." Her smile became a benediction.

As they dispersed, Deborah and Lapidoth withdrew to her tent. "Truly, husband, Yahweh's people seem no more of a single mind than when they crossed the Jordan." She sank cross-legged upon a mat.

Lapidoth folded his arms and said, "That is because Israel has no king."

"Yahweh is king!"

"You know what I mean. Ammon has a king, Edom and Moab have kings. Only Israel has no king," Lapidoth said.

"We have Yahweh," she replied doggedly.

"People understand better a king they can see. So do his enemies. As it is, anyone with strength and power and ambition could take over as ruler."

"That is not so. We have the laws!"

"*We need a king,* Deborah," Lapidoth said quietly.

Deborah sighed and bent her head. Her hands lay curled in her lap like a nest for baby birds. "Dear one, I must send thee from me again." She looked up swiftly. "General Barak must come! Only you can persuade him. Tell him the Lord will give Sisera into his hand."

"You shall have General Barak, Deborah." Lapidoth reached for her hands. As she rose he would have kissed them but she shook her head.

"Go quickly and return, that the war may be over and I may lie in thine arms and be Lapidoth's wife again!"

Two days later Lapidoth rode into Kedesh in northern Naphtali. His leather vest was stiff and stained white with salt sweat. Foam flecked the flanks and neck of his horse.

The house of General Barak dominated the center of Kedesh like a small fortress. Soldiers were everywhere, turning with frank curiosity as the heavily armed horseman rode through the streets.

Barak was sitting in his courtyard when a servant ushered Lapidoth into his presence. A pomegranate tree, bursting with green, waved in a slight breeze, creating an illusion of coolness above a carpet of sweet-smelling grass.

"Barak, son of Abinoam," said Lapidoth after an exchange of courtesies, "I bring you greetings from Deborah, prophetess of Israel."

Barak was tall and barrel chested. His hair was grizzled. Gray also covered his forearms and curled at the throat of his garment. His face was deeply seamed. "I have been waiting for you."

Lapidoth's brows shot up.

"Who is this woman who calls for a holy war? I heard the call. I did not choose to attend." The two warriors took the measure of each another across the platter of sweetmeats provided by Barak's servants.

Lapidoth could understand Barak's thinking. A lifelong soldier, he would not trust a prophet to know better than he the proper time to make war. Lapidoth drew a deep breath and launched into Deborah's message.

"Humph!" said Barak when he had finished. "So he's going to deliver Sisera into my hand, is he!"

"Barak, when I left Shiloh many were going home. Some feared to get involved in a war so near harvesttime. Some would not fight because they are engaged in trade with the Canaanites. I am no diplomat, Barak, but a soldier like yourself. Without the power of a national leader, I fear we cannot hold our people faithful to the call."

"Only a king could do that," said Barak.

Lapidoth hesitated. Finally he said, "Yahweh is king."

"Nevertheless, people need a king they can see and hear." Barak appeared lost in thought.

Lapidoth heard a bird call and saw it flutter the leaves of the pomegranate tree.

"Peaceful, eh?"

"Yes. And you have earned a soldier's pension. But it is not for us to ignore the call. Truly, Barak, Deborah speaks the words of Yahweh."

A slight smile hovered around Barak's lips. "Speak you as her husband?"

Lapidoth's smile was easy. "As a soldier, Barak. Has age weakened your insight as well as your faith? Do not you realize the threat beyond the borders of your own city?" Lapidoth rose and slowly circled the tiny garden. He could threaten the general. But Lapidoth was not given to threats he could not keep. And a lone soldier did not threaten a man who had a hundred at his call. "I am a man obedient to Yahweh. It is not easy to be the husband of a prophetess. Yet Yahweh put her in my keeping."

A sigh of forbearance escaped Barak's lips. "Very well," he said reluctantly. "I will journey to Shiloh with you. More than that, I will not promise."

People in the camps began to discipline themselves in a new routine. Deborah had called for sacrifice and ritual cleansing. No man was to go in to his wife or concubine until after Yahweh's war, or drink wine. Unleavened bread flavored with bitter herbs was to be part of every meal, to remind them that they must be ready to move upon the call of the Lord, even as they had waited to leave Egypt more than a century ago.

As Deborah strolled among the clusters of travelers, she sensed a difference in mood. The dissidents and malcontents had struck their tents and stolen away. Those who remained spent much time gathered together, as tellers of tales renewed the old stories of conquest. For some who had drifted far from Yahweh's teaching, the stories came to thrill them with a sense of pride in what had gone before, to imbue them with a sense of oneness with their brothers and sisters who spoke the language with different accents.

Toward evening on the fifth day, a flurry of excitement rippled through the camp. Captain Lapidoth was coming. With him was a man who could be no other than General Barak.

They left their cooking fires. When the two veterans appeared, crowds followed them to the tent of Deborah. She was waiting. With a triumphant smile, Lapidoth embraced her and presented General Barak. Deborah greeted him with a flashing smile and raised an arm to the multitude. "People of Israel, through Lapidoth Yahweh has brought us our leader!"

The people cheered. Barak shot a swift glance at Lapidoth, his mouth open in protest. Deborah stepped between the men.

"Barak, son of Abinoam, conqueror of Naphtali! When Joshua did lead the forces of Israel against Bethel, Debir, and Eglon, he destroyed them and many others. Yet Joshua died before all the tribes had secured their inheritance. For the tribe of Naphtali to secure its lands, O Barak, it remained for Yahweh to raise you up as commander!" Her words to him, meant for the people, exhorted them with her fervor. "It was you who secured for the Naphtalites the cities of Ramah, Rakkath, Kedesh, Hammath, Chinnereth, and their villages. Yahweh has blessed you according to his promise. 'O Naphtali, satisfied with favor, and full of the blessing of the Lord, possess the lake and the south.' This blessing, which Moses did pronounce upon the tribe of Naphtali, was accomplished through you!"

The multitudes began to sing and dance in the firelight, for now, as of old, Yahweh had chosen their leader. "Blessed be Deborah, prophetess of Israel, and General Barak, our deliverer!" they chanted.

Barak shot her a look of anger and turned aside into the tent. Deborah and Lapidoth followed. General Barak faced the prophetess. His words were cold. "I have not agreed to lead you people in this assault."

"Do not turn your back on Yahweh when he has called you!"

"It is easy for you to speak, Deborah of Ephraim. What do you know of battles? We are like a flea on Sisera's back. Do you think he needs these hills as much as we need his plains? Do you think he would consider us as rich a prize as, say, Philistia? What have we to tempt him? Hills too rocky to till and grass too sparse for flocks. You may well conceive that Sisera is preparing for war. But it is laughable to think it will be against the Israelites!"

"It is not for me to know the reasons Yahweh has set this before us." Deborah's stare drilled the commander.

"All the way from Naphtali, Barak, you heard the cries of the people," said Lapidoth. "We will leave you awhile to decide. Come, Deborah."

When Deborah and Lapidoth stepped outside, the people had dispersed. They walked a few paces in silence, then paused in the dappled moonlight beneath an oak.

"Oh, Lapidoth, what if he doesn't. . . ." Deborah came into his arms and they clung together, drawing strength from each other.

When they moved apart, Lapidoth kept her hand in his. "Dearest . . . there is finally news of Joash. He was taken prisoner."

"Oh, my poor Joash! What will become of him?"

"He probably went before Sisera."

Deborah bit her lower lip. Tears welled in her eyes. She did not ask further.

Lapidoth glanced toward the tent. "There's Barak." They went to meet him.

As they approached, Barak studied Deborah with a calculating stare. "I have seen the way the people look upon you, Deborah. I have heard your name on a hundred lips. Yahweh has not spoken to me, but I believe he speaks to you. I do not know how to choose the day when the angel of Yahweh will grant me success," he said slowly. "But if you will go with me, I will go, but if you will not go with me, I will not go."

And she said, "I will surely go with you."

"No!" cried Lapidoth.

Deborah turned swiftly to him. "It shall be so!" She faced Barak again. "But for this testing, Barak, you will not come home from battle covered with new glory. The Lord will sell Sisera into the hand of a woman!"

Barak looked strangely humbled. "I am old, Deborah, by the number of battles. Tell me what Yahweh would have me do."

"For the moment, rest. The women of Shiloh have prepared a place for you with fruits and vegetables, and sweetmeats and milk. Tomorrow we shall council."

Barak studied Deborah's calm face with wry amusement. "Were you so sure I was coming?"

Deborah smiled, a glint of her old mischief lighting her eyes. "Thus saith Yahweh."

He glanced helplessly at Lapidoth. "Is it permitted to pity one married to a prophetess?"

Lapidoth laughed.

"The time for humor will be after we have defeated Sisera," Deborah reminded them crisply.

Lapidoth heard Barak chuckle as aides escorted him to his tent. At last they were alone. Events were moving with such swiftness that Lapidoth did not know how to treat this prophetess-wife. As she stood in the tent opening, looking out over the people, he studied her profile. Her lips were parted, her body swaying slightly forward. For a moment he felt the old jealousy of Yahweh returning. "Deborah."

She turned to him. Something left or came back to her eyes, he could not be sure. His look carried the fire of his desire. He moved past her to pull down the flap of the tent, then seized her in his arms. Her arms went around his neck, and he could feel her sweet breath against his ear.

"Oh, my dearest, we cannot take our pleasure. Remember what happened to the family of Achan when they disobeyed Yahweh on the eve of battle."

"That old wives' tale? Doesn't a prophetess have any privileges?"

Deborah kissed him gently. "Being married to thee. It will not be long. Yahweh knows the mood of his people."

A night's sleep restored General Barak's pugnacity. When he met with Deborah and the appointed commanders he was in full fettle.

"All right." Barak strode up and down before the ranks of commanders, seated apart from the people under Deborah's oak. "Since Yahweh has chosen me to lead this campaign, I will assume the thoughts he has given me are his. Therefore, here is my plan. The only way to defeat the lion is to beard him in his den. Besiege Taanach. Do not let him use his chariots. We shall have people throughout the land make ropes and ladders for scaling, and the people who abide near the great cedar forests shall cut battering rams for the gates.

"All these shall be hid on Mount Tabor, which is across the Valley of Jezreel from Taanach, yet close enough to make the assault under cover of a single night. Against the might of their horses we shall trap wild animals, and set them before the gates."

"Nay, Barak." Deborah had set her face away from the general when he began to speak. Now she turned. Her eyes betrayed the piercing strength of an eagle which Lapidoth was so familiar with.

"It shall seem to be as you say."

Barak let out an expletive. "Don't muzzle the ox when it treads the grain."

She smiled. "Even an ox needs direction, good Barak. By day in every city we will seem to be laboring according to your plan, but it shall be otherwise. Men of Israel shall take this opportunity to disport themselves in Shechem, where Sisera has many friends. They shall boast loudly of our plan.

"But for thee, Barak, thus commands Yahweh, Lord God of Israel: 'Go, gather your men at Mount Tabor, taking ten thousand from the tribe of Naphtali and the tribe of Zebulun. By the thousands shall the tribes of Israel send their men after you, until they number forty thousand.' "

Barak listened intently. "Go on."

"And I will draw out Sisera, the king of the Canaanite armies, to meet you by the river Kishon with his chariots and his troops: and I will give him unto your hand."

Lapidoth turned a face of agony to Deborah. Sisera's forces would spare nothing to kill her. His lips compressed in a bitter line and he turned away.

31

THROUGHOUT THE LAND went the call to war, north to the hills of Galilee, south beyond the Canaanite stronghold of Jerusalem, and to the tribes across the Jordan.

In Shechem men boasted openly that Yahweh would bring down the walls of Taanach itself. Within two days, Gaius and Sacar had once again enriched their purses by bringing the news to Sisera.

At the same time, a caravan from Egypt was entering Taanach. Among the travelers were two Kenite metalsmiths who, soon with more business than they could handle, were regaled by rousing tales from the townspeople. Celebration was in the air. Sisera's troops had plundered an Israelite village. Heber and Jael learned of the foreign prophetess who had come to Taanach and tried to enchant their king. He had seemed to buy her threats. Now those upstart tribes squatting in their hills were learning what power was! What was the wilderness god of Deborah against El Baal? Hadn't Sisera triumphed?

And Jael and Heber, at their campsite in the midst of the caravan, were treated to another tale, more disturbing, of a retaliatory raid by Israelites against a Canaanite village. But the villagers somehow were warned, and soldiers had arrived secretly to protect them. And most astounding of all, they had captured the military commander and found that they had Joash, famed Habiru bandit, who had gone over to the enemy.

Joash! Heber shot a look at his wife. "And now the carrion feed on his body, no doubt," remarked Heber evenly, bending diligently over his grinding wheel.

Derisive laughter rippled through the crowd of peasants, all eager to share in the telling.

"Something like a carrion."

"Hush—Sisera might hear you!"

Heber looked up with a gaze of friendly stupidity. "You pose me a riddle."

"He is here, alive."

"In prison?"

"Oh, no. He lives in the palace, like a king!"

"With the queen, that is," someone added sotto voce.

"Sisera did not kill the man, then?" burst out Jael. "What generosity!"

"He put his eyes out and gave him to his mother for a plaything."

Jael gasped. Though she had never seen the king, she pictured the bestial face of a man who would do such a thing.

"Just ignore my poor wife." Heber smiled evenly. "She is unused to war. . . . There! Your tool is sharp as new, friend. I have need of replacing my pack straps. Is there a tanner nearby? These were made by a tanner in Naphtali. They lasted fifteen years. If I were near Naphtali, I would seek him out again."

"We have a tanner from Naphtali here. He is called Shamer."

"Shamer! The very one! Where is his shop?"

"In there." The man jerked a thumb over his shoulder. "Along the street of the chariots."

"Is one permitted to enter the inner city?" Heber inquired politely.

The two peasants looked at each other. "Eh, it would probably be better if the tanner met you here."

"Good idea! Is there someone who could fetch him?"

"I can get him."

Within an hour Shamer was hurrying toward the caravan grounds. A loud clanging ahead told him he had found the metalsmiths. "Heber! Jael!" He embraced them both. "What are you doing here? Did my—did Deborah send you?"

Heber stole a quick glance around. "Before I plague you with my problems," he said loudly, "take some refreshment with us. Here. Inside." The three slipped quickly into the small tent.

"It's been nearly four years since we met in Hammath," said Jael. "By your girth I think you have done well in Taanach."

Shamer's meaty hand closed around the wineskin Heber offered. "It wasn't bad until Deborah came. Eh, she launched a whirlwind all right. Did you know Joash?" he asked suddenly.

"Yes. We just heard. . . ."

Shamer's craggy head swung from side to side. "It would have been better to kill the man."

"Where is he now?"

"The king had him moved to the palace, is what I hear, next to the queen mother."

"Strange," murmured Heber.

"Not for one who would take the life of an innocent boy. Have you forgotten, old man?" snapped Jael.

"Of course not!" Heber turned to Shamer. "My son died with yours when Sisera's soldiers tried to steal Deborah."

"He was a hero," murmured Jael.

"I did not know," said Shamer. "Then my house is forever in your debt. What can I do now for you?"

"Lapidoth sent us for you."

"What?"

"Deborah proclaimed a holy war against Sisera. Lapidoth fears that when Sisera learns of it, he will kill you."

In spite of the seriousness of the pair, Shamer had to laugh. "Haven't you heard? It's over! That's how Joash was taken!"

"No, Shamer. This time all Israel will fight."

"But when? And how? Sisera has—"

"We do not know. We came as soon as Deborah sent out the call. Lapidoth knows how quickly Sisera's ears bring him news. Come with us now. Do not even go back."

"But—my tannery. Do you know how hard it is to get good tools?"

"We are talking about your *life,* Shamer!" cried Jael. "You must come now."

Shamer snorted and was silent a moment. "This may sound strange to you, friends, after you have risked yourselves, but I do not want to go. What is a man without his livelihood? What do I have in Hammath? Deborah belongs to the family of her husband and my son is dead. Here I have my work, a few friends and . . . and even though there is no priest of Yahweh in Taanach, Yahweh is here with me," Shamer added humbly.

"Then doesn't Yahweh call you to make war against your enemy? Do you not burn to avenge your son's death?" asked Jael.

"I am an old man. I would only be in the way."

"You can make harnesses for your own people, not your enemies!" cried Jael.

Heber stood up. "It is Yahweh's will. It is a *holy war*, Shamer. You cannot refuse!"

Shamer scratched his head with a great pawing motion. "Four years ago it was Yahweh's will that I come to Taanach, to keep peace between Taanach and Hammath. I lost my only son. And now you tell me it is Yahweh's will that I uproot myself once more, from the finest shop I've ever had, and return with you to fight this impossible war."

"Listen, after the war you can come back."

Shamer was silent so long that Heber finally said anxiously, "Well?"

"Joash must come, too."

Heber and Jael exchanged glances. "We can't even breach the inner walls! How shall we reach Joash?"

"When will Israel strike?"

"Deborah has not said."

"Very well." Shamer arose. "Set up shop here. I will see what I can do. If I could only take my tools. Oh, you have something—a broken pack harness—"

Heber smiled. "In truth I do. But it is a great unwieldy one. I can give you another—"

"No, give it to me."

Shamer hurried through the streets of Taanach, the harness coiled over his thick shoulder, the ends of it slapping against his leg. What was the matter with him? Why could he not hate Sisera? Indirectly the man was responsible for Gemalli's death, though he had most convincingly denied it, and he himself could not blot out the unutterably cruel scene in the metalsmith's shop where Joash had lost his sight. Alas, age had dimmed his hates as well as his desires. Well, in this as in all, he would try to do Yahweh's bidding.

As Shamer reentered the inner gates, Queen Mother Leah was leaning over the balustrade of her boudoir watching the colorful comings and goings.

"Joash, dear, come here. It is a particularly fine day." She turned back to the chamber, a smile playing about her lips. "Come now,

Joash, you have been my guest for over a week and have yet to utter a word. Did my naughty son take your tongue too?"

Joash lay on a couch piled with cushions. Beyond him a eunuch, Rab Saris, stood an indifferent watch. Joash threw an arm across his face. The tanned body looked paler, the muscles flaccid. Deep lines were etched around his mouth. Leah knelt beside him and stroked the lines with a rouged fingernail. Joash turned his face away.

"You were made blind because you would not see, Joash," said Leah in a light voice. "I wanted you to stay in Taanach . . . now, perhaps, you can be made to see." Her hand caressed him in rhythmic circles. "It will not be too bad. I will care for you."

Joash groaned.

While Leah abandoned herself to pleasure, Sisera met with his advisers and military commanders in the audience chamber below. Leaders of Gezer, of Jokneam and Jerusalem, and kings of all the lesser cities which had alliances with Sisera, had been summoned. To Beno's annoyance, Darkon had also been included.

"It is laughable," Sisera declared, "that these barbarians, living in hovels and tents, dressing in goatskins, declare war against me. Me! And at what a time. Just before our campaign against Phoenicia." He struck the hilt of his dagger and paced before the men. "Oh, these rabble! These carrion eaters!" He swung to Beno. "And what about their general? What did the Shechemites tell us?"

"That General Barak plans to lay siege to our city, lord, and run wild animals—"

Sisera cut him off with a shrill laugh. "And deprive us of our chariots, no doubt."

"You are now paying for allowing the so-called prophetess to leave the city alive," observed Darkon.

Sisera eyed him coldly. "Are you so sure of our gods, Darkon, that you would risk offending theirs?"

Darkon draped the fold of his black cloak more carefully on his arm before answering, "Take care. One would almost think you believe that Deborah's god is more powerful than El Baal."

Sisera's voice rose sharply. "For what good they do us, you could take all the gods and hurl them into the Great Sea. Enough. Shall we wait like sheep in the fold to be slaughtered? The Israelites want to meet us. Very well, we shall take time from our more important endeavors to oblige them." He glanced at Sem. "How soon can we be ready?"

"In a week, lord."

"Then we shall cross the Valley of Jezreel and coax them off Mount Tabor like lice from a dog's back. When they descend, we will squash them under our wheels!"

"Noble Sisera," Beno interrupted, "what about the tanner?"

Sisera grunted. "I don't intend to waste a good tanner. Oh, I suppose we'd better lock him up until it's over. Take care of it, Beno."

While Sisera spoke, the man whose fate was being summarily decided was at that moment hurrying toward the palace, as if to cooperate in his own incarceration.

Many a pleasant hour had Shamer spent in the cook yard of the palace, exchanging ribald stories with the laboring slaves, mending sandals and decorating bits of leather for their adornment, in exchange for well-cooked meals. And as he had worked, Shamer had told them the tales of Yahweh and the Israelites.

Shamer reached the cook yard this afternoon still lugging Heber's pack harness. In his turmoil he had not thought to go a few steps more and drop the harness off at the tannery. How could he, especially he, an Israelite, hope to free Joash, when Sisera would shortly learn of Deborah's call against the Canaanites? In spite of what he had assured the Kenites, he paled to think what Sisera might do.

"Here is Shamer," called one of the serving wenches. "Good morrow! Do you have a story for us?"

"How can I tell stories? I am dry as a thistle."

"Not for long!" She laughed and headed for the kitchen.

In the center of the cook yard were three great brick ovens, which had to be fed continuously as a never-ending round of breads and cakes were ladled into their recesses. A bench had been drawn beside one of the ovens, probably during the chill of morning. But in the heat of the cook yard in late afternoon, Shamer dumped his cumbrous burden and hauled the bench into a shaded area near the palace wall.

The wench returned with a bowl of wine. Shamer thanked her and forced a smile. Suddenly he had an idea. "Why don't you tell me a story? Tell me of Joash."

"Your Habiru? Oh, Queen Leah barely lets him out of her boudoir."

"But the man needs exercise."

An old woman, hunchbacked from many years' labor over her grinding mortar, leaned back on her heels, her pestle clutched in a gnarled hand. "He comes down at night. Haven't you seen him? Poor soul, out here stumbling around, waving his arms. And him such a fine-looking man before."

Two other scullery maids joined them. Both remembered Joash from the days of his youth, when he had the king's favor. Listening to their chatter, Shamer finished his wine and belched politely.

"I have not seen him for more than a week. Say, I have a story for you," Shamer said with relish, "but it's nearly evening now, and my poor stomach would perish without regular feeding."

"Oh, Shamer, I'll bring you a plate." The girl who had brought the wine hugged him. "You are like an old lion, shaggy and tired and waiting to be fed."

"Verily I am." Shamer smiled, pleased with himself.

An hour later the courtyard was deserted. An empty trencher lay on the bench beside Shamer. He heard voices approaching from one of the palace stairways that wound from an upper story down the outside wall. Sitting in the shadows, Shamer watched the eunuch Rab Saris guide Joash into the courtyard and then leave.

Joash ran his stick down and up the wall beside the staircase and made his way alongside the palace wall. He walked with his head slightly cocked, as though listening or counting. Before reaching the corner, Joash had his stick swinging up to anticipate it.

"Joash!" called Shamer softly.

He turned. "Shamer?"

Shamer came to him and embraced him. "How goes it with you?" He took Joash's hand and settled it on his sleeve. Together they began to circle the enclosed yard.

"Fine." Joash's voice was blurred. *He's full of wine,* Shamer realized. "I'm Leah's pet monkey. See this stick? My plaything. Be surprised. . . . Pet monkeys don't need much. . . . Shamer?"

"Yes."

"Shamer. They'll get you, too."

"Me, Joash? What are you saying?"

"Get you. Down below until after war—it's all over palace. Prattlers. Old Shamer's got to go, down below," he said in a singsong voice, "because of Deborah. All because of. . . ." His voice trailed off in a sniffle and he plodded on.

Shamer's heart skipped a beat. "Joash, do you trust me?"

He nodded. His fingers kneaded Shamer's arm.

"Then listen." Joash's head dropped on his chest and he stood perfectly still. Shamer glanced around fearfully. "You and I are leaving here. Now. Tonight. Remember the Kenites on Lapidoth's caravan? Remember Heber and Jael? They have come for us."

Joash sighed patiently. "Sisera'll find out, you know."

"Joash, pull yourself together. Yahweh is stronger. Yahweh *is* stronger! He will deliver us."

Joash lifted his face, as though listening. The eye sockets were two pits of blackness in the shadowed face. "Where are we?"

"In the courtyard of—"

"Not that!"

"Oh." Shamer glanced around. The ovens in the middle of the yard were between them and the bottom of the stairs where Rab Saris had left Joash. "Halfway around the wall."

"When I get back to the steps, the monkeykeeper fetches me. Here, monkey, monkey. . . ."

Shamer thought rapidly. Heber and Jael would not be expecting them tonight. But Sisera's guards might be waiting at the tannery. How could he manage with a drunken man? Probably the guards at the gates would not be alerted yet. He peered at Joash. "Are you ready?"

"Don't care. What's death, anyway?"

Shamer glanced around. He had come into the cook yard through the grape arbor that adjoined the larger landscaped courtyard around the palace. It was the entrance commonly used by tradespeople. His eyes fell on the forgotten harness. Shamer thought quickly. "Give me your staff."

Joash obeyed. Retrieving the harness, Shamer looped it around the staff. Settling one end of the staff on Joash's shoulder, he put his hand upon it, then took up the other end. "There. Joash, between us we are carrying a harness. Hold fast to the staff and walk as if you can see. I shall be before you. You will not stumble." *I hope.*

Shamer took a last look at the man behind him. "Pull your cloak around your face. And keep your head up!"

"Why bother with me?" Joash's voice sounded a bit more sober. But he did as he was told.

Shamer led the way across the courtyard toward the grape arbor. As they reached the shadowed wall, he saw a movement on the staircase. The arbor was still several paces ahead. Shamer's heart leaped. "Stop!" he hissed to Joash. "Not a move."

Rab Saris moved leisurely down the stairs. He reached the cook yard. Shamer heard him call Joash's name. He waited. His heart thumped like a mallet. Rab Saris called again. He advanced a few steps toward the ovens and turned in a slow circle.

When Rab Saris's back was to them, Shamer gave a sharp tug on the staff. Quickly the two men slipped into the protective blackness of the arbor.

By the time they reached the streets, they had achieved a sort of balance with the pole between them. By torchlight Shamer saw with relief that the gates were still open. But he was certain that the gates enclosing the outer city would be barred. He eyed the guards. What if they stopped him? What would he do? Before his courage failed, he began to whistle cheerily and marched through the gates into the outer city, giving them a careless salute as he passed. At the same swinging pace, he led Joash through the dark streets of Taanach toward the caravan grounds. When he saw ahead of him the flickering lights of a hundred fires, Shamer allowed himself a sigh that turned into a shudder of relief. Now to find the Kenites.

The city gates were still closed when the sun was at its highest the next day. Jael came back to her tent, with a basket of vegetables she had purchased, to report this gloomy fact to Heber. Within the tent, Shamer and Joash listened. "None may leave until Sisera marches."

"And when is that to be?" asked Heber.

Jael laughed shortly. "When he is good and ready. Oh, I can imagine he sits so proud in his palace, like a god in the gates of heaven! I spit on him!"

Heber glanced around uneasily. "Sh-h. Your tongue will get us all in trouble!"

At last Sisera was ready to march. As the great gates were unbarred and swung open, the chariots rolled forth. The teams pranced proudly, drivers controlling them with straps wrapped securely around an arm. Behind each driver rode a crack archer, muscular legs firmly balanced on the bed of the chariot. For two hours the charioteers maneuvered through the gates. Following them came a thousand armed foot soldiers.

In their wake the townspeople spilled out of the gates, waving and calling in holiday spirits. From the vantage point of the city could now be seen Canaanite legions weaving through the Pass of Megiddo to join Sisera's forces.

Leah and her handmaidens lined the parapet of the women's quarters to revel in the spectacle. Gay, tasseled banners flipped in the breeze as horses and chariots, the pride of her son's life, smartly took the field.

She picked out the proud figure of Sisera flying a bright red crest of feathers on his helmet, with similar plumes adorning the fore-plate of his chariot.

She said over her shoulder, her eyes still upon her son, "Fetch me a goblet of wine."

Sipping it, she said, "I suppose it's useless to hope for spoils. What could those peasants have?"

"There are always spoils of war, my lady," one of the maids replied.

They were silent a moment, watching the armies move in a broadening pattern upon the plain, like a slow mass of oil. Leah sighed.

"Shall I play and sing for you, my lady?"

"No." Leah's thoughts turned to Joash. She had not dared bring up the subject to Sisera before he left, indeed had avoided him, since it was she who had persuaded him to give Joash to her. Her spies had searched diligently. *Well,* she thought, *with my son away we will turn this place inside out until he is found.* She leaned over the rail.

A straggly looking caravan was snaking out of the gates and heading northwest. It was the caravan from Egypt, now bound for Phoenicia. She sighed again. Sisera had been most penurious with her this trip. She had not been allowed to buy nearly all that she had fancied. . . . Strange that Joash had not been found. And strange, too, that when the soldiers went to the tannery for Shamer, that odious peasant was also gone.

32

AND THE LEADERS OF ISRAEL trumpeted Yahweh's call. Armed with spear and dagger, bow and sling, leather shield and cudgel, with packs of food and heavy cloaks, the men of Israel left their homes at the heels of their elders.

More than one cast lingering eyes on the fields of barley. Would the rains come and ripen the grain while they were gone? Would they return in time to harvest? Would thieves and plunderers burn the fields and their homes in their absence? Still they came.

Barak moved out to rally the faithful of Naphtali and Zebulun and Issachar. Lapidoth, named leader of the Ephraimites, went forth from Shiloh. At his side was Deborah, and behind them, before the people, the priests bore the Ark of the Covenant.

All that day and the next streamed the legions of Israel. Down the dry slopes of the mountains to the valley of the Jordan, then north to the Sea of Galilee. At its tip the army moved west toward Mount Tabor, streaming up its slopes in a swath a mile wide, into the tall cedars at its crown. "Such legions I did not think dwelled in the hills of Israel," smiled Barak as Deborah and Lapidoth arrived. "Come, I want to show you something."

Barak led the commanders to his post at the pinnacle of Tabor. Through the forests they viewed the Plain of Jezreel. Among the web of dry creek beds the plain bristled with men and horses.

"My men have counted five hundred chariots and still more coming," said Barak.

Beyond the plain, the fortress city of Taanach rose at the southern pass of the valley fifteen miles away. Before it, the dry bed of the river Kishon stretched eastward toward Ephraim.

"And now?" Barak's wise eyes sought Deborah's. "They cannot climb Tabor with their chariots, but neither can we risk attack on level ground."

"We rest," smiled Deborah, "and wait upon the word of the Lord."

When all the forces of Yahweh had reached Tabor, they numbered forty thousand. As Deborah moved among them, she pondered why all had not answered the call. The clansmen of Reuben had come to the tribal confederacy. There was great searching of heart among them. Men of Gilead had stayed beyond the Jordan, silent to Yahweh's cry. And Dan, had the men of Dan gone over to the Canaanites? She had heard the rumblings that a wilderness god could not prevail in the cities. Had Dan heard, and believed? And Asher . . . were her sons so occupied with ships they forgot Yahweh?

Night after night the commanders gathered before General Barak: commanders of Benjamin, Ephraim, Manasseh, Zebulun, Issachar, and Naphtali. Deborah's soul blazed in humble pride for these men, their noble faces illumined by firelight as they discoursed with Barak, these brave leaders who heeded Yahweh's call. Among the commanders her gaze lingered frequently on the dear face of Lapidoth.

Nightly Deborah wandered among the flickering fires, and awaited Yahweh's command.

Sisera came out of his tent and looked up at the brooding mountain. He could see few Israelites, hidden in the trees and underbrush fifteen hundred feet above, but he could hear them as they sang and chanted prayers.

His forces had crossed the dry bed of the Kishon and advanced to within a mile of Tabor, forming a semicircle around its southern perimeter. Behind this line his tent was positioned on a slight rise. Around him ranged the tents of his advisers, lesser kings, and officers. Located well away were the tents of Darkon, his priests, and the comeliest of the temple virgins.

"What do you suppose they are waiting for?"

"Eh?" Sisera turned to Lieutenant Sem at his elbow. "I imagine they are wondering how it is we are here under their noses. The great General Barak," mused Sisera. "I fought him once before, Sem, when Jabin was alive. I'll warrant he curses the day he holed up on that hill!"

Barak was pacing back and forth. After three days, the men upon the mountain were growing restless. Were their flocks safe, their fields? Barak felt the same restlessness. Finally, noting that Lapidoth was watching, he strode across the few feet that separated their tents.

"I wish to speak to Deborah."

Lapidoth was surprised at the surly tone. "She is asleep."

"How long are we going to sit up here looking foolish?"

The tent curtain parted. Deborah, in a soft, clinging gown, her hair falling about her face, smiled serenely at him. Lapidoth went to her, encircling her waist with his arm.

Barak looked from one to the other. "That is a fine garment, Deborah—not at all warlike."

Deborah seemed amused. "Do you wear your studded girdle to bed, Barak? Shall I be a warrior in my own house?"

"Do not tease Barak," smiled Lapidoth. "Bring him some milk. Sit, Barak."

Deborah brought three cups of milk to the rug outside the tent. Barak shook his grizzled head. "I don't understand, Deborah. What are we doing here? There sits Sisera, more Canaanites joining him every day. His chariots run races under our feet and we do nothing. They hurl taunts at us and we do nothing. What does Yahweh tell you?"

"He hath not spoken."

"Then perhaps he means for us to take it from here."

"No. I should know if that were so."

"But. . . ." Barak's hands made swift, futile gestures. "This is no way to fight a war! Sisera cannot climb the hill with his chariots. We have four times his number of men and we would have the advantage. Neither can we descend to the plain. His chariots would cut us to pieces. And now that you have allowed him all the readiness he needs, there he sits, waiting for the hare to catch the fox."

"Trust in Yahweh, General Barak. He brought us here; he will surely bring us victory!"

"When will it be safe for us to leave?" asked Shamer as he walked with the Egyptian caravan bound for Phoenicia.

"It would be stupid to cross the valley with Sisera's legions out there," said Heber. "We'd never reach Shiloh in one piece. When we reach the western edge of Jezreel we will leave the caravan, circle through the foothills of Zebulun, and so reach Galilee. There will we be safe."

"Our people may already be at Mount Tabor," said Shamer.

Joash stumbled on a rock and cursed.

"Do you wish to ride for a while?" asked Jael. She could detect little of his former exuberance.

"I have my limbs!"

"Aye, and a sharp temper," retorted Jael.

"I'm sorry, Jael." Joash threw his head back. "I can feel the sea breeze. There lies west." He pointed.

"Yes. The world will not be all black, Joash," consoled Shamer. "Slip your hand through here." Shamer guided his hand through a pack strap of the ass. "Did I ever tell you the story of how Yahweh trumpeted down the walls of Jericho?"

And so the hours went. By evening, the caravan had reached the edge of the valley, where the hills narrowed into a pass through which the dry bed of the Kishon plummeted to the Great Sea. Here they camped with the caravan for the last time.

The following night found Heber and Jael, Shamer and Joash but a few miles northwest of Mount Tabor. The sinking sun cut sharp ridges in Tabor's western face as it sank over the Great Sea at their backs.

"The sky has such a strange cast," said Jael. "See how yellow it is."

On the day after they celebrated the Sabbath, seven days after they had reached the mountains, Deborah rose at first light and sought Barak.

"Up! For this is the day in which the Lord has given Sisera into your hand. Does not the Lord go out before you?"

The camp roused quickly. Deborah directed the priests to prepare a sacrifice of two unblemished rams. The dawn sky began to darken even while they chanted their songs of praise. Thunder rumbled over the mountains from the south. The earth trembled and the heavens touched the mountaintop.

"The Lord is marching!" cried the people.

"Tell your men to array themselves below the trees," Deborah commanded Barak.

Far below, the Canaanites saw them. Their eager shouts rose to the ears of the Israelites. As they harnessed horses to chariots, the first drops of rain began to fall. Within minutes the drops became a deluge.

"Bring the Ark!" cried Deborah. "The hour is at hand!" She ran to a promontory commanding a view of the field, the Ark and the priests beside her. The wind whipped through her garments and the rain plastered her hair to her face. She raised her arms. "Yahweh! Yahweh! Forward!"

Far below, Sisera leaped to his chariot. "By the gods!" he shouted hoarsely. "It is a cloudburst! Turn the chariots! Head for the Kishon! We must cross the valley before the flooding!"

Hearing Sisera's words, Darkon commandeered a place in a chariot. Even as the driver struggled to turn the horses, Darkon seized the whip and began lashing them unmercifully. In a mad scramble, the chariots raced over the rocky, clay soil for the foothills across the Kishon.

On Tabor, the Israelites watched as the foot soldiers abandoned rank and plunged after the chariots. With triumphant cries they raced down the hills in pursuit.

Through the blinding rain, slipping and sliding through the mud, the Israelites chased the retreating Canaanites. All about them chariots were toppling, their wheels sucked into the mire. Plunging, maddened horses flailed and struggled to be free of the harnesses imprisoning them to the iron chariots.

The rocky washes began to fill. The thin, clay soil could not contain the rain, and it rushed and sheeted over the ground. Loose rocks in the dry beds crisscrossing Jezreel shifted in the rush of water unfurling madly toward the Great Sea and bounded along, stoning the hocks of horses.

As the Canaanites fled they dropped spears and swords, which the pursuing Israelites quickly recovered.

Sisera's red-plumed helmet stood out momentarily in the blackened day and then disappeared as his chariot overturned and he plunged to earth. Struggling to his feet, he shook his sword at the sky and cursed the gods. The wind whipped away his words.

Darkon's chariot gained the banks of the Kishon ahead of the others. He leaped from the chariot and plunged into the river. His garments pulled as he struggled to cross. He gained the far bank, a high shelf which had been undercut by previous floods. Gasping and clawing, he struggled upward. Suddenly a great roaring sound came to his ears. He looked toward the mountains and saw a wall of water. Darkon screamed as he disappeared beneath its fury.

The next chariots to reach the river found a raging torrent, rocks like catapults hurtling on its crest. All day the battle raged, Israelites forcing Canaanites ever backward toward the river of no escape.

Sisera had lost his helmet. In a daze, he imagined he was surrounded by Israelites. They must regroup. Where were his commanders? In the blackness of the storm and mud he could not tell friend from foe. He heard the scream of a horse smote by a spear. He saw wheels spinning against the sky. He heard a wild, foreign chant rising upon the wind, and saw four priests moving through the battle as if it did not exist. They carried a box on poles. Madness. This was madness! Their god had unleashed demons!

Suddenly Sem was beside him. "It is a rout, sire! The troops are being put to death by their own swords!" A runaway horse careened toward them. In the wake of the horse, a giant of a man churned through the mud, cudgel in one hand and sword in the other. Lapidoth the Philistine!

With a howl Sisera leaped for him, Sem closing from the side with sword and dagger. Lapidoth struck Sisera a blow with the cudgel, at the same time parrying a thrust from Sem. Sisera reeled away. As Lapidoth leaped after him, Sem thrust the dagger through his armpit above his leather vest.

With a bellow of rage, Lapidoth turned and decapitated him. Sisera stumbled away in horror. "To Taanach!" he croaked. "To Taanach!" He threshed mightily with his sword, but there was nothing there.

Head down, Sisera bulled through the morass of mud-covered bodies. His men . . . must regroup. . . . He ran for hours. Behind him shouts and screams and the clang of metal striking metal carried on the winds, growing ever fainter.

All that day the wind howled and drove the rain over the valley. Jael stayed in her tent and Joash in another, on the side of a hill. Heber and Shamer, after counsel that morning, had left to locate the Israelite forces.

All day Leah waited, seeing only a vast grayness covering the plains. She peered out through the lattice. "Why is his chariot so long in coming?" she fretted. "Why tarry the hoofbeats of his chariots?"

"Are they not finding and dividing the spoil?" answered her ladies. "A maiden or two for every man; spoil of dyed stuffs for Sisera?"

"Spoil of dyed stuffs embroidered," responded Leah, "two pieces of dyed work embroidered for my neck as a spoil."

Vapor rose off the plain, steam from the bodies of fallen horses, fog from the sodden ground. Long lances of harsh light yellowed the sky. Daybreak brought an end to the storm.

For over an hour there had been no fighting. At the edge of the Kishon, the Israelites faced the unaccustomed sight of swift, rushing waters, as the river's brown mass roiled and tumbled toward the sea. Its progress was impeded by the bodies of men and animals caught in mangled chariots. Others had been spewed out like driftwood to join the fallen on the field of battle.

In the gray light, Barak, Ira, and Kanah moved among the men, searching for their own dead and wounded. There were no shouts of spoils, no plundering of bodies. This was a holy war. They were bound by the Law.

Jubilant soldiers streamed off the field, dragging their tired bodies up the hill to be met by a proud and fierce Deborah on the heights above them.

"Victory is ours!" Again and again the exultant cry rose to her ears. In camp, the women ministered to the returning warriors, binding wounds and tendering food and drink.

Deborah could see the fruits of victory below: a field fertilized with the blood of Canaan. Neither prisoner nor booty would be taken. And she who had never seen a field strewn with dead looked on as the Canaanites left alive were mercilessly slaughtered, and the horses, also. Deborah turned from the carnage, revolted. She found Phurah at her shoulder. "Though we take no spoils, could not the wounded and the animals be spared?" she cried.

Before Phurah could answer, General Barak called her name, his

voice ragged with exhaustion. With great effort, he climbed the last
rise. As he reached her, she noticed a long welt of congealed blood
on one forearm.

"General Barak. Yahweh blesses thee."

The furrows of his brow were reamed with sorrow. "Lapidoth is
sorely wounded, Deborah. We did not move him."

Deborah's hands closed into fists. "Where is he? I'm coming."
Suddenly she felt a restraining hand.

"No, Deborah," said Phurah. "You are still under the Nazirite
vow."

"He is not dead, Phurah! Let me go! I will go to him! Take me,
Barak!"

Barak turned and led her down to the field. Deborah's senses
reeled. Eyes frozen forever stared at her. Limbs jutted at skewed
angles from lifeless bodies. The noble head of a horse. A teeth-
baring grimace. A soft mist gleaming silver from the edge of a
jutting spear.

"Oh, hurry, Barak," she cried. In a quarter hour, she discerned a
knot of men gathered ahead of them. A path opened. Lapidoth lay
pillowed on a cloak and covered by another. His eyes were closed,
his bearded face gray, wiped free of mud.

Deborah gasped. It was all she could do to keep from flinging
herself upon him. She looked questioningly at Barak.

"Has he spoken?" asked Barak.

"Not moved," answered Ira. He moved around the silent circle to
take Deborah's arm.

Deborah leaned against him. Phurah's voice drifted remotely past
her: "See if he yet lives."

Kanah knelt beside the fallen hero. Deborah pressed her hands to
her face. She ached to hold his body, to beg Yahweh for his life.
How could this be happening? Kanah rose. "He is gone."

A wail keened from Deborah's lips. She threw herself forward,
but Phurah and Ira caught her before she could touch Lapidoth.
"You must not!" exclaimed Phurah.

"Then take the vow from me now!"

"Thou knowest I cannot! Thou must come before the Tent of
Yahweh. Deborah, Deborah, this is dangerous. You must not be
near the dead! Even thee! Yahweh will punish us all! Hasn't he given
us victory? Do not tempt his anger in the face of victory!"

Deborah bared her teeth. The cords of her neck stood out, her voice ringing in anguish. "Think you of victory when my Lapidoth is dead! How more could Yahweh punish me!"

"Here, let me take her. I am her father."

"Father!" Deborah found herself in his arms, felt his strength. "We have heard what you said. We will take her back to camp."

"You are Shamer the tanner, the one who was in Taanach?" asked Barak. "And this?"

"Heber the Kenite, friend of Lapidoth. We joined the battle yesterday afternoon."

Deborah flung an arm across her face. The image of Lapidoth, his eyes forever closed, scarred her brain. "Deborah. Deborah." Shamer's voice in her ear. Was she going mad? He led her, unresisting, away from the battlefield.

Ira and Kanah stared after her. Suddenly Ira called, "Heber! Did you learn anything of Joash?"

Heber left Deborah and hurried back to the soldiers. "He is with us, Lieutenant Ira. Sisera had his eyes put out."

An oath escaped Ira's lips. "Sisera! And who has seen Sisera this evil day?"

The hours passed as it rained without ceasing. Jael milked the goat and moved it and the two asses to a new patch of grass. Then she returned to the shelter of her tent, moving aside the curtain to sort out the sounds of the storm. Was it the cries of men she heard? And was that animals shrieking? Was the battle joined, she wondered, or was it only the storm?

She busied herself whittling a new tent stake to replace one which had splintered. Through the sounds of the storm came an occasional snore from Joash, asleep in his tent beside hers. His escape from the palace and then from Taanach had left him exhausted. *Surely no one will fight today,* thought Jael. She built a small, hot dung fire in the center of the tent. Then she took some of the goat's milk and poured it into a bowl, settling it near the fire to warm. Heber would be chilled when he returned.

Suddenly a voice spoke to her out of the gloom: "Who are you?"

She looked into the empty rain. "I am Jael, wife of Heber the Kenite." A soldier suddenly appeared before her. Jael gasped and scrambled to her feet.

"Between the Kenites and Canaan there is peace. I claim the hospitality of your tent." The man lurched inside. His eyes were bloodshot, his face streaked with mud. Wearily he looked at her. A slight smile curled a corner of his mouth. "Don't be frightened. I will not harm you. May I have some water?"

"Is the fighting—"

"I don't know. Who can fight in this?"

"Come in by the fire."

Jael placed a sleeping mat upon the ground and shook out a wool rug over it. She picked up the bowl of milk and offered it to him. "I had some milk warming for my husband."

"Thank you." The soldier's eyes closed as he drained the bowl. "Is it still the day the rain began?"

"It began this morning." Seeing his great weariness, she added, "Sleep, my lord."

He returned the bowl and stripped off his cloak, handing it to her, also. With a groan, he dropped to the rug. His eyes closed.

Jael walked softly to the tent curtain, the man's wet cloak still in hand. Suddenly she was startled by a noise. Joash was standing bareheaded in the rain, listening.

"What are you doing here? There's a Canaanite asleep inside!" she hissed.

"I heard Sisera's voice. . . ."

"It's a soldier. He's tired and confused. He fell asleep."

"It was Sisera's voice! Tell me, what does he look like?"

"He does not wear a beard, his hair is close cropped and blond, a very handsome—"

"I could believe Yahweh sent him!" Joash raised a fist.

"Is it he?"

"Yes!"

Sisera, Sisera! It throbbed in her brain. *My beloved son, Ehi.* She looked at Sisera's wet cloak. Deliberately she held it at arm's length and let it fall in the mud. "Wait here lest he waken," she told Joash.

"What are you going to do?"

Jael returned to the sleeping man. "Sisera?" she said softly. Slowly her face became a cold, closed mask. She fetched her mallet and the newly sharpened tent peg.

One in each hand she held them, and stood across the fire from the sleeping man. The flames flickered on the face of the handsome, exhausted king. With clenched fists, Jael raised her implements and offered them before the fire. She moved to Sisera's head and knelt there. By firelight she saw a faint pulse throbbing in his temple. With the delicacy of an artisan she poised the point of the tent peg atop the pulse beat and raised the mallet.

33

THE BODIES OF LAPIDOTH and his fallen comrades were consecrated and buried on the field of Jezreel. Deborah remained within her tent, receiving neither mourners nor food, or even her father. The time had come. Yahweh had fulfilled his part of the vow; now she must complete hers. Her head throbbed.

Deborah picked up a dagger. *Oh, Lapidoth, that Yahweh would let me use it to follow thee! Yahweh, thy will is hard! Didst have to take my precious husband?* Dropping the dagger, she broke into sobs.

"Blessed be Yahweh," she began to chant, "who hath again delivered the people of Israel. Blessed be Yahweh. . . ."

"Deborah, art ready?" called Phurah.

Deborah removed her cloak and unbound her hair. Dressed only in a dark shift which fell to her sandals, she stepped out to meet the priest.

Suddenly, a great confusion sounded in the camp. Heber's voice rose through the noise. "Hail! Hail! Everyone come!" Heber and Jael entered camp leading an ass with a body strapped over it. Behind them came a man whose face was hidden by his cloak.

Shamer went to the newcomers. At Shamer's voice, the young man pulled back his cloak. Deborah gasped. *Joash!* "Oh, Phurah, his eyes!"

"Yes. That's Sisera's work."

"It is a miracle!" Heber cried. Jael's face glowed ecstatically as her husband, spying Deborah and Phurah, pulled the unwilling ass to them through the multitude.

"Well, let us see the miracle God hath wrought," said Barak.

"I give you—King Sisera! Killed by my wife!"

A gasp went up from the people, then great shouts. Yahweh had done as Deborah had foretold. He had delivered Sisera into the hands of a woman!

237

Deborah stared at the body. Then she looked at Joash's sightless face and at the triumphant Kenites. She felt an immense weariness. She longed now only for it to be over.

General Barak knelt in the dust before her. "All has come to pass, prophetess of Israel, even as you have said. Blessed be Yahweh. From this day shall all Israel know from the lips of Barak the wisdom of Deborah, beloved of Yahweh." Barak seized her hand and pressed it to his lips.

Deborah gestured him to his feet. In an emotionless voice she said, "Let us dedicate our victory."

As the first stars rose in the east, the people gathered on the hill of Tabor. The priests lighted the sacrificial fires. Fourteen unblemished rams and two unblemished lambs were slain upon the altar and their parts thrown upon the fire. While the meat roasted, incense was thrown upon the flames. In the red smoke of the sacrificial offerings, the voices of the faithful rose in praise to Yahweh. Shadows of the flames flickered on their faces; sparks like fireflies danced upward as they sang their praises:

"That the leaders took the lead in Israel,
that the people offered themselves willingly,
bless the Lord!
Hear, O kings; give ear, O princes;
to the Lord I will sing,
I will make melody to the Lord, the God of Israel."

Deborah raised her arms:
"Lord, when thou didst go forth from Seir,
when thou didst march from the region of Edom,
the earth trembled,
and the heavens dropped,
yea, the clouds dropped water.
The mountains quaked before the Lord,
yon Sinai before the Lord, the God of Israel."

Phurah sprang up beside her:
"In the days of Shamgar, son of Anath,
in the days of Jael, caravans ceased
and travelers kept to the byways.
The peasantry ceased in Israel, they ceased
until you arose, Deborah,
arose as a mother in Israel."

Barak picked up the chant:
    "When new gods were chosen,
    then war was in the gates.
    Was shield or spear to be seen
    among forty thousand in Israel?"
Deborah's voice rang out:
    "My heart goes out to the commanders of Israel
    who offered themselves willingly among the people.
    Bless the Lord.
    Tell of it, you who ride on tawny asses,
    you who sit on rich carpets
    and you who walk by the way.
    To the sound of musicians at the watering places,
    there they repeat the triumphs of the Lord,
    the triumphs of his peasantry in Israel."
Barak's voice broke in:
    "The kings came, they fought;
    then fought the kings of Canaan,
    at Taanach, by the waters of Megiddo;
    they got no spoils of silver."
Then Deborah:
    "From heaven fought the stars,
    from their courses they fought against Sisera.
    The torrent Kishon swept them away
    the onrushing torrent, the torrent Kishon.
    March on, my soul, with might!"
And again Barak:
    "Then loud beat the horses' hooves
    with the galloping, galloping of his steeds."
Heber rose beside them:
    "Most blessed of women be Jael,
    the wife of Heber the Kenite,
    of tent-dwelling women most blessed.
    He asked water and she gave him milk,
    she brought him curds in a lordly bowl.
    She put her hand to the tent peg
    and her right hand to the workmen's mallet;
    she struck Sisera a blow,
    she crushed his head,
    she shattered and pierced his temple."

Deborah stepped before them all and lifted her arms above the fire.

"So perish all thine enemies, O Lord!

But thy friends be like the sun as he rises in his might!"

And the people's prayers swelled upon the incensed smoke and rose to heaven.

Suddenly Joash rose among them, in the billowing red smoke, his sightless face raised in wonder. "I had not sight while I could see," said Joash. "For your God is with you. He leaves you not without a leader. He has shown himself in the mighty miracles of his people. Truly you are the people of the one God. I, Joash the Habiru, shall be Yahweh's, too."

Shamer rose, tears streaming down his face, and embraced the young man. Joash clutched the side of Shamer's shaggy head to his shoulder. "From your tales, Shamer, such visions have come to the eyes of my mind! Blessed be Yahweh. He has given me new sight!"

In the bold glare of firelight, something about Joash's face, prematurely aged by mutilation and suffering, caught in the scattered threads of Deborah's memory. A woman, lines of suffering that would not give her peace, a woman . . . whose children were lost . . . Hannah of Harosheth.

"Joash."

He turned. He reached out. "Deborah. . . ."

"Thy mother, is she Hannah, and does she abide in Harosheth?"

"My mother, yes!"

"She awaits thee, Joash. Her arms cry out to hold one of her children again."

"Not like this. . . ."

"If he who was dead to her returns, shall she not rejoice, even in his infirmity?"

"I—I will think upon it."

Phurah stepped to Deborah's side. "It is time." At his signal, a hush fell upon the throng. It was time for the fulfillment of Deborah's vow.

Deborah knelt before the Ark of the Covenant on the altar. The dagger lay in her palm, hilt extended. Phurah stepped before her and took it. The people craned forward.

Phurah picked up a gleaming lock of her hair. He placed the dagger against her scalp and with a swift motion severed the lock.

The women gasped. He held the lock above the fire and threw it upon the flames saying, "Thy long hair, Deborah, is the visible sign of thy consecration to Yahweh." He cut another lock and continued, "It is the glory of thy head, and the product of thy body, which thou hast devoted to Yahweh."

The acrid smell of burning hair filled the air. Deborah closed her eyes. She heard the phrases. She felt the cuts as wounds in her soul. Finally he finished and Deborah rose. She turned to face the people.

Deborah's head gleamed obscenely white. Raw, red tufts sprouted from the naked scalp. Many of the people cast their eyes upon the ground before her shame. She appeared taller than ever. Her eyes dominated features emaciated by suffering. Her aquiline nose jutted from her face like a parody.

She felt the cold on her ears and neck and head. And now, she was truly alone. For what is woman without her crowning glory? And what did it matter, anyway? She had been forbidden to anoint her husband's dead body, the last and most sacred duty of a wife.

How completely separated she was from all that she loved on earth.

Phurah brought her a cup of wine, signifying the end of her vow. Barak came forth with her cloak. Tenderly he adjusted it about her face. He looked into her eyes. Her profound sorrow had taken her far away.

Jael stepped forward. "I will take care of her, lord Barak." Jael led her back to her tent.

And the people, warmed with wine and certain that they were once more Yahweh's beloved children, slept well upon the wet ground.

"What will become of Taanach without Sisera?" mused Shamer.

All day the clans had been leaving Mount Tabor. Among those who had elected to tarry another day, Shamer, Joash, Ira, and Kanah took their ease with Barak around a fire, drinking wine.

"It will become just another city-state of Canaan," said Barak. "Sisera had the power to bind Canaan into a single body. I doubt that Beno will be that strong. Without horses and chariots, none will be able to lead the others, or to hold the Valley of Jezreel." Barak's gaze rested on Shamer. He asked teasingly, "And what will you do without Sisera?"

"Humph. I would like to have my tools and my leathers back if I could get them," said the practical tanner. "Then I would reopen my old tannery in Naphtali."

"We'll send in an armed detachment with you," promised Barak. "It is the least we can do for the father of our prophetess." Barak turned to Ira. "And without Lapidoth, what of the caravan and your men?"

Ira leaned forward over his knees and trenched the earth with a stick. "We have decided to go on. The others have appointed me master in Lapidoth's stead." Ira's lips pressed into a sorrowful line. "I do not relish telling his friend Hamid that he is dead."

Kanah sighed expansively. "As for me, I shall be grateful to return to my little shop in Shechem. My workers have been too long without a master."

"A good worker works whether his master is present or not," observed Shamer.

Kanah's quiet gaze traveled to Joash. "And Joash shall come with me. Well did he serve me, and now I shall do the same for him."

"Well spoken," approved Barak.

Joash turned his face toward the voice of Kanah. "I could scarce strike fear in the heart of a bandit." His voice was firm, without bitterness. His hand reached out to find Shamer. "Shamer has offered me a job in his tannery. Tanning hides requires as much touch and scent as sight. And Yahweh gave me the gift of knowing his swift justice."

"What of Jezreel itself, General Barak?" asked Ira.

"The valley must not remain unoccupied," counseled Barak. "We must send people to settle villages on the fringe, so that we may put it under cultivation next season. That which is not used is soon lost."

Several heads nodded in agreement. "Yes, there will be more villages. And for the first time, Israelites will be farming the flatlands! Hear, hear!"

"Now perhaps Heber can be persuaded to settle down," said Ira slyly.

"Me, a farmer?" expostulated Heber. "Never! Besides," he said, "my wife has made my fortune. Who will not want their pots mended by the hand that slew Sisera?"

Guffaws of laughter broke out.

Hearing the laughter outside her tent, Jael turned to Deborah and smiled. "Men are like children. Give them wine after a battle and they are ready to play." Seeing the somber face of Deborah, her tone changed. "What are you thinking, Deborah?"

"Whither I shall go, now that Yahweh has no more need of me."

Jael was shocked. "Has no more need of thee? Did he tell thee?"

Deborah turned remorseless eyes upon her companion. "It was for this he called me."

"This and no other? How can it be? He will not leave thee desolate!"

Deborah said slowly, "I have not heard his call since the morning of battle."

The next morning the men were awakened by a cry from Jael. "Shamer! Heber! Awake!"

The men struggled out of their sleeping quarters. Jael stood before the tent of Deborah, a bowl of milk forgotten in her hand. "Deborah is gone!"

They did not know where she had gone, or when.

"How will she eat? How will she sleep? She has only her cloak, and food for a few days. And with her head shaven!" Jael began to wail. "O Yahweh, Yahweh, help us find her!"

Phurah joined them unobtrusively. "O Phurah," cried Jael, "do you know where she could have gone? Wolves, mountain lions. . . ."

"And men," added Barak somberly.

Phurah lifted his hands. "We must look for the hand of Yahweh in this. Do not seek her, but leave her to him."

34

Whither yahweh directed her feet mattered not. When Deborah stole away from camp, the people were once again united and trusting Yahweh, and for a time could be trusted to rid themselves of false gods. For a time. *They take and take,* she thought dully as she plodded onward.

She struck out in a northeasterly direction. From her girlhood home in Hammath by the Sea of Galilee she remembered climbing the hills and staring westward at Mount Tabor. Now she would keep Tabor at her back in the same manner. Confused by grief and weariness, she was seized with a great longing for her homeland.

Perhaps she was going home to die. For Yahweh had left her. In his glory she had seen men finally arise to be leaders again in Israel. Now she was through.

A great emptiness wandered in the void where her heart had been. Lapidoth . . . Lapidoth. . . . The sun rose higher. Her bare scalp itched and prickled under the wool cloak. She paused in a grove of tamarind trees and opened her packet, eating two biscuits and some dates. Finding a streak of green in the red earth, she followed the reeds to a glade and discovered a tiny spring. After bathing her hands and her face and head, she drank deeply, and refilled her waterskin. Then, spreading her cloak in the shade, she rested.

By midafternoon she was on her way again. Neither person nor beast did she see the whole day. She lay that night on a bed of weeds gathered into a springy pile beneath her. Wrapped in her cloak, she gazed at the stars. *From heaven fought the stars. . . . March on . . . march on. . . .* She slept.

Neither the second day nor the third did Deborah see another living beast. She had not taken a direct course, but skirted the hills that ringed Hammath. Somewhere north of Hammath her path led to Galilee.

Almost immediately she sighted peasants. Before Sisera's legions had made it dangerous, the road between Hammath and cities north had been well traveled. Deborah pulled her cloak about her face as a group of people came toward her, driving a few goats and sheep. They pulled off to the side of the path with all their animals when they sighted her. She heard their voices.

"It is Deborah. It is the prophetess!"

As she drew abreast they fell silent. A child began to cry and clung to his mother's skirts. She looked not upon their faces. Now the white limestone walls of Hammath shimmered in the distance. Above them she could see the dark green tops of cypress trees.

Old sights, old scents invaded her senses as she entered the unused tannery outside the walls of Hammath. Images of Gemalli and Shamer, of herself as a young girl, of happy laughter crowded her memory.

The following morning Deborah looked out the door to see a number of townspeople coming from Hammath. One of them carried a child. They called her name. The child was sick. Would she not pray for his recovery?

Would they not leave her alone! Deborah did not answer. When night fell, they went away. She took up her cloak and a staff and stepped outside. The people had left food at the door. She added it to her pack and set her face south.

A few miles below Galilee, Deborah crossed the Jordan at a narrow, marshy point and continued south on a well-used caravan road. Several days later, when she could see the ruins of Jericho rising in the west, she recrossed the Jordan. A town had sprung up near the foot of the old ruins. Here she came upon a caravan. Deborah was out of food, and therefore set herself by the gates of the town to beg with the unfortunates.

When she had been there less than an hour, she heard her name called in a musical, foreign-sounding tenor. She pulled her cloak over her face and bent her head upon her knees. A hand touched her.

It was Hamid. His great eyes liquid with sympathy, he raised her to her feet. "Deborah. Though Yahweh isn't my god, my prayers have been with you. We heard that you were wandering in the land. But must thou beg?"

"I do not wish the company of men."

"But where shall you go? Come with us!" he urged. "Ira is here. We have been to see Lapidoth's people. They grieve for you, Deborah. They want you to come home."

Deborah merely stared at him, waiting for him to be done.

"Will you at least drink a cup of wine?" Hamid led her to the shade of a palm within the gates, and spread his blue cloak upon the ground. He poured her some wine. "May I sit with you?"

She nodded.

"Remember Naomi and Elimelech of Bethlehem . . . kinsmen of Boaz the grain dealer? They went to Moab. Boaz learned that Elimelech and both his sons died of a plague there." Hamid shook his head. "If I were a believer of Yahweh . . . which I am not, which I am not . . . I would say that your god punished them for trying to outrun him."

But no pity stirred in Deborah's breast. Naomi deserved her loss. She gave Hamid her hand to help her rise.

"Thank you for the wine. I must be going."

"But whither will thou goest?" cried Hamid.

Deborah's eyes swept the horizon. They rested upon the eroded cliffs above the ruined city of Jericho. "There," she announced.

Hamid looked at the cliffs. *"Where?"*

"There." She took up her staff and began to walk away.

"Wait. Let me get you some food. Promise you'll wait!" Hamid disappeared toward the marketplace and reappeared within minutes with a large packet wrapped in linen.

"Thank you." She accepted the packet and turned away.

"Deborah . . . wait!"

She neither answered nor looked back.

All day Deborah climbed among the spired sandstone cliffs. *I will leave it to Yahweh whether I live or die,* she decided, as each step carried her farther from the unbearable face of civilization.

The wind had carved innumerable caves in the faces of the cliffs. Deborah explored one and then another. Finally she discovered one harboring a spring which pooled barely a handful of water. She knelt and scooped it up. It was pure and sweet. Here she would stay.

The third day of her retreat she peered out of her aerie and saw, far below, a shepherd with a staff climbing the cliffs. She hid within her cave. An hour later she peered out. The shepherd was gone, but in plain view a hundred feet below rested a packet. Deborah climbed down and found it contained food.

Thereafter, every second day someone brought provisions to the same spot. Weeks and months passed, and Deborah remained in her cave home. She spent long hours in prayer, but Yahweh had gone. Questions tormented her. On moonlit nights she walked near her cave, seeking answers upon the winds, but none came. Since Lapidoth's death she had felt no physical passion, and wondered at this. Perhaps physical passion, like other growing things, flourished when tended and died of neglect.

The dry season came, and nothing grew in the wilderness around Jericho. She hid from the parching heat. The silence was so absolute it became a palpable presence. At dusk she would venture forth to gaze at the tortured cliffs, mirrors of her own soul. Among the ghostly cliffs she could imagine huge, impossible cities reaching toward heaven and descending toward hell.

And her mind was tormented by Joash. He had suffered agony at the hands of Sisera. Yet Yahweh had used him, without doubt, to enable Jael to recognize and destroy the enemy. Did Yahweh, then, use pagans to accomplish his ends? And if he used them, did he not also love them?

But Yahweh had said, "Destroy the pagans who dwell in the land I give you." Yet Shamer had brought the light to Joash in the heartland of the enemy. She had heard Joash declare his power. Was Yahweh, then, truly the God of Joash? And of Hannah, his mother, who had come to her long ago in Shechem seeking his peace? And of pagan Jael? Jael, who had always declared her faith, the instrument of fulfillment of his judgment against Sisera. If pagans became believers, did Yahweh then accept them as his children? Did their faith cauterize that which had made them pagans?

The seasons came and passed. Deborah grew to look forward to the sight of the shepherd who faithfully brought food to the cliff. Then one day a different man threaded his way through the hills. He moved like an older man and stopped often to rest. But he did not stop at the usual place. On he climbed, pausing now and then to shade his eyes and seek out the higher path.

Deborah felt a curious mixture of fear and eagerness. She decided to meet the stranger, so she sat before the entrance of her cave and waited.

At last the man reached her. He rested upon his staff and pushed away his cloak. She recognized Boaz, the grain dealer from Bethlehem. He bowed low before her. "Yahweh bless thee, Deborah."

"And thee, Boaz," she responded. Her own voice sounded strange to her ears. She lifted her palm. "Please sit." Without thinking, she rose and cupped her bowl in the tiny spring until it was filled with water. She gave it to the man.

Boaz drank deeply. "Art well, prophetess?"

She smiled. "Only Yahweh knows."

"Yahweh has sent me for you."

Deborah's heart pounded unreasonably. "No, Yahweh is finished with me."

Boaz looked upon her with kindly eye. His hair had grown grayer, and he seemed heavier about the jowls. "Let me tell you all that has come to pass. Hamid followed you the day you appeared in Jericho. I was in Jericho, too, that day, bless Yahweh, and when Hamid returned he came to me. The caravan was about to depart, so I begged him to show me where you had gone. In these two years, Yahweh has been extremely generous, and I have been pleased to send thee sustenance."

Boaz waved aside her thanks. "Last year Naomi returned to Judah," he continued. "With her was a young Moabitess named Ruth, who had been married to one of her sons. Ruth insisted upon accompanying her. As you may know, Elimelech was my kinsman, and according to our Law, when there is no issue, the nearest kinsman must marry the wife of one deceased in order that his line be not extinguished.

"With no son to carry on the seed, Naomi sought my help in finding a husband for Ruth so that the name of Elimelech might continue.

"When I met the maiden, Ruth did delight my heart. In the years Naomi and Elimelech sojourned in Moab, Ruth learned of Yahweh and put away her own gods.

"So I have come to thee, Deborah. Ruth has borne me a son. Great is my joy, and greater still my joy yesterday morning when Yahweh told me in a dream that you should bless the babe."

Deborah shook her head. "It cannot be, good Boaz. Yahweh has been silent these two years."

"Perhaps Yahweh but allowed thee time to grieve and time to heal."

Deborah was silent a long time. She gazed out across the land of Canaan. In truth, if Yahweh had meant her to die, she would have perished before this. Finally she said, "I will come."

Boaz and Deborah came down out of the fastness of Jericho. At the base of the cliffs waited a servant with asses. Word had preceded them. The path to town was lined with peasants seeking a glimpse of the legendary prophetess.

In late afternoon they reached Bethlehem, a peaceful, sleepy village of whitewashed buildings gleaming on the sunny hillside. Boaz stopped before a cedar gate in a high wall spilling brilliant pink crepe myrtle. Inside the courtyard, water splashed musically into a limestone pool.

Naomi came hurrying forth with outstretched hands. "Deborah! Blessed be this house where thou hast set thy foot!"

"Naomi, is it you?" Gone was the sharp-tongued malcontent who had confronted her at the Feast of Ingathering so long ago.

"Oh, yes, Deborah. So many times I have rehearsed how to greet you. Yahweh punished my disobedience by taking away everything I held dear. Then, when I had nothing, he put it in my heart to return home. I was obedient to him, and he gave Ruth to cleave to me. And now, he hast made my heart full, for Boaz—"

"Peace, mother!" laughed Boaz. "Pray allow Deborah to refresh herself."

Boaz had generously provided new clothing and sandals for the prophetess, and Naomi pressed upon her her best embroidered veil. Deborah heard singing and returned with Naomi to the courtyard. Boaz was standing over a young bareheaded woman, the Moabitess Ruth, who held a babe upon her lap. Boaz looked up, his face lighted with joy.

"Ruth, here is Deborah!"

Ruth rose. Her face was fresh and sweet and shone with love. She dropped a shy curtsy and held up the babe. "His name is Obed."

Deborah opened her arms to receive the babe. She searched his sleeping face, the tiny, rosy lips. She felt the warmth and wonder of new life radiate from him to her. With a smile, she gave the babe back to his mother.

"Why hast thou come to Bethlehem, Ruth?" she asked.

"Because I love my mother-in-law. When my husband died, I wished to stay with her."

"What about your own people?"

"My people did not share love as Naomi and Chilion loved me. Naomi says Yahweh is the source of all love. It must be. I grew to love Yahweh because Naomi first loved me."

Unbidden tears misted Deborah's eyes. "And you a foreigner," she murmured. The icy dagger in her heart began to melt, releasing the pain in her breast. Suddenly she felt Yahweh near. His awesome power filled her. She swayed under its force. She closed her eyes. When she opened them she said, "Boaz and Ruth, thy baby is blessed. From the seed of his loins will come the first king of Israel!"

Boaz stared at her, stunned. "Is it true?"

"Thus saith Yahweh." *Thus saith Yahweh.* How good it felt upon her lips! Suddenly she felt imbued with a sense of urgency.

"Where is the Ark now?" she asked Boaz.

"In Shiloh. A temple has been built."

"Then I must go there."

"Not now!" protested Naomi.

"On the morrow. Good Boaz, I must leave you. I shall return to bid you good-bye." Swiftly Deborah turned and let herself out the gate. She went through the drowsy streets of Bethlehem almost at a run, and up a hill beyond the gates.

She reached the crest and waited breathlessly, joyfully, trying to still the panting pounding of her heart. A bat shot across the evening sky. A fragrance of oleanders and acacia and myrtle drifted to her nostrils. She paced upon the hills as of old, unaware of the passing of the night. She gazed back upon the sleeping city. Soft, dark blue shadows and pewter-colored walls anchored the star-filled night, fading as she followed the dome of heaven from the deep blue west where night was disappearing to the violet paling before a new dawn.

In the lush chill, deepest shadows, a mystery throbbed. At once she felt the presence of Yahweh, and finally, his voice.

My peace I give unto thee, Deborah, she heard. *For thou hast served me faithfully. No more shall ye fight. Peace, and understanding, and wisdom. In my name thou shalt henceforth deliver these things to my people. I am Yahweh.*

Deborah fell to the grass and wept.

Epilogue

LITTLE IS KNOWN ABOUT DEBORAH, prophetess of ancient Israel, except that she rose to leadership at a time of great crisis and the people followed her into battle against King Sisera and the Canaanites.

Judges 5 tells us she arose as a mother in Israel. This chapter is thought to be the oldest piece of biblical poetry extant, probably written at the time of the events it chronicles, possibly by one of the participants.

Judges 4, written centuries later, tells essentially the same tale and elaborates slightly, adding that Deborah was married to a man called Lapidoth and lived and judged in the hills of Ephraim before calling the holy war.

Judges 5 tells us the kings of Canaan fought at Taanach, by the waters of Megiddo. The area in which the battle took place is variously referred to as Megiddo, Armageddon, the Plain of Jezreel, of Esdraelon, or of Kishon. While scholars are unanimous as to its location, there is no corresponding unanimity on the actual date of the battle. A commonly accepted date is 1125 B.C.

At this time, according to Judges 4, Jabin was king of Canaan, residing in Hazor with Sisera as his commanding general. But in an account of an earlier time, Joshua 11:1–10 records that Jabin, king of Hazor, fought with horses and chariots against Joshua and was slain by him.

Archaeological evidence, which points to Hazor being razed in the 1300s B.C., supports the Joshua account. Additionally, no other Canaanite save Sisera is mentioned by name in Judges 5. Therefore it is probable that Jabin ruled from Hazor during the preceding century, and it is possible that in 1125 B.C., Sisera was chief king of Canaan, rather than merely general of the army.

In the matter of placing Sisera's fortress at Taanach, near the battlefield, rather than at Megiddo or elsewhere, I was guided by the fact that the ruins of ancient Megiddo have been dated as existing since 1300 B.C., while the ruins of Taanach are not that old. Taanach was thought to have been occupied at the time of the battle.

Taanach and Megiddo were both fortress cities built on opposite sides above the Pass of Megiddo, which was a critical juncture on the main caravan route from Egypt to Phoenicia. Taanach seemed a logical choice for a king's fortress.

A question still lingers in my mind. After the Israelites' victory upon the Plain of Jezreel, why did they not pursue their advantage and occupy the city of Taanach (or whatever city had been the historical base of Canaanite operations)? As far as can be determined, there is no historical evidence that they captured any city after this enormous victory. I wish I'd been a flea on the wall of a gossipy marketplace about that time, and listened to the tales the people told!

Another point which should be mentioned is the historical precedent for fictionally relocating the Ark of the Lord from one town to another. The Bible places the Ark at Shiloh (1 Samuel 4:3), at Kirjathjearim (1 Chronicles 13:5), at Jerusalem (1 Chronicles 15:3), at Gilgal (Joshua 4:11–19), and at Gibeah (Judges 20:26–29). For a brief discussion, see John Bright's *A History of Israel.*

After the war, according to the King James Version of Judges 5:31, "the land had rest forty years." Josephus, a Roman historian who lived about the time of Christ, wrote in *Antiquities of the Jews* that Deborah lived forty years after the battle, during which time the Israelites were at peace. Some scholars believe Deborah was judging in Israel during those forty years. How young she must have been when God called her!

Since scholars are pretty much in agreement on the date of the battle of Jezreel, this affords an interesting supposition: Could Deborah have actually known Boaz, Naomi, and Ruth?

Well, the Book of Ruth, whose story occurred ". . . in the days when the judges ruled . . ." (Ruth 1:1 KJV), chronicles the ancestors of King David as being Jesse, his father, and Obed, his grandfather. Obed was the son of Ruth and Boaz, and grandson of Naomi. According to *The New Westminster Dictionary of the Bible,* at age thirty, David became king of the southern kingdom of Judah. The referenced edition of the Revised Standard Version of the Bible places this at 1012 B.C. and David's birth at 1042 B.C., a mere eighty-three years after the battle of Jezreel. Thus it is possible that, around the year 1125 B.C., Deborah could have met Ruth, the new mother of a very special baby boy, who was destined to be the grandfather of King David, first king of all Israel.

CHRISTIAN HERALD ASSOCIATION AND ITS MINISTRIES

CHRISTIAN HERALD ASSOCIATION, founded in 1878, publishes The Christian Herald Magazine, one of the leading interdenominational religious monthlies in America. Through its wide circulation, it brings inspiring articles and the latest news of religious developments to many families. From the magazine's pages came the initiative for CHRISTIAN HERALD CHILDREN and THE BOWERY MISSION, two individually supported not-for-profit corporations.

CHRISTIAN HERALD CHILDREN, established in 1894, is the name for a unique and dynamic ministry to disadvantaged children, offering hope and opportunities which would not otherwise be available for reasons of poverty and neglect. The goal is to develop each child's potential and to demonstrate Christian compassion and understanding to children in need.

Mont Lawn is a permanent camp located in Bushkill, Pennsylvania. It is the focal point of a ministry which provides a healthful "vacation with a purpose" to children who without it would be confined to the streets of the city. Up to 1000 children between the age of 7 and 11 come to Mont Lawn each year.

Christian Herald Children maintains year-round contact with children by means of a *City Youth Ministry.* Central to its philosophy is the belief that only through sustained relationships and demonstrated concern can individual lives be truly enriched. Special emphasis is on individual guidance, spiritual and family counseling and tutoring. This follow-up ministry to inner-city children culminates for many in financial assistance toward higher education and career counseling.

THE BOWERY MISSION, located at 227 Bowery, New York City, has since 1879 been reaching out to the lost men on the Bowery, offering them what could be their last chance to rebuild their lives. Every man is fed, clothed and ministered to. Countless numbers have entered the 90-day residential rehabilitation program at the Bowery Mission. A concentrated ministry of counseling, medical care, nutrition therapy, Bible study and Gospel services awakens a man to spiritual renewal within himself.

These ministries are supported solely by the voluntary contributions of individuals and by legacies and bequests. Contributions are tax deductible. Checks should be made out either to CHRISTIAN HERALD CHILDREN or to THE BOWERY MISSION.

Administrative Office: 40 Overlook Drive, Chappaqua, New York 10514
Telephone: (914) 769-9000